A CIRCLE OF FIRELIGHT

Curtis Edmonds

Scary Hippopotamus Books
Trenton, New Jersey
http://www.scaryhippopotamus.com

ALSO BY THIS AUTHOR

Rain on Your Wedding Day

Wreathed

Lies I Have Told

If My Name Was Amanda

And I, according to my copy, have done set it in imprint, to the intent that noble men may see and learn the noble acts of chivalry, the gentle and virtuous deeds that some knights used in those days, by which they came to honour, and how they that were vicious were punished and oft put to shame and rebuke; humbly beseeching all noble lords and ladies, with all other estates of what estate or degree they been of, that shall see and read in this said book and work, that they take the good and honest acts in their remembrance, and to follow the same. Wherein they shall find many joyous and pleasant histories, and noble and renowned acts of humanity, gentleness, and chivalry.

— William Caxton, Preface to *Le Morte d'Arthur*, by Sir Thomas Malory (1485)

DEDICATED TO
KATIE AND STEPHANIE
WITH HOPES AND PRAYERS
FOR SUNSHINY DAYS
AND SWEET DREAMS

A THOUSAND MIDNIGHTS

The river in my dream is deep, with a swift current. The water is silt-brown and scored with deep ripples. It moves at the speed of a thoroughbred racehorse in full gallop, running through a narrow gorge cut into the gray bedrock. Plumes of white foam lap against the far bank.

The near bank is carefully tended, with short grass and well-trimmed rosebushes. A dirt road, smooth and even, runs parallel to the river, shaded by a line of tall sycamores. But the far side is a wild, strange place, a landscape of tropical flowers and thick, green vines hanging from live oak trees, at once inviting and forbidding.

There is only one way across, and that is the bridge that looms ahead in the distance. It is both familiar and ominous, a wide antique arch spanning the rushing river. In the half-light of dusk, the pale-yellow limestone glows softly. It does not take long for me to close the distance. The two steel lampposts that flank the bridge on this side cast a cold pool of light. I take a tentative step onto the cracked paving stones. I feel for the hilt of my sword.

I have walked the dirt road toward the bridge for a thousand midnights and have never once crossed to the other side. As always, a guardian waits at the center of the bridge, tall, ragged and silent. As always, he is wearing a long black leather duster, with dark tattered robes underneath. All I can see of his face is his green eyes, flashing in the near-darkness. He leans on a rough-hewn staff of wood, a foot taller than his gaunt frame. He waits for me to make the first move, with a patience tinged with malevolence.

"I am Ashlyn Revere," I say, "and I wish to cross."

The guardian does not answer, as always, and when I draw my sword from my scabbard and point it in his general direction, he does nothing. Night after night of slow patient experience has taught me that I cannot taunt him or distract him. I know I must defeat the guardian in order to cross, but I have never learned how; it's a puzzle I can't solve. It does not matter what incantation or weapon I use. He can move that long black staff swifter than my eyes can follow; he can use it to parry any edged weapon or block any missile weapon, and if I get too close to him, he can use the staff to beat me senseless. Magic is even more worthless—he can dodge or withstand any spells I can bring to bear.

I could walk away, but I never do. Something keeps driving me forward, across the bridge, and not knowing what that might be is, in its own way, as frustrating as my failure to defeat the guardian itself. I can choose *how* to fight, but not *why*, for reasons I can't even begin to understand.

I dip the point of my sword toward him, in an ironic half-salute. He nods his head slightly, in his only outward show of emotion. I feint twice to the right and then try a slashing move at his knees. He blocks the slash with the staff, hard enough that my sword arm tingles with the impact. I try the same move again, and he blocks it the same way.

This time, I try the same feint, but instead of slashing at his knees, I go for his neck with a vicious backhanded slice. The guardian raises his staff to block my blow, shattering the sword at the hilt. In one smooth motion, he lowers his arm, bringing the end of the shaft crashing down on my shoulder. I fall to one knee, and just barely stop myself from pitching face-first onto the limestone pavement.

The guardian goes back to his post, leaning once again on his staff, waiting on me to make the next move. A hot wave of emotion flares through me, sharper than the pain in my shoulder. I make my way to my feet. I taste frustration, sharper than acid, in the back of my throat. *Most people*, I think, *have recurring dreams about fun things. I am not that lucky.*

I throw the shattered hilt of the sword at the guardian, as hard as I can. He blocks it, almost negligently. He takes two careful steps toward me and then lashes out with the staff, slamming it into my injured shoulder.

I manage to keep my footing and stagger away from the blow, to the low wall on the side of the bridge. My hands find purchase on the top of the wall, where I steady myself for a moment. I hear, rather than feel, the impact on the back of my head, and then pitch forward into the dark river.

I open my eyes, expecting to wake up in my room, turn over, and go back to sleep. But all I can see is the silt-brown flow of the water, and all I feel is the current carrying me into the depths of the river. I cannot tell in which direction the surface lies. Some nameless obstacle careens against me, sending me spinning farther in the murk. I am drowning, and I don't know what to do.

In my panic, I see a flash of white and make a grab for it, hoping that it is a rope or a branch I can use to climb out of the rushing water. It is instead a hand that grasps my wrist, but instead of welcoming flesh it is brittle bone. I struggle to get away, but the bony hand will not let go. It pulls me farther down, into the absolute blackness of the river bottom.

I AM ASHLYN REVERE

I open my eyes, just a crack, and see thin strips of light on the ceiling. Morning sun rolling in through the blinds, the tentative first wave of August sunshine. I lift my head from the pillow a tiny fraction, to read my bedside clock. Seven-forty-six, and I reach a practiced hand for the snooze button. I press it, and feel a shock of excitement, like a current of psychic voltage rush from my finger to my brain and back again, completing a circuit.

This is it. This is the big day. The one you've been waiting for.

I sit up straight and swing my feet over the edge of the bed. I take a deep breath to burn off the last few scraps of sleepiness. In a few short minutes, I will be on my way to Manhattan for the job interview that I hope will change my life.

I am lost for a moment in indecision and anxiety over what to wear. I have had about twelve job interviews over the last two months, since I graduated from college in June. I usually wear my charcoal J. Crew tweed dress to interviews, but the fabric is too heavy for August. My beige pantsuit has a stain on the jacket from a lunch interview at an Italian place in Morristown. The light gray suit, I decide, is the best

15

alternative, with a white silk blouse to make it look cooler and more relaxed. I study myself in the mirror and see split ends and un-plucked eyebrows and a button on my jacket hanging by a thread. I don't have the time to fix any of it, so it will have to do. I make my way downstairs.

My sister Penny is downstairs ahead of me, tucking into a bowl of cornflakes piled high with bananas. "Looking swanky," she notes, with that special bite of angst and sarcasm you can only master when you're in high school. She is reading on her Kindle—no telling what, but I wouldn't be surprised if she were re-reading *Pride and Prejudice* for the nineteenth time.

"Leave your sister alone," Mom says. "Ashlyn, I have French toast cooking for you on the waffle iron."

"On the what?" I ask.

"I saw it on the Pinterest, and thought I'd try it. You need lots of protein before your interview."

I have a horrible vision of dripping maple syrup all over my light gray suit, but when your mother makes you a special breakfast, you eat it. "That sounds good, Mom," I say. "Thanks."

My mother spends her life running off inexhaustible reserves of nervous energy. The word *relax* is not in her vocabulary. She is typically fidgety and restless, over-involved in every school event, every soccer game, every class project. As a strategy— if not as a survival method—I have schooled myself to under-react around her, not to show her the side of my personality that matches hers, not to let her jittery approach to life overwrite mine. I am nervous now—

about the interview, about whether I'll be late, about whether I'll make enough to cover both rent and student loan payments—but I can't share my anxieties without her amplifying them.

"So, tell me again about the interview," she says. "I know you're meeting with someone in publishing, but I don't know what you'd be doing, exactly."

"It's an editorial assistant job," I say. "It's mostly reading the manuscripts people submit, at least at first. But there's lots of room to move up in the organization."

"You're going to be a book editor soon, I just know it," she says. "Just like Jackie O."

I have never heard of Jackie O, whoever he may be, but I wouldn't tell her that for the world. The green light goes off on the waffle iron, and she takes two slices of bread off it and slides them onto a plate. It's not bad, if you like your French toast crisp. My younger brothers clomp down the stairs, and Mom doles out more cornflakes. Dad follows close behind them and makes his way to the Keurig to fill up his travel mug for his drive to work.

"How soon will you know if you got the job?" Mom asks.

"Not right away," I say. "They're interviewing people all week. It's a competitive process."

The last two words come out a little tense. I have been living at my parents' house since I graduated from the University of North Carolina in May. After three months spent churning out resumes and obsessing over the details of my LinkedIn profile, I am no closer to achieving gainful employment. This is the first interview in weeks where I think I have a legitimate shot at getting an actual job, and I don't intend to waste it.

"Do you want any more French toast, dear?" Mom asks. "There's a couple of slices left."

"No, thank you."

"Can I have them?" Penny asks. Penny has the appetite of a Burmese python.

"Do you know how to get there?" Mom asks. "You don't want to miss the interview because you're running late."

"It's in Lower Manhattan, so I'm driving to Jersey City and taking the PATH train from Journal Square. I should make it there in plenty of time."

"Wait a second," Penny says, around a chunk of French toast. "You're going to New York?"

"What if I am?" I reply.

"Does that mean you're moving out of my room? You and all those old books, I mean."

"I am not living in *your* room. I am living in *my* room."

"Girls," my father says, not looking up from the coffee maker. This has the subtext of *this is the thousandth time you have had this argument, and everyone else is tired of hearing it, so kindly shut up.*

"And I don't know where I would live," I say. "If I get the job, I'd be working in Manhattan. I'd love to live there, but it's so expensive."

This is a polite understatement. There is no way I can afford to live in Manhattan on an editorial assistant's salary. Even Brooklyn is too expensive. I can maybe just manage Hoboken if I can find a roommate. But whatever the sacrifice is, I'm ready for it. Anything that gets me out of this house is worthwhile. I dearly love my parents and my siblings. But I worked my tail off through four years of undergrad to earn my independence, and it is tremendously frustrating that I am still far away from achieving it.

"Where in New York?" Penny asks.

"Over by Madison Square Park."

Penny takes a bite of waffled French toast. "It's a perfect day to explore the city, and you get to go while I have to stay here. It's so unfair."

I have heard those three words from Penny my whole entire life. It is unfair that I am four years older than her. It is unfair that she didn't get to take over my room when I went away to college. It is unfair that I am healthy, and she is sick.

Penny was born with cystic fibrosis, a genetic disease that causes the buildup of thick, ropy mucus in her lungs. It impacts her breathing, and requires her to eat a great deal, even by hungry-teenager standards. She is on a detailed medication regimen that's more complicated than integral calculus. Every time she leaves the house, she runs the risk of developing a bronchial infection—which can put her in the hospital for a week. That, in turn, limits her options as far as work and going to college. And unless she can get a lung transplant, she is going to die before she's forty.

I know this, and she knows this, and we have both internalized it, but she cannot stop herself from bringing up the essential unfairness of things. I learned long ago not to respond to her when she acts this way, but I never stop feeling bad about it.

"Penelope Dawn Revere," Mom intervenes. "Do not talk with food in your mouth."

"Sorry, Mother." Penny takes another bite of French toast and gives me a calculating look.

"It's okay, sweetheart. Ashlyn, do you need to leave right this minute? I can fix that button on your coat before you go. You want to be sure to make a good first impression."

I know she means well. I know that. But if I let her do this one thing, she's going to notice more, and it's going to make me that much more nervous and I'm already nervous enough. "I really do need to go, but thanks. If I leave now, I should be there in plenty of time," I tell her. She wishes me good luck and gives me a hug. Penny doesn't say another word to me; she just goes into the bathroom for what I presume is a good sulk.

Dad walks out the door with me and gives me a quick hug on the driveway.

"So this is the big interview," he says. "Do you know who you're talking with today?"

"Probably not anyone you've ever heard of," I say.

"Come on," he says. "Give me some credit."

Behind the cool accountant façade that Dad displays to the world beats the heart of a paladin, and his preferred reading material reflects that. His high-fantasy paperback collection isn't just organized, it's cross-referenced in triplicate. Of course he knows who the top editors in the genre are. I let loose a sigh. "His name is Gary Baxter," I say.

"Gary Baxter? He runs Berserker Books. They published Hal McAllen's series, the one about the invasion of Utopia."

"That's him," I say. "Berserker got bought out by one of the big conglomerates."

Dad's eyes wrinkle a bit. "Your mother, for some reason, is under the impression that you are going to be editing literary fiction, not pulp genre trash."

"You love pulp genre trash," I say. After I devoured all the Harry Potter books, he set me loose on his classic high-fantasy paperback collection. This was much to the despair of my mother, and eventually, the University of North Carolina English department as well. I mean, it's not *that* big of a stretch to compare and contrast Virginia Woolf with Ursula Le Guin.

"Don't get all judgmental on me," I say.

"I am not being judgmental. Not one bit. Your mother, however, is more than a bit judgmental about people who mislead her about things like this. As you should already know."

"If I get the job, I'll explain it to her. If I don't, then there's nothing to worry about." Except being unemployed for the foreseeable future, that is.

"You'll do fine," he says.

"I'm so nervous," I confess. My father is as restful as my mother is worried; he has to bear my anxieties as well as hers. "What if I'm not who they're looking for? What if I say the wrong thing? What if come across the wrong way?"

"Relax," Dad says. "You are going to go in there and be very impressive. And if this publisher won't hire you, there are other opportunities."

"What other opportunities? I have sent out endless résumés into the screaming void. This is the only shot I have right now. If I don't get this job, I'm going to be stuck here forever, living in the same room, dreaming the same old dreams."

"That wouldn't be so bad, you know. Some of us have been stuck here for a long time ourselves."

"This isn't about you. It's about me. And I have to do this. I have to get it right, and I'm nervous, and I'm babbling, and I *know* I'm babbling, and how am I going to talk to a total stranger if I can't talk to you?"

He doesn't respond. He takes a deep breath, and then another, and waits for me to do the same.

"You know what I'm going to say, don't you?" he asks.

"That I should try to control my emotions."

"I am not telling you not to *feel* your emotions, sweetheart. But you don't have to *display* them when they come to the surface. It's okay to feel nervous, but you shouldn't act nervous. Okay?"

"Okay," I reply, sounding more confident than I feel.

"You got this," he says.

Dad is getting gray now, with a network of wrinkles around his eyes from a lifetime of staring at balance sheets. He has a fine analytical mind, I know. If he says I am going to do fine, I have to believe him.

"I got this," I repeat.

"You'll get the job. Don't worry. Remember who you are. You are Ashlyn Revere."

"I am Ashlyn Revere," I say.

Dad gives me another hug. "I love you. Good luck. Knock 'em dead."

"I love you, too."

He gets into his car, gives a little wave, and drives out carefully, and then he is gone, on his way to remunerative employment. I want to do that, too, so much that something catches in my throat. But the only way to make that happen is to ace this interview, and to do that I have to control my emotions. I am not doing that so well at the moment.

HEAR THE SIRENS

I am in my hand-me-down Honda and trying to make the left turn onto the highway, but the guy in front of me is texting someone and doesn't know that the light has changed. I honk at him in a friendly way, but when we get to the next light, he picks up his phone again. I decide that turning right is the better part of valor. That puts me on Amwell Road, which I can take all the way to New Brunswick where it crosses Interstate 287. I'll catch the Turnpike from there and cross the bridge to Jersey City.

I think about switching on the radio, but I don't want the distraction. I want to focus on this interview. Mr. Baxter is going to ask me about my background and experience, and I don't have a lot of either. I don't know where I want to be in five years, and I never remember what my worst trait is, other than being a nervous wreck about job interviews.

It does not take me long to drive out of town and through the fields and woodlands of Central Jersey. The summer sunshine promises to be blazing. Traffic is light at this hour of the morning. The strip malls replace the woodland as I get closer to New Brunswick.

Once I move out, I think, *this is the way I'll come back to visit.* Whenever that is, wherever I go—I will come back. I'll spend summer Sundays in New Jersey, sitting on the back porch, watching Dad vulcanize innocent hot dogs and hamburgers, while my brothers wrestle in the tall grass, and Penny complains about Mom and Mom complains about Penny. I love my family, and I want my independence. Why can't I have both?

I slow down for a red light and hear a loud coughing sound from the rear of the car. I tense up and my foot hits the brakes hard, harder than I'd intended to, and I lurch against the seat belt. I look up, and my car has stopped fifty feet short of the intersection. The driver behind me blasts his horn, loud enough to make me jump half out of my seat. I look in the rearview mirror and see Penny emerging from the floor of the back seat.

"What the actual hell," I say. "You scared me to death."

"Sorry," Penny says. "I didn't mean to. Are we almost there?"

I suppress a scream. There is no good reason for her to be in the back seat of my car, and all sorts of good reasons for her to stay home. She must have snuck into the car while I was talking to Dad.

"Why are you back there? Do you not know that I have a job interview today?"

"You're going to Manhattan, and I was going to be stuck at home all day, doing nothing. I never get to go anywhere or do anything fun."

"I am not going to Manhattan for *fun*," I say. "I am going on a *job interview*. I don't have the time or the inclination to babysit you."

"But you're stuck with me," she says. "You can't just drop me off here, and you don't have time to drive back home and drop me off there. I'm coming with you whether you like it or not."

"You are *so* not coming with me to the job interview." I have a sudden vision of shaking the hand of Mr. Baxter and having to explain, exactly, who this teenager is with me, and why she is wearing a surgical mask.

"Of course not. I'll just sit in the lobby or something and wait for you to be done. I've got three Regencies loaded on my Kindle, so I'm okay waiting for as long as you want. After that, we can go and have lunch. There's a Shake Shack across the street in the park."

"I can't believe this," I say. "You are out of your mind. Don't you care if I get this job or not?"

"Of course! I want you to get the job, so you can move out and I can get my room back. It'll be fine. Do you think we can get *Hamilton* tickets? Probably not. But Hamilton is buried in Manhattan, right? We could go see his grave. Make a day of it. Doesn't that sound like fun?"

"First of all, that was never your room. Second, I am calling Mother and having her meet us at Jersey City, so she can pick you up."

"Won't work," Penny says. "She said she'd be leaving right after we did, to take the boys to Flemington to get school clothes. She's halfway there by now, which means it will take her forever to make it to Jersey City. And you don't have the time to sit and wait with me, and you can't leave me there all alone. Anyway, I already texted Mom and told her where I was, so she wouldn't freak. She thinks you invited me along."

"You did not."

"I did. And that makes you responsible."

Penny knows she has me over a barrel. I have always shouldered more than my fair share of household responsibility, over and above the traditional big-sister role. Mom and Dad have been so consumed with Penny's needs that I was forced to become far more self-reliant than most kids my age. When my twin brothers were born, I had to take on a good bit of the baby care responsibilities, too.

But mostly I was responsible for Penny. I had to help with her cystic fibrosis treatments, holding her hand to calm her down. Every time I played with her, I had to pay attention to her breathing, and keep her from getting too excited. When I woke up in the middle of the night, I checked to make sure she was okay before I could go back to sleep. Even when I was in Chapel Hill, I texted Penny every so often to make sure she was all right. Responsibility was a habit that I couldn't drop.

But if I have to play the part of the responsible child, then Penny has to play the part of the sick child. "Setting aside the obvious risk of infection,", I explain, "we're going to have to walk from the parking garage in Jersey City to the train station and then walk across the World Trade Center station to where the subway is. Are you going to be able to walk that far?"

"You did not just say that to me," she says. "My own sister, doubting my abilities. Anyway, I have all my bases covered. I've got a mask, and hand sanitizer. This time of day, there shouldn't be a lot of people on the train. And my lung function is really high right now. It should be safe for me to go."

"You still have to walk through the subway station. You know what can happen when you get overexerted."

"I brought my portable oxygen concentrator. And we don't have to take the subway. We can take a cab or an Uber. My treat. I still have all my birthday money from Aunt Iris. I even brought all the medication I'm scheduled to take."

I am cornered. There is no way out. I am going to have to drag my sister to my job interview. Not only is this deeply frustrating, but it pushes me back into my old role of being responsible for Penny. It's wrong to resent her, I know that, and I don't want to have that emotion, but I can't help feeling it, either. I want to tell her how I feel—how important this interview is to me, how annoying she is being right now, how I don't need the additional stress right at this moment—but saying anything at this point is going to lead to another of the knock-down drag-out fights that we had so many times when I was living at home. I grip the steering wheel and force myself not to say anything I can't take back.

I pull up to the light at Easton Avenue, in the left lane to make the left turn which will put me on the interstate. I look ahead to check the light, which is still red. A bright-blue Volvo in the northbound lane on Easton is stopped, trying to make the left turn. It moves forward, just a touch. A gray van—a glazier's van, with a sheet of glass mounted on the outside—is heading south on Easton. I watch as the van clips the front fender of the Volvo and flies into the air.

Pain. A deep core of pain, that expands and radiates throughout my body. A vast expanding universe of pain. Broken glass everywhere. A trickle of something runs down my cheek, but I can't brush it away. My left arm is enveloped in pain, and I can't move it. I can't move my right arm at all.

Penny is in the back seat. I can't hear her, and I can't turn my head to see if she's all right. Somehow not knowing how Penny is feels worse than the pain.

"You're going to be okay, lady. Stay with me."

I hear the voice, low and confident. I know I am supposed to say something, but I can't. I whimper, and that seems to be enough.

"Okay okay okay. Everything's going to be all right. We called nine-one-one, okay? They're sending an ambulance. The hospital's just down the road."

I am crying. I can feel it, the salty tears stinging at a cut on my face. I open my eyes, and all I can see is the spiderweb constellation of what used to be my windshield.

"It hurts," I say, and I am surprised I can say that much.

"I know you're scared," the voice says. I don't know who it is, some stranger, some good or at least concerned Samaritan. "Is there anybody I can call?"

"I need help," I say, and it comes out as a cough.

"Okay. What's your name, sweetheart?"

"Ash," is all I can say. My breath is getting shallower. I think about ashes, and dust.

"And you, in the back, what's your name?"

Penny is not answering. I let out a wordless moan. The pain is growing, becoming malignant.

"You hear the sirens, Ash? They're coming. They're almost here. You're okay, sweetheart. They're going to take you to the hospital. All you gotta do is..."

OR 12

"Sinus rhythm returning to normal," a voice says.

"Good. Breathing is shallow and regular. Right pupil is blown. Pulse-ox?"

"Still low."

"Okay, keep her on oxygen. Can you hear me, miss?"

The lights overhead are dazzling, and I snap my eyes shut. The horrible wrenching pain is back. I try moving my arms and legs, but I can't. "It hurts," I say, because it does, and because I cannot bring myself to ask if I'm paralyzed.

"I know it does," the second voice says. "You're being very brave. We're going to try to make you better. You understand why you're here?"

"Car accident," I say.

"That's a good sign, then."

"Pain," I say.

"Just hold on a little longer," the first voice says.

"Okay, listen," the second voice says. "You're at Robert Wood Johnson Hospital. I am your trauma surgeon. My name's Anne Dixon. We're taking you into the operating room. Just be patient, all right?"

How is Penny? Where is she? All I can say is "Sister," and I hope that is enough.

31

"The girl in the back seat is your sister?" This is the first voice. She sounds concerned, and so is probably a nurse. "The ambulance driver found your phone. Your mom and dad are on their way. Just relax, okay? We'll get started soon."

"How?" I can't get the rest of the sentence out.

"If you're asking about your sister, she's fine. Just relax. We'll take good care of you."

I don't know whether to believe this or not. But if Penny is here, they're caring for her, too, and there's nothing I can do to help. And I have my own problems at the moment.

I open my eyes, but all I see is a spinning universe of ceiling tiles. It's disorienting, so I close them again. There is a searing pain on my left side, and when the cart hits a bump in the hallway, the pain radiates in every direction. I try to concentrate on breathing, which is the one thing I know I can do for myself.

When we stop, I look up and see another doctor, probably an anesthesiologist, with kind eyes and a purple surgical mask. "I'm going to put the mask over your face now," he says. "I need you to relax, and try to breathe normally."

"Wait," I say. He just said something important, and he doesn't realize it. He doesn't know. "Penny," I explain.

"Penny?" he asks.

"Cystic."

The anesthesiologist's eyebrows raise up. "Your sister?"

"There was another girl in the car," Dixon says,

"They're looking after your sister. Don't worry. Breathe deeply when I put the mask over your face."

I try telling him that Penny has CF, but it comes out as a hiss.

"I know you're worried about your sister, but you should calm down. If you start hyperventilating, I can't give you the anesthetic."

I sink back into the bed. The doctors have to know, and I can't find a way to let them know.

"Relax," the anesthesiologist says. He puts the mask on my face, and I can't move my arms to stop him. "There you go."

I breathe in, as slowly as I can. I try to blot all the sad and scary thoughts out of my mind, like the pain I feel, and the deep concern I have for my sister, and the job interview I was supposed to have in New York, and I realize, *oh God, I'm not going to make it there in time,* and I take one last deep breath.

NEUROLOGY CONSULT

Dr. Drew Kingman hustles his way into the emergency room, half out of breath. He is running a bit late—not his fault, there is a track repair issue on the Northeast Corridor that caused his train to leave the station late from Newark Penn. He ran flat-out from the New Brunswick train station after he received the text about the accident. Two victims. Neurology consult.

Louise Parker is there, emergency room nurse, short, spare, and competent. "White female, age eighteen or so. Brought in unconscious. Car accident—a glazier's van pancaked on top of them. There's a lot of superficial cuts, but they look worse than they are. The other victim went to OR."

"Head injury?" Kingman asks.

"Looks that way."

Kingman does his initial round of checks. No bleeding around the skull. He gently lifts her eyelids, and both pupils are dilated. "Did she throw up?" he asks.

"In the ambulance."

"Okay. Definite head injury, I'd say. Take her down for a CT scan so we can see how bad."

"What about her breathing?"

Kingman stops, listens, and hears the wheeze in her lungs for the first time. He hadn't noticed. He checks the monitors, and the pulse-ox is low.

"Doesn't sound right," he said. "If her brain stem was damaged, she'd be struggling to breathe on her own. It would be a really high-pitched sound. That sounds more like she has TB or double pneumonia, or else she's a dedicated three-pack-a-day smoker. Put her on oxygen for the time being, see if you can get her stable enough for a CT."

"Yes, doctor."

"How bad was the other victim?"

"Worse. White female, twenty-three or so. She was in the front seat. They took her up to OR 12. Dixon saw something on the X-ray she didn't like."

"Did she call in Torrez?" Dixon is a trauma surgeon, and a good one, but if the other victim has a skull fracture serious enough to warrant emergency surgery, that means there needs to be a neurosurgeon in the operating room. Torrez is on-call, and he has the best hands.

"No. Livingston." Thoracic surgeon, chest-cutter.

"Did she not have a head injury?"

Parker puts the oxygen mask over the girl's face. "Probably. She was a mess."

Kingman watches the oxygen monitor, which is starting to trend in the right direction. The patient sounds like a retiree on emphysema, but she couldn't have that at her age. "Check her for pneumonia and TB," he says. "I'm going to OR 12, see if I can help."

Parker frowns. "Dixon won't like that. She's not your patient."

"I got called in to consult, I'm going to consult."

Kingman heads toward the operating suite, hangs up his lab coat, scrubs in, puts on a mask, and announces himself. "Kingman, neuro. How can I help?"

"A little busy here, Dr. Kingman." Dixon has a good bedside manner for a surgeon, but she saves it for patients.

"You called for a consult, I'm here."

"That was before the X-ray showed she had a shattered rib poking her pericardium," Livingston says. "Suction."

"Skull fracture?" Kingman asks. Obviously, keeping the patient from having a fatal heart attack in the emergency room takes precedence over anything else, but an untreated skull fracture can be every bit as fatal.

"Depressed fracture, longitudinal," Dixon said. "Not serious enough to warrant surgery, at least not right now. Let us account for all these broken ribs and get her stable, and you can check her out."

"Was she conscious when you brought her in?" Kingman asks.

"Yes," This is Patel, the anesthesiologist. "Conscious, although she'd passed out at the scene. Very agitated, though. Worried about her sister. Wouldn't stop talking about her."

"That's not what she said, doctor." This is an ER scrub nurse; one Kingman doesn't recognize with her mask on. She is tall, with pale skin. "She said 'cystic,' not 'sister.' Whatever she meant by that."

"Cystic," Kingman repeats. "Why would she..." *Oh, wait. Yeah. Cystic fibrosis. The sister, that's why she's having difficulty breathing.* "Cystic fibrosis—never would have thought of that. Be right back."

"Thanks for the visit, Dr. Kingman," Dixon says. "Stop by anytime."

A Large Black Rabbit

I lie alone in the quiet darkness, listening to the silence.

I am afraid to move. I do not know where I am or why. I lie still on the cold ground, wondering if I can move or not, and willing myself to find out. I try to move my arms, and do so successfully, which is reassuring. I sit up and hug my knees close to my chest.

I feel no pain, for which I am grateful. It is dark and quiet and peaceful. I can make out the form of a creature next to me, who appears to be a large black rabbit. I consider picking him up and cuddling him, but that would wake him.

I get to my feet and take a good look around. I am under a spreading ash tree in the predawn quiet. A green meadow stretches in every direction as far as I can see, dappled here and there by the white blossoms of wildflowers.

The rabbit wakes from its sleep, its ears twitching. "Are you all right, Lady Ashlyn?" it asks. The rabbit has a kind voice, with a cultured mid-Atlantic accent.

"I'm not sure," I say. "Where are we?" *Obviously, someplace where rabbits can talk,* I think.

"That should be left," the rabbit says, "as an exercise for the student."

"I'm not a student anymore," I said. "I graduated. Cap and gown, the works."

The rabbit twitches his whiskers. "Nevertheless. You must work it out for yourself, or it will not mean anything to you. Where do you think you are?"

"I have no idea," I say. "I was injured in a car accident. The last place I remember was an operating room in the hospital. I went under anesthesia."

"That is where you were," the rabbit says. "Where are you now?"

"I don't know," I say. "I mean, I see the tree, and the meadow, and the flowers. Could be anywhere, I guess. Do you know where we are?"

"I cannot give you the answer," the rabbit says. "What else do you see?"

"I see a talking rabbit," I say. He is solid black, dark as the dark places, with deep glossy fur. There is a faint touch of pink about his ears, but otherwise he could have been carved out of ebony. His eyes are wide, even darker than the rest of him, if that's possible. He has a serious expression on his face, which is all that's keeping me from giving him a hug. I think we could both use one.

"So you do. What conclusions do you draw from that?"

"We're not in Kansas anymore?" I guess. "Although, you know, if you said we *were* in Kansas, that would be kind of comforting. At least we would show up on GPS."

"Please try to stick to the facts. What else do you see?"

I look down to see what I'm wearing. I have my comfortable old Carolina-blue hoodie on, and a fresh pair of blue jeans, and the black Chuck Taylor sneakers I wore in high school. I am not wearing my light-gray suit, and wonder what became of it.

"The sun is coming up," I say. "There are plants, so that implies an oxygen atmosphere. I don't think it's the real world, but maybe it's modeled on someplace in the real world."

"What do you mean by the *real* world?" the rabbit asks.

"A meadow like this in the real world would have ants. And mosquitoes. And fences. This place doesn't have any of that. It's like reality, but it's better in a lot of ways, so that makes it different from reality."

"What is reality?"

That is an unexpectedly deep question for a black rabbit to be asking. "Is this that David Foster Wallace thing? Where the fish don't know what water is?"

"How would a fish learn about water?"

"You pull the fish out of water, it will learn pretty quick," I say.

"Just so," the rabbit says.

"I'm a fish out of water?"

"Perhaps not. A fish out of water would be struggling to get back into the water. And if it stayed out..."

"It would die. Is that the answer? Am I dead?"

The rabbit twitches his nose.

"Oh, come on," I say. "That's a simple enough question."

The rabbit still won't answer. I take a deep breath and consider. Of all the possibilities, *dead* holds the least amount of appeal. I decide against it. If I'm wrong, well, there's nothing I can do about it, so there's no need to worry. Or I don't think so.

"I don't think I'm dead," I say. "If I was dead, I'd be either in Heaven or Hell. I'm not wearing a white robe, and I don't have angel wings. I don't see Saint Peter or Grandma Ruth anywhere around. Doesn't sound like Heaven to me, and there's no fire or sulfur or eternal punishment that would tell me if I was in Hell. And I am just fine with that, because either Heaven or Hell would mean that I was dead, and I don't feel dead. The logical conclusion is I am dreaming now. It fits with the known facts, and most importantly, it means that I'm not dead. As a theory, it has that going for it."

"Well reasoned," the rabbit says.

"It also means that if I want to leave, all I have to do is wake up."

The rabbit looks concerned. "If I may be so bold as to make a suggestion," he says.

I give the rabbit the same quelling hand signal that Mom gave me when I was twelve and I was trying to tell her something important about *Dragonriders of Pern*. "Okay, Ash," I tell myself. "Wake up. Wake up. Wakey, wakey, eggs and bac-ey. Wake up wake up wake up." But nothing happens.

"As I was saying. Do not try to wake yourself up."

"Why not?"

"All you are doing is causing yourself stress and anxiety, for no good reason. You are here because this is a calm and tranquil place. Embrace that."

I suddenly feel tired and achy all over. I find a comfortable shady spot in the meadow and sit down. "So, what can I do here? Walk around? Maybe leave and find a nice warm coffee shop somewhere?"

"You should rest," the rabbit says. "You have been through a traumatic experience. You must recover before you go anywhere. That would be the responsible thing to do."

"What about Penny?" I ask.

The rabbit twitches his nose again. "Penny is your sister?"

"Yes, she is. She was in the back seat of the car when I had my accident. I think she was hurt, too, and she has cystic fibrosis, and I'm worried about her. Do you know what happened to her?"

"I do not," the rabbit says, not unkindly. "I am sorry."

"Can I see her? Here?"

"You may see images of other people from time to time. But they are illusions and memories, not flesh and blood. You may see your sister or your parents, but only as reflections, not as they are. What happens to you, or your sister, on the mortal plane depends on factors outside my control, or yours. You should rest."

"How am I going to get any rest?" I ask. "It's the first thing in the morning."

"Is it?" the rabbit asks.

I lie back down on the grass. The sun wheels over the meadow, far faster than it ever does in real life.

The sky above turns blue, and then red, and then twilight gray. The rabbit settles in beside me, quite close, and I give him a good cuddle at long last.

At the edge of the meadow, just as the sun goes down, a long unbroken line of campfires blaze into life. I close my eyes and go back to sleep.

A Very Sick Young Lady

"Let's start with the good news," Kingman says to the couple in the waiting room. They are ashen with fear and worry, holding each other's hands like refugees.

"Any good news would be welcome," Mr. Revere says.

"The good news is that just before she went into surgery, Ashlyn told a nurse that Penelope has cystic fibrosis. We didn't know that at the time. We wouldn't have known how to treat her in the emergency room. Ashlyn saved us a lot of time figuring that out— although of course you told us when you got here."

"She is the responsible one," Mrs. Revere says.

"The other good news is that the X-rays came back negative. Penelope doesn't have a skull fracture. There is evidence of a severe concussion on the CT scan, but it doesn't look like there's going to be permanent brain damage. Still, she hasn't regained consciousness, so we'll have to keep her here to monitor her."

"It's not safe for her to be here," the husband says. "I don't know what you know about CF, but she's going to catch an infection if you're not careful."

"Unfortunately, we don't have a lot of choices. I made the decision to put her on a ventilator."

"We'd hoped to avoid that," the wife says, and underneath the worry on her face, Kingman sees the strain of nearly two decades of CF treatment. "We've seen instances in other patients where they go on a ventilator, and they can't breathe independently afterward. Penny has worked so hard to stay independent; I'd hate to see her lose that because of a car accident."

"I understand, ma'am," Kingman says. "Believe me, I don't want to keep her on the ventilator longer than necessary. I'd rather see her breathe on her own. But with a concussion, at least we know this way we can keep her breathing while her brain heals. And since she's in ICU, it's a more sterile environment, so we shouldn't have to worry about infection. It should just be temporary, that's what I hope. I'm going to consult with her pulmonologist in the afternoon; he's on a flight to Seattle for a conference at the moment."

"What about Ashlyn?" the wife asks.

"Your daughter Ashlyn," Kingman says, "is a very sick young lady." *Sick* is not the right word, and Kingman knows it, but he can't think of anything else as accurate.

The parents tense up at this, as Kingman knew they would.

"The primary concern that the trauma surgeon had was with her internal injuries. Those were the most serious initially—the collapsed lung, and the splinter of bone near the heart. Both arms were broken, and the right collarbone. She's going to need some reconstructive surgery on her left wrist.

Ashlyn...should make a complete physical recovery from the trauma. Eventually."

Kingman waits a long moment for the parents to take a breath before he explains about the brain injury.

PAIN AND GRIEF AND HEARTBREAK

I wake up under the spreading ash tree. The rabbit is still asleep, and I do not have anyone to talk to or anything to do except think about my situation. It feels odd to fall asleep in the middle of a dream and then wake up again in the same dream. My guess is that I am not really waking up and going to sleep, but instead slipping in and out of REM sleep, which seems reasonable enough.

I decide to do a little exploring, just in the local area. There's a wide, marshy pond, with a small white gazebo near the shore, and I watch the water lapping quietly against the bank. I kick off my sneakers to do a little wading, but the water is bone-cold. I jump back almost instinctively, but this is the first actual sensation I have felt since I arrived here. I put my feet back in the water, and the cold travels up my leg, as though my blood vessels are drinking in the chill. I check to see if my feet are turning blue, and that is when the skeletal hand reaches out of the water.

A wave of terror courses through my system. I try to move, but my feet are frozen in place. The bony hand grasps my left ankle and pulls me deeper.

This is just a dream, I tell myself. *A scary dream, where I am being dragged into the depths by a skeleton.* And I remember that I had this dream, just last night. I had been able to wake up from that one. Here, I am not so sure I can.

The skeleton grasps my ankle. I try to yank it back, but my legs are frozen, and I can't get them to move at all. I lose my balance and fall, with my rear end bumping on the shoreline. The skeleton drags me closer to the water. I grab hold of one of the posts of the gazebo, and scramble, crab-like, out of the water. It is just enough to keep the skeleton from pulling me in the rest of the way. The skeleton keeps tugging at me, but after a couple of minutes of futility, it lets go. I scoot myself farther away and clutch my frozen legs to my chest.

The hand retreats into the tiny lake, and I breathe a strangled sigh of relief. The rabbit hops over to me, concern on his little furry face. "What is wrong?" he asks.

I point towards the water. "There was a..."

The water of the pond ripples and a fully-formed skeleton arises from the lake. There is a crown of magnolia flowers on its head, pale against the whiteness of the skull. The skeleton holds out its bony arm, beckoning me back into the water.

"I see," the rabbit says.

"That's all you can say? I almost drowned."

"You would not have drowned," the rabbit says. "You would have just died. If that is any consolation."

The skeleton is still beseeching me to come into the water.

"So that thing out there just literally tried to kill me?"

"Not in the way you mean that, no. She is not a murderer, or even malevolent. But if you seek her out, you will die."

I scuttle backward, trying to keep as much distance between myself and the skeleton as possible. My legs are still ice-cold, and I would run out of the meadow if I could move them.

"Okay, wait. I almost drowned in another dream, last night, and I didn't die. If it gets me now, that doesn't mean I am going to die in real life, right?"

"Last night, you were in perfect health, lying on your own bed," the rabbit explains. "Right now, you have been injured in an accident. A symbolic death could become real enough."

I was surprised by the skeleton grasping my ankle, and then frightened when it came out of the water. Now I am absolutely afraid. Did the surgery go wrong? Is this how I die? Here, in my dreams, with a skeleton carrying me to the bottom of a pond? I hug my icy legs closer to my body.

"I don't want to die," I tell the rabbit.

"Please do not be frightened," the rabbit says. "It is all right, whatever happens. If it is your time to go, I will go with you, and comfort you as best I can in your journey. And of course, you can always choose to go, if you want."

My teeth are chattering, and not with the cold. "Why would I choose to die?"

The rabbit looks at me, kindness in his round eyes. "Because there are worse things."

I remember my friend Mark from high school, who walked in front of a train two weeks before graduation. I remember my Grandma Ruth in her nursing home bed, staring at things that just weren't there. I remember my roommate Laura from college, whose mother had breast cancer and fought hard through chemotherapy, just so she could see Laura graduate. And I remember the long passage from the emergency room to the operating room, the bright lights in my face, the strained tones of the doctors, trying to reassure me, although what they were trying to reassure me about I do not know.

Am I going to be okay when I wake up? Am I going to be paralyzed, or worse?

The skeleton stares at me with its unseeing eyes, beckoning me onward. It takes a step closer, out of the water, and it is wearing the exact same pair of shoes on its bony feet as I had been wearing. Not just the same model, but the same scuffs and wear. I swallow hard and turn toward the rabbit.

"I don't want to go with her," I say.

"Then do not. It is your choice. But consider that even if you leave here, and go back to your own place, you will be facing a great deal of pain and grief and heartbreak. There is one way to avoid all of that."

The skeleton takes another step closer. I feel the pain and fear of the accident all over again. I struggle to breathe. I feel the fierce fiery bloom of pain in the middle of my chest. I know l will bear the scars of the accident for the rest of my life, however long that is. I have no idea whether I will pick up a real book again, or work for a living, or walk.

50

The skeleton reaches down and touches my face, its bony hands gentle against my cheek. The pain recedes, vanishes. If I go with the skeleton, I will not have to worry about any of that, or anything else, ever again, because it would all be over.

And I don't want it to be over. I don't know how badly injured I am, or how much pain I am going to have to endure once I wake up. It doesn't matter. I am not going to willingly choose to end my life here and now. There's a big wide world out there full of college basketball games and strawberry milkshakes and high fantasy novels, and I'm not going to turn my back on all of that just yet. Not while there's hope.

"No," I tell the skeleton. "No way. Not today."

I pull back from the skeleton's touch and heave my body backward. Life and heat return to my legs. The skeleton turns its eye sockets on me, something close to a sorrowful expression in its manner. It sinks soundlessly back into the water of the pond, without as much as a ripple.

"Are you quite all right?" the rabbit asks.

I stumble my way over to one of the benches in the gazebo. "You might have mentioned that there were skeletons in the pond," I say. "That would have, like, been useful." I am starting to have some real concerns regarding the rabbit's commitment to my personal safety.

"You have to understand the symbolism of this place before you put yourself in more danger. You are in a weak state. Rest, and pay attention."

"Pay attention to what?" I ask.

"Paying attention to your surroundings would be a nice start. You do not yet know what you do not know."

"Wait. Of course I don't know what I don't know. Unless you're saying that there are things that I don't know that I should know, but still don't know. I think I just gave myself a headache."

The rabbit, for once, looks at a complete loss. "Perhaps I can simplify. This is a dangerous place, but it is more dangerous because the dangers here are so different than the dangers you experience every day in your own place."

"Even if that's the case, it doesn't tell me *why* I am in mortal danger here." *Or whether the rabbit is part of that danger or not.*

"You are a human," the rabbit explains. "You are, if you'll pardon the expression, part body and part spirit. Part material and part immaterial. You can travel in both realms. And both realms can be dangerous, especially if you are not prepared."

"But my body is here, now," I say. "Some material part of me must be here."

"Look at yourself," the rabbit says. "A close look. Go on."

So I do. At first glance, my body is not any different than it always is. I am wearing what I usually wear—blue jeans and a light-blue UNC sweatshirt. Somehow, my sneakers are back on my feet, although

I'm not sure how or when that had happened. I have the familiar pattern of moles on my left wrist that has always been there. But my fingernails look different. I'd painted them a bright scarlet for the job interview. But here, my fingernails are plain and unpolished.

"Do you see what you expect to see?" the rabbit asks.

"Let me think for a minute. This is an immaterial realm, or so you have said. That implies that the clothes that I am wearing are not real. They represent my real clothes, in the real world, the same way my body represents my body in the real world, but they are not real themselves. That's why my sneakers got back on my feet when I got out of the lake."

"Correct."

"Let me try something." I hold my left hand out in front of me and pass my right hand over it. A ring appears on my finger—the silver-and-emerald ring my parents gave me when I graduated high school. I wave my right hand again, and the ring vanishes. I pass my hand over it again, and the ring reappears.

"Cool," I say. "I can do magic."

"That is not magic," the rabbit says, with a tinge of frost in his voice.

"Well, magic in the sense of an illusion. Because everything here is an illusion, isn't it?"

"No," the rabbit says. "It is not. That is why it is dangerous. There are things here that will test you. You can run from them, or you can fight them. It is better to fight them, if you can, and if you have the heart for it."

"What about..." I incline my head toward the pond.

"Perhaps not," the rabbit says. "That is a fight you would not win."

"And what about you?" I ask.

"What about me?"

"Well, you just said this is a dangerous place. Are you part of that danger?"

The rabbit twitches his whiskers. "I am no one you should fear. I am also no one you should cross. I will help you, if I may, and protect you to the extent that I can. But you will need to learn to fight, and quickly."

"So, what am I supposed to do?" I ask. "I've been fighting one of those things—there's a guardian by some bridge somewhere—for years now, and I've never once won. I've fought for so long that I've forgotten why I'm even doing it. So fighting doesn't work for me. And you're going to teach me how to do that? How to fight whatever else it is I have to fight? Don't take offense, Mr. Bunny Rabbit, but you don't inspire confidence as a mentor here."

"I will ask you, please, not to refer to me as a *bunny*." The rabbit's voice is frosty again, "Show some respect, if you do not mind."

"Can I ask you a question, then?"

"You have done little else since coming here."

"What am I supposed to call you, then? What's your name?"

The rabbit wiggles his ears. "I cannot tell you my name, for I do not have one that you would readily understand. You may call me by any name you like, so long as it is proper and respectful."

"How mysterious of you. Maybe you're a secret agent. Rabbit. James Rabbit."

"If you must."

"All right then. Fine. You should have a nice rabbit name. That means *Watership Down*, then. I would go with Fiver, but you're a little big to be the runt of the litter."

"You are not serious."

"Blackavar, maybe? Although he got his ears ripped up. Your ears are just fine."

"I would hope so."

There is one other book I remember that features a rabbit; I have read it a thousand times to my little brothers. *I am a bunny*, I quote to myself. *I live in a hollow tree.*

"Nicholas," I say. "Perfect. It suits you."

"If you are thinking that I am Santa Claus," the rabbit says, "I am sorry to disappoint you. I am nothing of the sort. I am here to guide you, and to be your companion on the journey to come. If you will have me, of course."

"The journey to come?" I ask.

"Yes. We cannot stay here. It is safe now, but it will not be for long. We do not have much time for me to tell you everything you ought to know."

SCARLET KNIGHT

The first thing I learn from Nicholas is not sword-fighting but instead is the inverse square law.

I spent four years at the University of North Carolina, and in all that time, I did not learn one thing about the inverse square law. It works like this: the sun, the earth, and the moon all have gravitational attraction, which means that they all pull things toward their centers. The earth exerts the biggest pull because it's closest to us. The moon is smaller and farther away, so it has a tiny pull on the tides. The sun is huge, but it's so far away that it doesn't pull us in, which is overall a good thing.

The same law applies in the realm of dreams. I have the most control over the things which are close to me. This means I can wear any clothes I want to, and I can change them instantly. All I have to do is concentrate. To start with, I try out the jumpsuit that they were wearing in the last *Ghostbusters* movie. This is utilitarian but not flattering, so I switch to a *Firefly* costume, complete with long brown coat. I ask Nicholas to set up a mirror so I can admire the effect, and I look *incredible*.

"We do not have a great deal of time for vanity," Nicholas says. "You have enemies here, although you

56

do not realize it. If they find you, and you are not prepared, it may go ill for you."

"Spoilsport," I reply.

I cross my arms and blink, and instantly I am wearing a *Sailor Moon* outfit, complete with short blue skirt and long white gloves. My hair shifts into these long pigtails, so I shake my head to coil them into a set of Princess Leia cinnamon buns, and it works.

"Can I change the color?" I ask.

"Of course," Nicholas says. I try long, dark hair over the black-leather getup that Scarlett Johansson wears in the Marvel movies and feel deliciously indecent. Then I switch over to a *Lord of the Rings* elf costume, and sure enough, my ears get all pointy. I am so pleased with the effect that I change over to a form-fitting blue *Star Trek* uniform, with Vulcan ears and a chili-bowl haircut.

"Enjoying yourself?" Nicholas says dryly.

"Immensely." I am not that much into cosplay, but if I were, this would be heaven. I try the Queen Elsa transformation from *Frozen*, where she changes her hairstyle and her dress all at once (although I don't sing the song).

"Impressive," Nicholas says.

"I know. I wish Penny was here to see it," I say, and then immediately feel guilty. I don't know where Penny is, and Nicholas won't tell me, so the only recourse I have is to feel guilty about it, and that's frustrating.

"Can we, perhaps, choose something practical for the next phase of the lesson?" Nicholas asks.

"You got it," I say. The princess dress falls away, and I find myself in a kind of urban-ninja getup—black T-shirt with the Punisher symbol tucked into dirty black jeans and scuffed black work boots. I look like an extra in a zombie movie.

"That will do," Nicholas says. "What do you know about weapons?"

As it turns out, I do not know as much about weapons as I thought I did. I can manifest a sword well enough, but I have next to no idea how to fight with one. I try a lightsaber next, but when I go to slice something with it, it doesn't do anything. It's just a fancy flashlight.

If the lightsaber is difficult, handguns are impossible. The inverse square law bites you in the rear with projectile weapons. In the real world, you use gunpowder to move the bullet incredibly fast out of the barrel. In the dream world, you have to use your mind to propel the bullet the way you want it to go, and the farther away the bullet gets, the less control you have over it. Then I try a longbow, Katniss Everdeen-style, and that is even more embarrassing. I am strong enough to pull the bow back, but the arrows simply will not fly. This means that, when I go to fight the guardian to cross the river, I am going to have to do it up close and personal.

"Perhaps we should start with something simpler," Nicholas says. "Something that you will not hurt yourself with. Like a stick."

"I am doing the best I can here. If I can't use regular weapons, what other alternative is there?"

The rabbit looks thoughtful for a long moment. "There is someone who can help you, in ways that I cannot. He can determine what an appropriate weapon would be for you, and he can teach you how to use it. But he and I are...not friends. You will have to decide whether or not you can work with him."

"So how do we find him?"

"It is not that easy," Nicholas says. "There are two ways. We can start walking away from the park, toward the river. It will take some time, and we will doubtless run into trouble on the way."

"The hero's journey," I say. I'd taken a folklore course at UNC. "Any way we can, you know, short-circuit that?"

"We can," Nicholas says. "But it will be upsetting for you, you see. It has to be."

"What do you mean, *upsetting?*"

An air horn goes off, loud and insistent. I see a vast heaving sea of faces and lights. I see the court, and everything becomes clear. I am at Rutgers, in the basketball arena; I can tell from the big scarlet R at half-court. The Scarlet Knights are wearing their home white and are pushing the ball out of the backcourt. The Rutgers point guard has the ball and is trying to drive down the lane, but he can't find a clear path and throws it out to the perimeter. The shooting guard steps back to take the three, which misses long. The Tar Heels center gets the rebound and heaves the ball down the court. The Carolina guard gets the easy layup.

I look around me. I don't recognize whoever it is to my left. Dad is to my right, on the aisle. There is an empty seat between us, with a blue parka with pink stars on it.

"Where's Penny?" I ask.

Dad can't hear me or isn't paying attention.

"Penny! Where is she?"

Dad looks over to me but doesn't say anything. Penny should be there. She always sits in between us when we go anywhere, which isn't that often.

"Where is she? Dad!"

Dad doesn't say anything. He doesn't recognize me. I push past him. Penny has to be around somewhere. I run down the stairs towards the court, screaming her name. I'm responsible for her. She could be lost and having trouble breathing, and nobody here knows how to help her. I get to the railing and turn around. There are ten thousand faces and none of them are Penny and I don't know where she is.

I turn around, and a police officer is at my elbow. He is tall and forbidding in his blue uniform, and I take a step back. He has a short scruffy red beard and pale blue eyes. He takes my arm, but in a nice way, to get my attention.

"We found your little sister. She's okay. I can take you to her."

"Oh, thank God." My knees turn to butter. I stagger, and the arena starts to spin in a way that arenas are not supposed to.

"You're going to be okay. Everything's going to be okay."

The air horn blows for the end of the timeout.

And then, just like that, I am back in the meadow.

"Everything's going to be okay," the police officer repeats, although he is no longer a police officer. He had been just over six feet in his police uniform, but now he looks half a head taller, swathed in a black leather and chain mail getup. His red beard is longer now and forked. His muscles are ropy and lean, and he carries a long sword in a sheath. His scarlet gloves are studded with wicked-looking metal rivets on them. A long, immaculate red duster trails behind him.

I sink down on the gazebo bench. "Is Penny okay?" I ask.

"No," the tall man says. "You are both in grave danger."

"You just said that she was okay. What's going on?"

"I apologize for the deception. I had to tell you that your sister was all right to get you to calm down. It was the best way to get you out of the situation that *he* put you into, to frighten you." He cocks his thumb in the direction of Nicholas, who is cowering under the opposite bench.

I hurl a few choice words in the rabbit's direction.

"It was necessary," Nicholas whimpers. "He would only come if he thought you were being threatened."

"Is Penny okay?" I ask.

"Nothing has happened to her that I know about," Nicholas says. "The best way to get *him* involved was to put you in an environment where you were in an intense state of fear. I surmised that a threat to your sister would accomplish that."

"You got that right." My entire body is shaking with stress and residual fear.

"I would be happy to dispatch this rodent for you, Lady Ashlyn," the tall man with the red beard says, "if it were possible, which, *unfortunately*, it is not."

"Can you two quit sniping at each other and concentrate on, you know, actually *helping* me?" I ask.

"Lady Ashlyn," the tall man says, "do you know *anything* about your companion?"

"Well, now that you mention it, no," I say. I had not given it any thought.

Nicholas twitches his whiskers. "I am fulfilling my role, as you are fulfilling yours."

"And your role is?" I ask the tall man.

He pulls himself up to his full, impressive height. "I am Sir Roland Hargrove of Summervale, Warden of the Western Marches, and I am here to protect you," he says. "To the best of my ability, which is formidable. I cannot protect you from yourself, mind you, but I can stop outside forces from harming you, with sufficient warning." He glares at Nicholas, who is still hiding under the bench.

"And your role, Nicholas?" I ask.

"I am a comfort," the rabbit says.

Sir Roland grunts. "Oh, come on, rodent. You can do better than that."

Nicholas hops out from under the bench and into my arms. "It is true."

"Not complete, though," Sir Roland says. "It is enough for now. You have summoned me, and I am here. What would you have me do, Lady Ashlyn?"

"Some answers would be nice," I say. "What do you mean by 'Summervale,' and why do you call me Lady Ashlyn? Why don't you like Nicholas? And what's going on with Penny, and why am I in danger, and what can I do about it?"

"I can answer the last question for certain," he says. "You can fight. That is all you can do. If you want to escape this place, and this rodent, and rescue your sister, you can fight. There is no alternative."

"Nicholas said you could get me a weapon," I say.

"Well, he's right about that," Sir Roland says. "I *am* a weapon. If you have enemies, I will fight them."

"That is not why I summoned you, Sir Knight," Nicholas says. "She faces a long and difficult struggle—both in Summervale, as you call it, and in her own place. She will need to learn to fight if she is to succeed."

"Lady Ashlyn is no fighter. She never has been. She needs my sword to defend her."

"Ashlyn has to learn how to fight for herself. And quickly. You could teach her, if you would."

Sir Roland considers this for a long moment. "Stand up," he says.

Nicholas hops out of my lap, and I stand up. I think I look like a fighter in my urban-ninja getup, but I know Nicholas is right. I don't know how to fight, not in this world I don't. I haven't had to fight in the real world, ever, but it looks like I might have to.

Sir Roland gives me an appraising look. "You are not strong enough," he says. "You need far more training than I can give you in a short time. And I do not think you could use any weapon I gave you effectively. But your rodent friend has a point. Whether you are ready or not, you are going to need to fight, and fight hard. There is no alternative."

"Both of you are talking about fighting," I say. "But I don't know who I am supposed to fight, or why, or what I should be fighting with."

"Well stated, Lady Ashlyn," Sir Roland says. "I do enjoy a challenge, you know. We can begin."

"No," I say. "Not until you tell me about Penny. Not until you tell me why we're both in danger."

"Very well," he says. "Your sister is somewhere within the Eastern Marches, across the river. She is held captive by a nameless, shapeless entity that wishes her ill. You must cross the river and rescue her, before it is too late."

"That just tells me why Penny is in danger. You said we both were."

Sir Roland nervously adjusts the fit of his long scarlet gloves. "If you have to rescue her," he says, "that puts you in the same amount of danger. I would have thought that would have been obvious."

Nicholas makes an amused little snort at this.

"Fine, then, rodent. Do you want me to tell her? Or would you rather have the honor."

"I would not dream of interrupting you," Nicholas says.

"Tell me what?" I ask.

"Very well. Lady Ashlyn, as long as you remain here, in my domain of the Western Marches, you are under my protection. I do not say that you are *safe*, necessarily, but if you are in danger, I can protect you. Once you cross the river, my powers are weaker. As you grow closer to the Eastern Marches, you run the very real risk of falling into the hands of the Dark Lord."

"The who now?" I ask.

Rise and Fight Again

"When you say *Dark Lord*," I ask, "what specifically are we talking about? Is he like Evil with a capital E, or is he just kind of moody every so often?"

"Yes," Sir Roland says.

"No," Nicholas says.

"I would appreciate some consensus on this issue," I say.

"He is the enemy," Sir Roland says. "My enemy, and yours. He is the source of all your dark thoughts and negative emotions. He is anger and fear and hate, all put together. He must be destroyed. And you, Lady Ashlyn, are the only one who can destroy him."

"You have got to be kidding me," I say.

"I am completely serious," Sir Roland says.

"You are always completely serious," Nicholas replies.

"This is the plot of all the third-rate fantasy novels I've ever read," I say. "The chosen one has to confront the Dark Lord. I mean, *come on*. This is ridiculous."

"The Dark Lord is quite real," Sir Roland says. "And the danger you are in, and your sister is in, are also quite real. The only way to eliminate that danger is for you to defeat him. There is no alternative."

"And here my mother told me that I was wasting my time reading all that genre fiction," I say. "Let me tell you something, Mr. Knight, and Mr. Bunny Rabbit. No, thank you. You want me to rescue my sister, I can see that. But going up against some random Dark Lord, because I am in some unspecified, danger, I'm saying that's a hard pass. Do you hear me on this?"

"I thought," Nicholas says, "that we had agreed not to use the term *bunny*."

"Yeah, yeah, yeah," I say. "Sorry. But my point holds. I don't have any interest in going after some random Dark Lord because it's a plot point or something in some fantasy novel I read once. If the mission is saving my sister, that makes sense to me. I'm ready to go. But don't just stand there and tell me that there's some Dark Lord out there I have to defeat just because you say I have to. That's not reasonable."

"You are making a mistake," Nicholas says. "You are viewing this realm through the lens of your own perception, which in turn is colored by your experience. If you have spent your time reading fantasy fiction, well then, this realm may appear to you as a scenario out of one of those volumes. But that does not make the Dark Lord any less real, and it does not alleviate the danger that he poses to you and your sister."

"It still doesn't make any sense," I say. "How come I am the one who has to fight him? Sir Roland is a foot taller than I am, and he knows how to use a sword. Let him do it."

Sir Roland makes a minute adjustment to his gauntlets. "I have battled the Dark Lord often, but every conflict between us always ends in a draw. I would destroy him if I could, but I cannot. The only one who can defeat him—the one who can *destroy* him—is you."

"This is getting ridiculous. Let's just assume for a second that there's an actual, real Dark Lord out there, and I have to fight him for whatever reason. Which I kind of doubt, but okay."

"You are having a conversation with a knight in armor and a talking rabbit," Nicholas says. "Why is it so unreasonable for there to be a Dark Lord?"

"It just sounds so contrived," I explain. "Look. I have read every fantasy novel that there is. And all of them have some sort of big bad character. A Dark Lord. A White Walker. A Wicked Witch. What have you. And then the hero—or the heroine, depending on what kind of book it is—is the Chosen One who has to defeat the Dark Lord. There's like a million variations. Call to Adventure. Refusal of the Call. All that good stuff. So here you guys are, telling me that I have to destroy the Dark Lord. That's Storytelling 101, right? That's all this is, a story I am telling myself to distract myself from the reality that I'm in a hospital bed somewhere. Right?"

"Wrong," Sir Roland says.

"The Dark Lord is a symbol," Nicholas says. "But he is a very powerful symbol, of something very real. He is the personification of the negative aspects of your personality. That makes him powerful."

Okay, that sounds sort of worrisome there. "Just how powerful are we talking about here?" I ask. "Because, believe it or not, I have a lot of negative stuff going on here."

"He is only as powerful as you allow him to be, Lady Ashlyn. If you are willing to fight him, you have a chance. If you show him weakness, though, he will corrupt you. If you allow him to grow stronger, he will destroy you utterly."

"The rabbit is correct," Sir Roland says. "For once."

At least the two of them agree on something. "If the Dark Lord is a symbol of negative emotions, then what about positive emotions?"

"That would be my master, the Lord of Light," Sir Roland says. "He is far from here."

"And not likely to show up, then?"

"As you say."

"And that makes Nicholas..."

"Your friend and guide," the rabbit says.

"Oh, come now," Sir Roland says. "He is far more than that, Lady Ashlyn."

I give Nicholas a searching look, but he just scratches himself with a back foot. I take a deep breath.

"But what about Penny?" I ask. "If the Dark Lord is just a part of my personality, how is he some kind of threat to her?"

"I do not believe that he is," Sir Roland says. "The Eastern Marches are home to many a dark and evil force. I do not know the true nature of the entity that has captured your sister, except that it is not the Dark

Lord. But the longer she is in its clutches, the worse it will be for her. You should leave as soon as we can get you some training."

"So I'm in danger from the Dark Lord, and Penny is in danger from something else, but we don't know what. This doesn't sound like information I can do a lot with."

"I do not know what has happened to your sister," the rabbit says. "I suspect what has happened, as usual, is more complicated than what the knight is telling you. But if you cross the river, the Dark Lord will seek you out. And it is possible that the Dark Lord may use your feelings for her against you, so be on your guard."

I sink down on the bench of the gazebo. It is a calm place, a quiet place, and I do not want to leave. It may be that the Dark Lord is a serious threat to me, although I don't understand how or why. I figure that it can't hurt for me to protect myself, either way. I don't want to seek out danger or fight anything if I can help it. Staying here seems as good of a strategy as any, and I could do just that if I only had myself to worry about.

"I will cross the river into the Eastern Marches to rescue Penny," I say in a still, small voice. I am not exactly sure how I am going to do that, but she is my responsibility. I will figure something out. "If I have to defend myself, then I will, but I need your help to do that. If you're both willing."

Sir Roland sits next to me on the bench. Nicholas hops back into my lap.

"It is a hard thing that you will have to do," the knight says. "I do not envy you. But you have made the right decision."

"I will go with you," Nicholas says. "I will be your guide, and assist you as I may."

"What do I have to do?" I ask.

"You will need to travel," Sir Roland says. "Cross the bridge into and find where your sister is being held captive. Rescue her if you can. It will be a hard journey, with many dangers, and will require a level of courage from you that you haven't yet mastered. But you will."

"So when do I leave?"

"First we train," the knight says.

We start off with hand-to-hand fighting, which proves that I have no real idea of how to punch anyone and less idea about how to defend myself from being punched. The experience at least is not all that painful. When Sir Roland conks me on top of the head, it stings for a moment, but I am able to jump back into the fray and get hammered again.

Sir Roland tries to punch me, and I finally manage to slip his punch and counterpunch, the way you do in video games. He grins at me and then does a Chuck Norris-style roundhouse kick that connects with my ear. I am flat on my back, staring into the endless blue sky, and all of a sudden, I cannot get up anymore.

"Are you ready to get up?" Sir Roland asks.

"No," I say. "I am the opposite of what ready is. I would just like to lie here and bleed awhile. Metaphorically speaking, of course."

"This is not working," Nicholas says.

"She is getting better," Sir Roland says. "Marginally. Use makes master. Shall we continue?"

I bite back a sarcastic reply and pull myself off the ground. Penny is somewhere in the Eastern Marches, and no matter how ridiculous this all sounds, the only way I am going to rescue her is to learn how to fight. Sir Roland tries to kick me in the ear again, and this time I remember to duck.

Now we move on to swords. Sir Roland's sword is commonplace, nicked and dull and utilitarian, but effective. I pull the best sword I can think of out of my imagination—the "Green Destiny" from *Crouching Tiger, Hidden Dragon*—and it is a beautiful, gleaming thing, inset with jade. But it is lightweight and strong. I raise it high above my head and charge toward Sir Roland with all my might. He raises his blade against it, and I am left with a hilt with a shattered edge.

"Pretty blade," Sir Roland says. "But pretty doesn't count for much."

"You've got to be kidding," I say. "That is a legendary blade. They fought a whole war over it in the movie. How does something like that just *break*?"

"The blade is nothing," Sir Roland smirks. "Your mind is *everything*. Train your mind, and the sword will follow."

I come up with a plainer blade, lighter and needle-thin. I decide to try circling around Sir Roland, with some vague idea of getting him to lunge at me, which would open him up for a counterattack. I get about halfway around, and then he fakes a lunge, takes a step back, and watches as I stumble forward. He smacks me on the back of my head with the flat of his blade, and I fall face-first into the dirt.

"I could teach her to fall down like that," Nicholas says.

"Give it time," Sir Roland says. "She is getting better. At least she isn't giving up."

"Is that an option?" I guess, although I know what the answer is.

"Once more into the breach, Lady Ashlyn," Sir Roland quotes, and raises his sword, waggling the point a little in my direction.

I am overcome with a desire to wipe that smirk off the knight's face. This time I wait for him to make the first move. I parry his attack, but my blade shatters again. Sir Roland raises his sword and takes a step toward me, intending to mow me down with the flat of the blade again. I drop the hilt of my sword and focus my mental energies toward stopping him. "*Expelliarmus*," I shout.

A red jet of flame sparks toward Sir Roland and snaps the sword from his grip. His empty hand flies into the air, and the momentum swings him around, unbalancing him just enough that he spins around and drops, rear end first, onto the grass of the meadow.

I look down and find that I am now wearing a black robe and a blue-and-gold striped scarf. In my hand, I find an eight-inch wand—not just any wand, but *my* wand, the one I created in my (thankfully) unpublished Harry Potter fan fiction. It is just as I imagined it would be, made from cherry wood, with a unicorn-hair core and a golden four-leaf clover stamped on the base. I wave it in the air and shout "*Lumos!*" and the end of the wand flares into light.

Sir Roland gets up onto his feet. "What enchantment is that?" he sputters.

"The potentially useful kind," Nicholas says. "Can you use it to do anything else?"

"I'm not sure. Let's see." I point my wand at Nicholas. "*Geminio!*"

Nothing happens.

"What was that supposed to accomplish?" Nicholas asks.

"I was trying to make an exact duplicate of you," I say, a bit disappointed.

"That would perhaps not be wise. Maybe something else?"

I try some simpler spells. I can send out green sparks, but I cannot summon anything heavier than a pine needle. I suppose that just reading books doesn't substitute for an actual magical education.

"You have to figure out a better weapon than that," Sir Roland says. "It might work, once, to surprise someone, but you're not going to be able to fight the Dark Lord's minions with just green sparks."

"Wait a second," I say. "Minions? What sort of minions are we talking about, exactly?" I am picturing the tubby little yellow characters that look like allergy medicine.

"Will you show her, rodent?" Sir Roland asks. "You did such a good job of disturbing her last time."

"I would not dream of denying you the opportunity," Nicholas says.

"Very well. Are you ready, Lady Ashlyn?"

"You keep asking me that," I say.

"It is fortunate for you that I do. The Dark Lord will not show you any such courtesy." Sir Roland claps his hands. Nothing happens for a long moment. I look around and don't see any kind of minion. And then I spot it, a dark dot in the sky. The dot circles around, getting closer, until I see its true shape and scream in pure fright.

"Is there a problem, Lady Ashlyn?" Sir Roland asks.

"That...that is a flying monkey," I say, nearly choking on the words.

"Observant," Nicholas says.

"No no no no no no. You do not understand. That is a *flying monkey.*"

The monkey swoops down from the sky and lands in front of me, and then sits there, chittering at me, and beating its wings. He is wearing the classic uniform, complete with blue-and-red fez. I can hear my metaphorical heartbeat surging in my ears.

"Okay," I say. My teeth are chattering, and I have to stick to one-syllable words. "Make that thing go away. I mean, right now."

"You are afraid of him?" Sir Roland asks.

"*Of course I'm afraid of him,*" I shriek. "Hello? Flying monkey."

"From your childhood," Nicholas says. "An old fear."

"It's from a movie. My mom plays it every Christmas." The monkey flaps his wings, and I manifest a new sword. "You stay away from me, Mr. Flying Monkey. You got that?"

The monkey yelps defiance, takes to the air, and charges at me from above. I flail at the monkey with the sword, mostly by instinct. I just clip him, but it is enough to bring him to the ground. The monkey clenches his little paw and shakes it at me.

"Nicely done," Sir Roland says. "Now move in for the kill."

"Excuse me?" I say. "The what?"

"You have to kill it," Nicholas says. "Just stab it in the heart."

The monkey flaps its wings in rage, but my sword has severed an important part of its wing structure, and it cannot get airborne. It is not—to my relief—a *talking* monkey. I know I couldn't stab a talking monkey. I am not at all sure I can stab this one.

"Can't you just wave your hand and make him disappear?" I ask.

"Finish him," Sir Roland says. His face now is almost as red as his beard.

I look at the monkey's adorable embroidered vest, and drop my sword. "Sorry," I say. "Can't do it. Not in cold blood, not like that. I don't believe in killing things for no good reason."

Nicholas waves a forepaw, and the flying monkey disappears. "You will have to face horrors much worse than this," the rabbit says. "And they will do their best to destroy you. You will have to fight them, and kill them if necessary."

Sir Roland spits into the dirt. "If you can't stab a wretched little flying monkey, how will you save your sister?"

"I will fight much worse things than this to save my sister," I say. "But not in cold blood, not for no reason."

"I understand what you are feeling," Sir Roland says. "You are feeling strong emotions—fear, pity, even love. And those emotions have their place. But you have to keep them under control, especially here. If you can do that, you can accomplish what you need to accomplish."

"I can feel my emotions," I say. "But I don't have to display them."

"Very well said, Lady Ashlyn. Although it is not always easy to do that."

"I know."

We spend the afternoon and evening working on swordplay. I learn about the importance of keeping my guard up when Sir Roland leans in and slashes me hard on the shoulder. It stings like crazy, but only for a second, and the cut heals itself instantly. This is comforting, in an odd sort of way. "Does this mean that I'm invulnerable?" I ask. It would be nice to have a superpower.

"No," Sir Roland says. "It just means that I am trying hard not to hurt you. Not everyone will be as courteous."

"You call this courtesy?" I ask.

Sir Roland beams again, his smile splitting his face as suddenly as a hatchet would have. "I do indeed." Then he hits me with the flat of his sword, knocking me face-first into the dirt. I bounce right back up again, though, and swing my sword around in a wide arc. The point catches Sir Roland on the inside of his elbow, and he howls in pain.

The sun is setting behind the trees by the time Sir Roland sheathes his sword. "You have learned much, Lady Ashlyn. "I am not altogether sure that you are ready, but there is no time."

"I don't think that I'm ready, Sir Roland," I say. "I will do my best. But I had hoped to train a little longer."

"I would like that, Lady Ashlyn. But you must rescue your sister, and therefore I must take my leave of you, and return to my own place."

"What is that like?" I ask.

"It is a fair land, with many wonders. You have been there before, many times, although you do not remember."

"I have?"

"You have," Sir Roland says. "We have had many happy adventures together, you and I, especially when you were little. But they all fade away in the morning, and the memories pass with time. And as you get older, the dark thoughts and the dark memories begin to take over, and dreams become confused and frightening. That is what you have to face, and what you can destroy, if you are strong enough."

"I will do my best," I say. "I have to try—if not for me, then for my sister. But it's scary. I don't know where I'm going, or what I can accomplish."

"You have a guide," Sir Roland says. "You will know what to do when the time comes. And I have a gift for you, to help you on your way."

"Well, thank you," I say. "I don't have anything for you, though."

"Don't feel bad," he says. He hands me a sword with a white hilt, sheathed in a jet-black scabbard.

"I think we've established that I can't handle one of these very well," I say.

"Read the inscription on the scabbard," the knight says.

Draw Dyrnwyn, it reads, *only those of noble worth, to rule with justice, to strike down evil. Who wields it in good cause shall slay even the lord of death.*

I'd held the Green Destiny in my hands, but I'd never felt its power. This sword *is* power.

"Draw it," Sir Roland says. "See what happens. But carefully."

I draw the sword from its scabbard. It is a black sword, and its blade gleams in the sunlight. At the tip, it has a bright blue flame, just like a pilot light. I hold the sword above my head, and dancing blue flames ripple along the edges.

"You are familiar with the blade?" Sir Roland asks.

"Definitely. From *The Chronicles of Prydain*. But can I actually use Dyrnwyn? You know, with the noble worth thing?"

"The sword sufficed for an Assistant Pig-Keeper," Sir Roland says. "If you use it for a good purpose, it can do you no harm."

"You cannot give her that sword," Nicholas says. "It is far too powerful for her to use. The damage she can do is incalculable—not least to herself."

"Bite me," Sir Roland says.

"Oh, I have been longing to," Nicholas replies.

"Okay," I say. "Okay okay okay. You two are the *only people I know* in this whole ridiculous place, and you won't stop sniping at each other. Can we please stop it? Okay? For me? I am not asking for much here."

Sir Roland and Nicholas stare at each other, and Nicholas blinks first. He hops over to his spot under the gazebo bench. Sir Roland walks over to me and puts a reassuring hand on my shoulder. "I wish there was more that I could do to guide and protect you, Lady Ashlyn; I wish you a pleasant journey and a successful one. Goodbye."

"Goodbye," I say, and Sir Roland walks down the path to the wooded fringe at the end of my consciousness, where he fades away, and then disappears.

"We have a long journey tomorrow," Nicholas says. "Best you get some sleep."

I lie down in the soft grass of the meadow, Nicholas by my side. In the distance, a ring of campfires crackles and snaps. I yawn deeply and draw Nicholas close to me, feeling his soft warmth.

STANDARD PROCEDURE

Kingman has a nasty little habit. He rationalizes it, the way everyone else rationalizes their nasty little habits, but he knows that it is... well, not *wrong*, but unprofessional.

So there he is, in the stairwell of RWJ University Hospital, standing in a corner, iPhone in hand, looking up Ashlyn Revere's Instagram profile.

This is not cool, and Kingman knows it. There is no reason for a doctor, a medical professional, to go around snooping on patients on social media. It's not what you're supposed to be doing, and who knows what Hippocrates would have thought.

What Kingman tells himself is that he's trying to build rapport with a patient. That's what he would do with any other patient who was not lying insensate in the intensive care unit. Yes, he's talked to her parents, and gotten an idea of who they think she is, but looking at her Instagram gives him an idea of how she wants to present herself. A few selfies, but not many. She's smiling in the few that she's posted—at graduation up at Chapel Hill, at some rock concert somewhere, along the beach at Point Pleasant. Some pictures with friends, at restaurants and bars. Not much with her family. A couple of professional pictures, of course—the father said she'd been looking for a job.

Ashlyn Revere is tall, taller than Kingman, who is just five-seven. In the pictures, she has a heart-shaped face, framed in ash-blonde hair. *Jolie blonde,* as they would call her back home in Kingman's native Louisiana. She has a little crease between her eyebrows, and Kingman wonders if it's a result of stress or if maybe she needs glasses. Kingman flips back through earlier pictures, some of which show Ashlyn in a Carolina-blue uniform; she'd played varsity field hockey for two years before a wrist injury in her senior season. Young, bright, athletic, headed for a job interview in New York.

Kingman puts his phone in the pocket of his lab coat and walks up the last flight of stairs. Ashlyn Revere is still in intensive care. Her blonde hair has been shaved off, and her skin is winter-pale against the white sheets, except where the bruises show.

Kingman has been working for twelve hours, and he's bone-tired and ready to take the train home—in fact, he started taking the train to work because he'd fallen asleep in the car in the middle of Route One. He should have left already, but he had to check on Ashlyn Revere before he left. Dawson is the ICU nurse tonight, and he's looking relatively unruffled. "How's she doing?" Kingman asks.

Dawson waves towards the EKG. "I think she just went to sleep again," he says. "Probably the best thing for her. There's been quite a lot of activity, though, although it kind of looks weird, somehow. Can't put my finger on it."

"Intracranial pressure?" Kingman asks. This is the crucial factor. Ashlyn Revere has a subdural hematoma, a giant crescent-shaped blood clot inside her skull, and it's got the potential to squeeze the life out of her brain. The pressure is already high, and it needs to come down. Kingman has ordered putting her into a medically induced coma to do just that.

"Stable," Dawson says, which means that it's not going up, which is good, but it's not going down, which is bad. But all the other vital signs look good, Kingman thinks, or at least what's good for someone who's nine hours out of serious thoracic surgery.

"I think she's stable enough," Kingman says. "We can try to bring her temperature down." This is the standard procedure for brain injury; you bring the body temperature down to just a little over the standard for hypothermia. It can bring down the intracranial pressure. If she'd just had the head injury, it would have been done first thing, but Dixon's surgical judgment had been right; removing the splinter of rib near Ashlyn Revere's heart had to take priority.

"All right, doctor," Dawson says. "I'll take care of it."

That is it, all that Kingman can do for her. He decides to take the elevator, so he doesn't run the risk of falling asleep walking down the stairs. He crosses Easton Avenue and makes his way up to the train platform. He doesn't have long to wait for New Jersey Transit to send the next one, and he's asleep before his rail car crosses the bridge over the Raritan River.

TO STRIKE DOWN EVIL

I wake up the next morning, and the good news is that I am not sore after a full day of training and swordplay, the way I would be in the real world. And I don't have to shower or wash my hair or even brush my teeth, so that is nice. The morning air is a little chill, so I wear my favorite red flannel shirt, sturdy khaki slacks, and tan Timberland boots. I put on the sword belt, with Dyrnwyn hanging from my left hip. I do not feel stronger or more confident with the sword. I am unprepared and very much alone. I remember my Tolkien and put on a long coat of lightweight silvery chain mail under my shirt. It is comfortable and comforting, and I like the subtle jingle that it makes.

I look down at the sword belt and notice that there is a slim pocket stitched into the belt, just to the right of the scabbard. I manifest my eight-inch cherrywood wand, and it fits perfectly in the pocket.

And I remember something from a book I'd loved when I was a kid, something I hadn't thought about in years, and I wonder what would happen if I try it here. I slip the wand out of its pocket and wave it where I think the horizon might be, out there in the gloomy darkness. Nothing happens.

I try again, but this time, I hum a tune while I wave the wand. It is a simple tune, an old Cat Stevens song called "Morning Has Broken," of all things, that my mother sang to me when I didn't want to get out of bed in the morning. I concentrate on the song and wave my wand in time with it. And this time it works, and the horizon begins to glow with the first thin yellow light of dawn.

I follow that up with the tune that they use in the Looney Tunes cartoons to signify morning, but I don't know any more of that particular piece of music than a couple of bars. I think for a second, and then a new song pops into my head—the "Dance of the Sugar Plum Fairies." This time, I don't just think about the music; I actually *hear* it, as though the meadow is wired for sound. I wave my baton in the general direction of the sunrise, and the thin pink line on the horizon explodes in a vibrant explosion of color. Clouds gather around the sun, glowing in a thousand subtle shades of pink and orange. It is a gorgeous, operatic sunrise, and I am creating it.

As the last strains of Tchaikovsky fall away, the colors start to fade, the clouds scud away, and the sun shines a dull yellow in an empty blue sky. I wave the wand around a little, but I can't make the scenery change at all. I consider waking Nicholas up to see if he can help, but he is still snoozing contentedly on the bench of the gazebo.

What else can I do? I ask.

Yeah.

I draw on every car ride with my dad spent listening to the classic rock station, and point my wand to the sky. The music blares out, loud and funky—*1999*, by Prince, off the album of the same name. And *just like that*, the sky turns purple, and the stars come out and trace all these groovy psychedelic patterns across the sky. The moon rises—two moons, in fact, both of them vibrating with the rhythm of the music. I jump up and down with pure glee, singing along with the familiar words. I spin around and catch sight of the rabbit, now wide awake, staring at me with a disapproving look on his furry face.

"Stop that," Nicholas says. "Right now."

I don't care. I keep dancing, until the last words of the song trail off, and all of the purple leaks out of the sky.

"Are you quite done?" the rabbit asks. There is something like a note of panic in his voice.

"I didn't know I could do that," I say. "That was awesome."

"You literally could not have done anything more dangerous," the rabbit says. "You just wrote *Ashlyn Revere is here* in hundred-foot letters across the sky, for the Dark Lord to read. We have to go before his minions close in."

"Where?" I ask.

"We have to get across the river. Now."

He darts off down a path that I hadn't noticed before. I sheathe my wand, gather my sword belt around my hips, and take off after him on a dead run. All I have learned so far about my power in this world is that I still have a lot to learn.

The woods surrounding the meadow are bleak and gray, with leaves of muted reds and yellow, and an occasional chill breeze shakes the branches in the canopy. Nicholas darts from place to place with the speed and cunning that you'd expect from a rabbit; I try to follow as best I can without running directly into trees. But I am slower than Nicholas, and when I trip over a tree root and fall on my face, he is not exactly comforting.

"We need to *hurry*," he says, using just the same inflection that I've heard ten thousand times from my dad, whenever he was trying to get me to put the book I was reading down so that he could bundle me into the minivan so we could go to the grocery store.

I scramble to my feet, with a mild curse under my breath for all the intrusive tree roots and the annoying rabbits of the world. "It would be helpful if I had some idea where we were going, and why we were going there."

"The Dark Lord has his minions prowling the Western Marches."

I ask simple questions, and all I get is doubletalk. It's beyond frustrating. "Could you please explain what, exactly, you mean by *minion*."

My knees buckle under me, and I hit the ground again. I let loose another curse at whatever traitorous tree root that must have tripped me, but then I look up and see a large black beast blocking the path ahead. It looks something like a low-slung panther, but with six legs. I manage to get up to my knees, but the beast dashes toward me and knocks me down again.

This time I hit the ground rolling and use my momentum to leverage myself upright. I draw my sword across my body, but the beast smashes into me a third time, and I can't do anything useful with the weapon. I am flat on my back breathing hard. Now the beast is on top of me, and there is no mercy in its obsidian-black eyes. The beast raises a silver-tipped paw and slashes down at my ribcage, but its claws slide off my chain-mail armor. Score one for *mithril*. The beast whimpers in surprise and pain, and I roll towards its injured paw and manage to get out from under it and onto my feet in a heartbeat. I stand with my guard up, ready to defend myself if the dark, sinuous thing pounces.

I get my first good look at it. The beast is long, from its prominent fangs to the end of its long tail. Its fur is sleek and black, and it moves with catlike grace. Its misshapen head is crowned with short horns tipped with silver and supported by a thick neck and hulking shoulders. Its six legs end in thick, meaty paws, with curving silver talons.

"You're doing very well," Nicholas says, which would be much more encouraging if he wasn't hiding under a thorn bush.

The beast circles to the left, keeping its dark eyes on me, staying just out of reach of a sword lunge. When the beast lashes its tail and snarls, it does not move from its position. I come to the late realization that the beast is now blocking the path we were taking through the woods. I take a tentative step, and the beast does not move. I can see the long muscles in its back bunch, as if coiling for a spring at my throat. I keep my guard up, as Sir Roland taught me. The tip of my sword burns with a pale blue fire.

The beast makes its leap, and the sword blazes into bright orange flame. The edge of the sword meets the beast at his nose, and I hold firmly to the hilt. The beast's momentum thrusts me back three steps, and I struggle to keep my footing. I take another step back and lunge, striking the beast in the face with a clumsy backhanded stroke.

I realize why I am at a disadvantage. The beast is on all sixes, and is low-slung. To attack it, I have to swing my sword with a downward stroke. But all the time I was sparring against the very tall Sir Roland, I was aiming upward, the better to knock his block off. I have no idea how to fight something that is shorter than I am. I can't lower my sword to slash at it, because that would mean letting my guard down, and the beast will be at my throat. I have to find some way to protect myself.

Ashlyn, you idiot.

I thrust my left arm out and manifest a round shield, and then go into a defensive crouch. The beast blinks, once, and then springs at me. Raising my shield arm, I thrust Dyrnwyn up at the beast, catching it under its middle left leg, and feel the sickening scrape of its bones against the steel. The beast howls in pain as its claws scrabble uselessly at the shield. I give the sword a quick twist and pull it out, flames glistening down its length. The beast falls hard on the forest floor, with its wound giving off puffs of black smoke. I steady my shield and slash at its neck, but the beast dodges the blow. I circle to my right again, and this time the beast, slowed by its wound, lets me get on its flank. I keep my shield up and connect with a long raking cut on the beast's left side. A thin line of black flame runs across the beast's body, and it rolls over on that side to smother the fire.

I know what I have to do, but I am afraid to do it. The beast has to die. I know I cannot leave it behind in its wounded state; it will track me down and find me at some point where I am vulnerable and not expecting it. But I have never killed anything, unless you count that one squirrel that I accidentally ran over on the way down to Chapel Hill my sophomore year. If I kill the beast, I will cross a line that I can never uncross.

The beast is lying there, vulnerable, whimpering in pain. It would be right to kill it, and might even be merciful. I could slay the beast if it was still springing at me—if it was a question of defending myself. I am still breathing hard after fending off its assault, and fear and adrenaline are coursing through my system. But no matter how much the beast frightens me, I can't murder it. Even if maybe it deserves to die. I step around the beast's body, check it to make sure that it won't get up anytime soon, and head for the path that leads to the river.

It turns out that I am a poor judge of how badly a beast can be wounded and not fight. A quick heartbeat after I turn my back on the injured beast, Nicholas emerges from under his thorn bush, rushing past me and leaping into the air. I turn my head to see the rabbit knocking the pouncing beast off to the left before it can land on my back. The beast swipes its silver claws down my spine, but the *mithril* coat keeps it from ripping my flesh. I breathe a small, grateful prayer, and raise my sword. While Nicholas scrambles out of the way, I bring my sword down across the beast's wide back, just as it struggles to its feet. The blow catches the beast squarely, sending lines of flame up and down its spine. The beast rolls over again, and this time I strike my sword deep into its chest. The beast's long body shakes in pain and then lies still. I pull Dyrnwyn away from the beast, and its flames rush to consume it, leaving behind a column of thick greasy smoke. The sword's fire flickers out, and I sheathe it.

"Nice shield," Nicholas says.

I look at the shield closely for the first time, and it has red and white circular stripes, with a white star in the center on a blue field. "How about that," I say.

"We still need to hurry," Nicholas says.

"Give me a second." I am still breathing hard, and the cold air knives through my lungs.

"You were asking what the Dark Lord's minions look like," Nicholas says.

"Yeah," I say. "Figured that one out."

THE RESPONSIBLE ONE

We make our way through the forest. I am keeping my head on a swivel, looking out for beasts. After what seems an age of walking, we find a broad dirt road, stretching in both directions, dark and empty. Nicholas lets me slow to a quick walk, which I accept gratefully but silently.

"Are you feeling all right?" Nicholas asks.

"I'm fine," I say, to be polite. I am thinking about the beast and the smell that it made when it burned. "Are we close to the bridge?"

"Not that far," Nicholas says. "Summervale is a big place, you know."

"I had no idea. Why is it called that again?"

"I believe that you gave it that name, when you were small. It is just a name; you can change it if you like."

"Because this isn't summertime. It was summertime back in the meadow, but all of a sudden, it's getting cold. What caused that?"

"I do not know," Nicholas says. "You are correct that the weather is most unusual. I cannot tell if there is anything to worry about."

"I don't understand anything about this place," I say. "Sir Roland said that he was the warden of the

Western Marches. Are there Eastern Marches? Is that the Dark Lord's territory? Do I have my own territory? How does that work?"

Nicholas wiggles his ears, which I now realize is how he displays annoyance. "You are applying your own conventions to this realm. They are not appropriate. There are no fixed borders and very few permanent landmarks."

"So why did I show up at the meadow?" I ask. "That's not something I remember from any dream."

"It is a peaceful place," Nicholas says, "and my home."

"Oh. I didn't realize that."

"This is still a world of your own making," Nicholas replies. "You are using your own memory and consciousness to fill in some of the blanks. There are rough analogs between your world and mine, but they are much more different than they are alike. The sooner you realize this, the sooner you can deal with the things around you effectively."

"Well, then, how come you were able to put me in the basketball arena like that?"

"Simple—I have access to your experiences and memories, to an extent. However, they are necessarily incomplete and fragmentary, and I do not always have the frame of reference to interpret them correctly. For example, there is a large section of your experiences that seems to be related to a talking yellow sponge and his starfish friend, which I cannot even begin to understand properly."

"Television," I say. "Animated images projected on a glass screen. It's a form of entertainment."

"That is meant to be entertaining?" Nicholas asks. "How?"

"It's designed for kids," I say. "Look, as much fun as it would be to keep having this conversation, how do we get to where Penny is?"

"We will walk, and walk quietly. This road leads to the bridge, and then we can cross the river to where Penny is being held."

After a thousand midnights, I have never learned how to defeat the guardian of the bridge. This time, my sister is depending on me to find a way across. I pick up the pace, hoping that I will figure it out this time.

We are walking more slowly now. The cold north wind is blowing more stiffly as the sky darkens. Even with the moonlight, the walk is getting more difficult.

"Do you think we can stop for a bit?" I ask.

"If there were any place to stop," Nicholas says, "I would suggest it."

We look at each other for a long moment, as if we were both daring each other to conjure a hotel out of thin air, complete with clean sheets and room service. But I am too tired to make the effort, and Nicholas, for whatever reason, doesn't choose to try. I shrug and head down the road. There doesn't seem to be anything else we could do at that point except walk, and worry about how I am going to get us across the river.

After another half hour or so of walking, I see a mailbox. It is an ordinary enough mailbox; it had been painted black once, but the color has chipped off here and there. Someone has built a frame around it— nothing fancy, just two boards, placed to resemble an A-frame log cabin, with old rusted Virginia license plates nailed to each side. And there is a small track leading off the dirt road, into the woods.

"This way," I say.

"If I may ask," Nicholas says.

"This is my grandfather's cabin," I say. "Well, I mean, it's the mailbox. The cabin is this way."

"Are you sure?" the rabbit asks.

"I don't know," I say. "The real cabin is way up in Sussex County. Which I know doesn't mean much, from a geographic perspective. And Grandpa Ray isn't there anyway; he's in a nursing home in Hackensack. But that's the mailbox. The way I figure it, worst case scenario, it's a place to lie down for a little while."

"That is far from the worst-case scenario," Nicholas says.

"That mailbox is here for a reason. I say we check it out."

The cabin looks as it always has, with Grandpa Ray's old GMC truck rusting quietly out front. Ray Revere grew up in a little town in southwestern Virginia and worked his way through Virginia Tech to get an electrical engineering degree. He'd spent his entire career at Bell Labs, trying to make telephone switching systems more efficient. But part of him had never left the mountains, and he'd built this cabin up in the Jersey highlands. Most weekends, we would get up early and make the drive north to visit Grandpa Ray and Grandma Ruth. Grandpa Ray and Dad would disappear into a sheet-metal shed out behind the cabin and tinker with car engines or whatever other piece of machinery they had. Penny would sit on the porch and breathe in the mountain air that everyone thought was good for her, and I would wander through the woods and meadows, wondering what my friends were doing. I have happy memories associated with the cabin—mostly because Grandma Ruth was a pastry chef—but it always represents utter crushing boredom in my mind. Although, considering how eventful the past couple of days have been, utter crushing boredom sounds pretty good right at the moment.

"Can we go in?" Nicholas asks.

I walk up the stairs to the porch, and lift up the corner of the doormat and find the key there, just where it should be. I open the door and Nicholas hops inside.

"It looks empty," he says.

I take off my sword belt and stack it on the porch with my round shield. "We should check the kitchen," I say.

I edge to the right because I don't want to startle anyone. Grandpa Ray is at the breakfast table, with his usual coffee mug, with the old "Bell Systems" logo. I can't help myself. "Is that coffee?" I ask.

"Not really," he says. "I wish I could offer you some, though. Come sit down."

I give him a hug, first. He is the first non-fuzzy friendly face I have seen.

"You look good," he says.

He looks good, too, and that breaks my heart. This is the Grandpa Ray I remember, the one who remembers me, the one whose mind has not yet been corrupted by Alzheimer's and age. His wide smile and courtly manners are back, as though time never touched him. For the first time since the accident, I feel a measure of peace.

I sit down from him across the table. "It's good to see you here."

"I understand you were in a car accident. You and your sister, both."

"This van just flew into the air and landed in our laps," I explain. "There wasn't anything I could do."

"How bad was it?" he asks.

"I hurt all over," I say. "They took me to surgery, but I don't know why."

"I understand," he says. "You must have gone through a horrible shock. Would you like to lie down for a while and rest?"

"I feel better just being here," I say. "Seeing you."

"It's the mountain air that does it," he says. "Perks you right up. Will you be staying long? You and your rabbit friend there?"

Nicholas hops up onto one of the chairs. "We do need to be going," he says.

"But you just got here," Grandpa Ray says. "You can wait a while longer. Relax."

I look at Nicholas, but he has a blank expression on his face. I cannot tell if he is anxious to be going, or if there is something desperately wrong about this situation that I do not understand.

"What do you know about your sister?" Grandpa Ray asks.

"I don't know," I say. "They wouldn't tell me anything about her."

"Typical," he says. "Doctors. They don't want to worry you, so they don't say anything. They don't realize that it's worse not to know sometimes. Do you think she was hurt bad?"

"I don't know," I say. "I tried to tell them about her cystic fibrosis, but I couldn't get the words out before they put me under for surgery."

"They'll check her medical records, don't worry," he says. "What I can't figure out is why she was in the car with you."

"I was on my way to the city for a job interview, and she snuck in my car so she could tag along."

"And you didn't take her home?" he asks.

"Well, no," I say. "I couldn't. I had to make the job interview. I couldn't turn around, and I couldn't leave her by herself at the train station in Jersey City." I had forgotten all about the job interview, which had been the most important thing in the world at the time. How did that happen?

Grandpa Ray takes a long swig of whatever it is that looks like coffee, but isn't. "You could have called whoever it was that you were interviewing with. Explained the situation. They would have understood, don't you think?"

"I told them I would be there," I say. "I couldn't go back on a commitment like that."

"You have a sister with a serious disease," he says. "You can't just go and take her into New York on the train. She could catch pneumonia. You know that. They would have rescheduled. They might have thought better of you for it."

"It was an important interview," I say. "And I never asked for her to come. She snuck into my car. It's not my fault that she decided to ride along."

"But you're the older sister. You're supposed to be the responsible one. If you had turned the car around, you could have dropped her off and still made it to New York later that afternoon, and then you wouldn't both have practically gotten killed in that accident."

I feel a brief stab of guilt, as sharp and painful as a shard of bone. "It wasn't my fault," I say. "Not the accident. That wasn't."

"How can you say it's not your fault?" Grandpa Ray demands.

"We should leave," Nicholas says. "Right now."

I glance over at Nicholas, who is not his usual unruffled self. In fact, he is looking distinctly ruffled. But if there's a danger here, I don't recognize it, and I need to set things straight with Grandpa Ray first. "The accident wasn't my fault. I was stopped at the light. The van just fell on top of us."

"But you didn't have to go that way," Grandpa Ray points out. "You could have driven north and taken 78 to Newark. You could have taken the Northeast Corridor train from New Brunswick. If you had done either of those things, you and your sister wouldn't be in intensive care right now."

"*It wasn't my fault*. And even if it was, it's over now. It's done."

"What are you going to do about it?" Grandpa Ray says. "You need to make this right."

"I'm on my way to do that," I say. I try standing up, but I somehow cannot manage to get up from my chair. "I have to rescue Penny. She's somewhere across the river, and I need to find her, and get her out of whatever danger she's in."

"You can't do that," Grandpa Ray says. "You'll never find her, for one thing. And you'd be too close to the Dark Lord. He's too strong, too powerful. You'd just get yourself captured like your sister. You'll never make it."

"What did you just say to me?" I whisper.

"Ashlyn, listen. You're better off staying here. This way you won't get into any more trouble. And you can think about what you've done."

"Grandpa Ray would never tell me that I couldn't do something."

"Well, you can't just waltz into the Eastern Marches. You'd never get across the bridge, even. It's not possible."

Somewhere, I find the ability to stand up.

"My grandfather *loves* me. He *believes* in me. He would *never, ever, not even once* tell me that I couldn't do anything, no matter what it is. I don't know who you are, or what you are, but you are not Grandpa Ray. You can't be."

"He is not," Nicholas says. "We should go."

"You need to sit down, young lady," the thing that looks like Grandpa Ray says. "Let me tell you something. You're out of your mind if you start listening to...him," he splutters in Nicholas's direction. "Do you even know what he *is*?"

I still do not know what Nicholas is, exactly, but at this moment, I do not care. "He's my friend. And you aren't. I'm leaving, and you can't stop me."

The not-Grandpa Ray thing struggles to his feet. "You need to think about what you're doing, Ashlyn. Don't go and make another rash mistake. Sit down, and let's talk this over like reasonable beings."

I take a tentative step toward the door and find that I cannot take another.

"You have to control your emotions," Nicholas says. "You have to stop listening, and then walk away."

I try taking another step, but I am only able to slide my foot a little. I close my eyes and think about the real Grandpa Ray, my family, and all the happy memories I have associated with this cabin. I take another careful step backward, my eyes still closed shut, and then another, ignoring the ranting voice in the kitchen as best I can. I feel the rough wood of the door against my back, and then turn and open the door. I collect my sword belt and shield, and make my way down the stairs, heading back to the dirt road.

I take one quick look back and see the figure of my grandfather on the porch, shaking his fist at me, but I cannot hear him any longer. I turn my back and head toward the bridge that will take me across the river to rescue my sister.

SILVER BELL

We make our way back to the dirt road and walk in silence through the dark forest. As the first light breaks, I see the river just ahead, the dawn sunlight sparkling on the surface of the water.

"Not too much farther," says Nicholas.

Across the river lies the Eastern Marches, looking at once familiar and unfamiliar. If the Western Marches are experiencing the chill of an early fall, the eastern lands are deep in the grip of November. The verdant leaves of the live oak trees are brown and withered, and the tropical flowers are nowhere to be seen. But I am not here for the scenery. I am here to save Penny. But first, I have to cross the bridge, which is in its old familiar place.

"Any advice?" I ask Nicholas.

"The guardian is not truly your enemy," the rabbit says. "Your enemies are fear and doubt and anger. If you can overcome those, you can overcome the guardian."

"Control your emotions, yeah," I say.

"I hope," Nicholas says, "that a reference to one of your experiences in your waking life might be helpful at this point."

I stop walking and get down on one knee to make glaring at the rabbit easier. "Just what experience are you talking about?"

"The Penn State game," Nicholas says.

"The Penn State game *was not my fault.*" Opening game of the season my senior year, Big Ten—ACC showdown, and I'd missed the tying shot in the last minute—in what turned out to be the last game of my college field hockey career.

"I made no such suggestion," Nicholas says. "I am merely pointing out that having more control of your emotions could have helped you in that contest."

"I saw an opening and tried to slam the ball into the goal. It hit the post. Bad luck."

"You swung at the ball hard enough to hurt yourself."

"I jammed my wrist. I missed the rest of the season with my arm in a sling. It was worth it, or it would have been worth it if I'd made the shot."

"The lesson is clear," Nicholas continues. "You made a bad decision and let your temper get the better of you. I know that you *can* control it; you were able to do that just now when we escaped from the Doubt."

"The what again?"

"The being that resembled your grandfather. He was a representation of your doubts, just as the black beasts are a representative of your fears. If you wish to avoid such dangers, you must control your emotions."

"That's not the easiest thing in the world," I say.

"Indeed. But I have mentioned, more than once, that this is a realm where symbols have immense power. You interpret your fears as large beasts, but that is not what they are. They are symbolic of what you are thinking."

"What does the guardian symbolize?" I ask. "And if you tell me it ought to be left as an exercise for the student, I am going to lose whatever control I have over my emotions."

Nicholas twitches his whiskers. "It is complicated. Crossing into the Eastern Marches means leaving behind a part of yourself while taking the next step into the wider world. You may not have been ready to do that before."

"But now I have to. To rescue Penny."

"That, and to confront the Dark Lord."

"Not interested in doing that," I say. "Not now, anyway. Sufficient unto the day and all that good stuff."

"All the same, he is still there, on the other side of that river, and if you cross it, it will be hard to avoid him."

"One way to find out."

I rise to my feet and walk to the two steel lampposts that flank the bridge entrance, as familiar to me as my own heartbeat. I am keyed up and nervous, but underlying that is a deep layer of fear and agitation, and under that is an even deeper knowledge that I have no idea what I am doing.

The guardian waits for me in the center of the bridge, his green eyes flashing. The chill fall wind makes his leather duster billow behind him. As always, the first move is mine to make, and I put my hand on Dyrnwyn's hilt.

A few fine flakes of snow begin to fall, swirling in the brisk autumn wind.

I plan my attack. I will make a quick slash, take two steps back, and then parry the blow from the guardian's staff. Except that it might be better to use my shield, and let the shield absorb the first blow, so I can counter-attack. The shield is strapped to my back, and I reach around my left shoulder with my right hand. But my right hand is gripping the handle of the sword, which comes out of the scabbard when I reach.

I can now either drop the sword, or sheathe it, or do without the shield. I move the sword to my left hand and reach around for the shield, and somehow manage to turn myself around a hundred and eighty degrees. I turn back around while trying to fish the strap of the shield loose from my shoulder. I manage to get the shield halfway down my arm, but the strap gets caught on the edge of my left gauntlet. I switch the sword back to my right hand, somehow get the shield unstuck, and at last I am ready to face the guardian.

Who is laughing at me. Great big heaving waves of laughter. Perfect.

"It's not funny," I say, although I know that I am wrong, and it is probably hilarious.

The guardian's hood slips off, revealing a shimmering cascade of blonde hair. Her laugh is silvery and bright.

"I am sorry," she says. "I know I should not laugh at you, Lady Ashlyn, but you looked so ridiculous."

"You're a woman," I say. I hadn't known. I'd fought the guardian for years, and had never even thought about her being a woman.

"What else should I be?"

She is tall and muscular and her face is plain and wide with a strong chin.

"I hadn't thought about it," I say. "I was focused on crossing the river."

"Which I cannot let you do, Lady Ashlyn. As you know."

"I need to cross," I say. "I have to rescue my sister. She is trapped in the Eastern Marches, and it's my responsibility to rescue her."

"The East is not safe," the guardian says. "I would have explained that, but every time you see me, you come at me with a sword, or arrows, or whatever else you have armed yourself with."

"I don't care that it isn't safe," I say. "I can protect myself. And once I rescue Penny, I'll come right back, I promise."

The guardian leans heavily on her staff. "Words are wind. If you want to fight me, I am prepared, but I would rather you just went on your way."

I draw the sword Dyrnwyn, its point awash in flame. "I will pass, whether you will it or not."

The guardian takes a step backward. "That is a very powerful blade," she says. "I do not know where you acquired that, but you need to be careful with it. You do not know what it can do. Or, rather, what you can do with it."

"One way to find out," I say, and take a tentative step forward.

The end of the guardian's staff lashes out, but I block it with the shield. I take another step forward and feint right. Fire ripples up and down the blade.

"You cannot cross," the guardian says. She swings the staff at me again, quick as a snake, but it clatters off the shield. "It's not safe. You need a guide."

"I have a guide," I say, and make a backhanded thrust with the sword. The guardian blocks it and then strikes me on the shoulder with the other end of the staff. The *mithril* coat absorbs the worst of it.

"I don't see any guide," she says. She makes a broad sweep with the staff, but I duck under it in time.

"Nicholas!" I shout. "Get out from whatever bush you're hiding under and help me convince her." The guardian's staff slams against my shield, and I take a step backward.

"Who is Nicholas?" the guardian asks.

"He's my friend," I say. I try the backhand slash with the burning sword, but she blocks me again with the staff. "He's, you know, a black rabbit."

"A black rabbit?" the guardian asks.

"Well, yeah." I raise my shield to block a blow, but it doesn't come.

The guardian takes a step back and then takes a deep breath. "You might have mentioned that sooner. Quit cowering, Atropos, and get out here and face me."

There is a long pause, and then Nicholas slowly hops onto the bridge and makes his way to where we have been dueling. "Lachesis," he says. "Well met."

"You are Lady Ashlyn's guide? You? You should not be within a thousand miles of her now."

Nicholas twitches his ears. "Lady Ashlyn is recovering from injuries caused by a serious car accident in her own world."

"That makes no sense," Lachesis says. "She is supposed to go to New York and do badly on her interview, and then take a job closer to home. That is the plan."

"That's a lousy plan," I say. "What do you mean, I am *supposed* to do badly on my interview? Who do you think you are?"

"She is a Fate," Nicholas says. "She weaves the strands of your life into a coherent whole. But she could not anticipate your accident; it was not part of her plan. That is why she will not let you cross; if you enter the Eastern Marches, she loses more of her ability to control what happens to you."

"She is not ready for the temptations ahead," Lachesis says. "I cannot let her cross, not alone."

"I will go with her," Nicholas says.

"That is not a comfort," Lachesis replies.

"It may be for her. You know that is my role."

"Your *role*. Do not make me laugh, Atropos. I know what your role is, even if Lady Ashlyn does not."

"Would you mind telling me, then?" I ask. "Because he hasn't really been all that forthcoming about it, and I wouldn't mind knowing."

"He is a Fate, as well," Lachesis says. "Atropos. You understand?"

I don't quite understand, but I don't want to admit that. "Either way, he's my guide, and I need to rescue my sister. Can you let us across? Please?"

"Atropos. Can you keep her safe? Will you?"

"I cannot promise anything," Nicholas says. "What happens to her is outside my control, and yours, now. As hard as it is, you are going to have to let her go."

"Are you going to let her go?" Lachesis asks.

"Not unless I have to. You know that."

"If either of you could give me some kind of clue as to what you are talking about," I say, "that would be nice. Really, it would. Because you are both giving me a headache."

Lachesis lowers her staff, just a fraction. "You may cross, Lady Ashlyn. I will trust in your common sense, and in the abilities—if not the wisdom—of your guide."

"Okay, wait a second," I say. "I have been trying to cross over this river for years now, and all of a sudden, you let me go now? Without a fight? Just because Nicholas—I mean, Atropos—is with me? That was the answer all this time?"

"It was never about an answer," Lachesis says. "I am not a puzzle for you to solve, child. I am here to guide your path, to help you make choices—and that means to keep you away from choices you should not make."

Despite the cold north wind, I feel a hot blaze rise in my throat. "You don't have the right to do that," I say. "You don't get to decide what I do and don't do. I make those decisions, and so far, I've made mostly right ones. I don't need you, or anyone else, holding me back or protecting me."

"You have no idea what is across this river," Lachesis says. "The Eastern Marches—the land across the river—are a place of great danger. I am not protecting you from yourself. I am protecting you, as best I can, from people and situations that can scar you down to the soul."

"Then why let me cross at all?"

Lachesis leans on her staff, suddenly looking much older. "I would not," she said. "But I have no choice. If your sister is in danger, you must go to her. As you say, she is your responsibility. But she is more than that. She is the beat of your heart, and you are the breath in her lungs. You may cross."

I know what she says is true, but it doesn't lessen my anger. "You kept me from becoming everything I could have been, all this time," I say. "What would I be, now, if you had helped me?"

"Come here, child," Lachesis says. "Come here. You are right to say that I have not helped you in the past. But I will do so now. I have something for you."

I walk over to Lachesis, who towers over me. Her plain face is drawn and sad. "You must not trust Atropos," she whispers. "He will guide you faithfully, but do not let him choose your path. You understand?"

"If he can help me rescue my sister," I say, "that is all I care about."

"More than just her life is at stake," she says. "Here. Take this."

It is a sleigh bell, attached to a rich and soft black velvet ribbon. The bell does have any markings on it, but I recognize it anyway. I put the bell up to my ear, and shake it. It does not make any noise, and I am not surprised, having read that particular book to my little brothers at least a thousand times.

"I can hear it, wherever you are," Lachesis says.

I put the ribbon around my neck. "So this means I will see you again?" I ask.

"If you are in danger, yes," she says. "Go. Follow the rabbit. Rescue your sister. And come back safely, you understand? Go."

PERSUASION

"So, tell me about this Atropos thing."

"It is not a *thing*," the rabbit sighs. "For better or worse, it is my job."

The snow is falling thicker now, and Nicholas has to hop over the snowdrifts. Even wearing my green plaid winter jacket over my red flannel shirt, and a pair of my dad's old Carhartt work gloves, I am still shivering.

"It's been a long time since I've studied Greek mythology, but I'm pretty sure there are three Fates."

"Yes," Nicholas says. "Clotho is the first; you will not meet her, I daresay. Lachesis is the second. She weaves together the strands of your life. And I am the third. Atropos."

"And the third fate is responsible for taking a giant pair of scissors and cutting my life short, is that right?"

"You remember correctly," the rabbit says. "Although it does not have to be scissors, technically."

"And when, exactly, were you going to explain this? You know? The part about you being the one who is responsible for killing me?"

"It does not work that way," Nicholas/Atropos says. "I am not here to murder you, if that is what you want to hear."

"As helpful as that information is, it not exactly what I want to hear." I had trusted Nicholas, from the moment I first arrived in Summervale, and all this time he had the power to cut my life short, and he never said anything, not even once. He let me think we were friends, but we never were. How could we be? "I want to hear why you wouldn't tell me that you were, what, the personification of my actual death, or whatever you are actually supposed to be."

"Technically, as a rabbit, I cannot be a personification of anything. The word you are looking for, I think, is *symbol*. As I have been trying to explain all along."

"Nicholas, for the love of God, if I get any more ridiculous pedantry from you, I am going to scream."

"Please do not scream," Nicholas says. "You might attract another of those beasts. And it is because of those beasts—and other creatures of the Dark Lord— that I have not been entirely straight with you about my role."

"You can't pin this on the Dark Lord," I say. "You should have told me what you were from the beginning."

"And what would you have done from the beginning, knowing who I am? You might very well have run off into the forest, and what would have become of you then? Lady Ashlyn, I understand that you do not fully realize this, but your life has been in danger from the moment you arrived. All I have been trying to do is help you, and to comfort you at a difficult time."

I throw up my hands. "A difficult time? *A difficult time!* I am literally dying over here, and you think it's just a difficult time?"

"It would be difficult for me as well," Nicholas says. "Your death is my death. It is the destruction of Summervale. I do not want your death, but it is inevitable. And I have much less control over the timing of your death than you suppose."

"This is not a comfort, Nicholas. You understand that, right?

Nicholas twitches his whiskers. "If death comes, I will comfort you, if I can, and if death is delayed, I will guide you faithfully."

"How do I know that?"

"Because we are here."

I look around and don't see anything other than dead leaves and the gray sky. "Wait a second. We're here? How'd we get here so fast?"

"Some of us," Nicholas says, "are not nearly as fascinated by the prospect of trudging through the snow for hours as others might be."

"Here" turns out to be a narrow country lane, paved with flagstones. Tall evergreen hedges flank the pathway on either side, trimmed with new-fallen snow. At the end of the lane is an imposing English manor house, its roof half-hidden in snow. A thin plume of black smoke rises from the chimney.

"Your sister is inside," Nicholas says.

"Wait a minute," I say. "How do you know she's in there? There could be anything inside that house. Like, I don't know, a bear or something."

"What is in there," Nicholas says, "is much worse than any bear."

I feel a cold shiver down my spine that has nothing to do with the arctic weather. "What specifically are we talking about, here," I say.

"Look at the door."

I walk up the steps to the porch, keeping an eye out for anything that might decide to burst through the hedge. The front door is black, newly painted and glossy, and the brass knocker is shaped like a mermaid.

"I don't get it," I say.

Nicholas hops onto the porch. "Technically, that is not a mermaid. It is a siren."

I take a deep breath, remembering the sound of the sirens that came to rescue me after the car crash. But that is not what Nicholas is talking about. "The sirens are beautiful women," I say, "who sing so seductively that they lure sailors to their deaths."

"Not women, not exclusively, but yes. The siren is likely trying to entice—or seduce—your sister. You will have to use your powers of persuasion to counter whatever he or she is telling her."

"Great. Thanks. You have my back in there, right?"

"No, Lady Ashlyn."

I squat down to put myself on Nicholas' level. "What are you talking about? You're my guide, right?"

"I am, and I have guided you here. But I cannot enter the house. I will wait here for you."

"Look here, Mr. Bunny Rabbit."

"I *thought* we agreed not to use that word."

"Nicholas, you will explain right now what is going on, in words I can understand, or I am going to open that door and throw you to the siren."

"You would not dare, and even if you did, it would make no difference. I would simply bounce off the door. That house is a part of your sister's consciousness. I have no place there. The Dark Lord himself could not enter your sister's plane of existence. Only you can go inside. Only you can rescue your sister. I would help if I could, but I cannot."

"Great. So what do I do? How do I rescue her?"

"When you open the door, you are choosing to enter your sister's plane of existence. I cannot tell you what that will be like, as I only have your plane of existence for reference. What I can tell you is that just as you choose to enter her plane, she may choose to leave hers to enter yours—or she may not."

"In English?"

"You cannot rescue her by force," Nicholas says. "You will have to use persuasion. You will have to convince her to leave the siren and come with you. And it will be difficult, because the siren has its own powers of persuasion, and has had longer to convince your sister of whatever it wants her to hear. So talk to her, listen to her, and figure out how to get her to choose for herself what she needs to do."

"That's good advice," I say. "I think I can do it. But don't forget that I'm still mad at you. When this is over, we are going to have a long talk."

"That will be lovely." Nicholas hops off the porch and starts nibbling on a holly bush.

I bring down the siren-shaped knocker, hard. No response. I reach to lift the knocker again, and the door opens, revealing the figure of an English gentleman.

"State your business," he says.

He is long and lean, with a dark complexion and fever-bright eyes. His black hair cascades down in carefully coifed ringlets. He is wearing a heavy coat over a dark maroon waistcoat, and patent-leather boots shined to a mirror-bright finish.

"Hi there," I say. "My name is, um, Lady Ashlyn Revere, and I am looking for my sister, Penny, and my friend thought that she might be here."

"You are intruding on my privacy," the gentleman says, in an accent straight out of a BBC serial drama. "My privacy, and that of my guest. Not to mention that you've decided to pay a social call dressed in such outlandish attire."

"The jacket? It's a little cold outside, you know. Actually, if I could come in for a minute to get warm—that's quite the fire you have going on back there."

"Mister Darcy!" a high-pitched voice says. "You are being most terribly rude to our guest, and on such a snowy day."

Darcy—and that is plainly his name—grimaces, but opens the door and grudgingly lets me in. Penny is there, standing behind Darcy, and she dodges around him to give me a smothering hug. "It is you! I thought it might be. I am so pleased to see you, sister dear."

Penny is using a phony English accent and is wearing a rich red velvet dress trimmed with black embroidery, complete with a lace bodice that is suitable for ripping, if one enjoys such things. Her hair is usually lank and stringy when it isn't a mass of tangles. Now it is artfully teased and crimped, with cascades of flowing tresses framing her long face. And she is wearing makeup, which is what makes my jaw drop the most. Penny has never had any interest in makeup that I know about. But here she is, looking like she has just stepped off the cover of a Regency romance novel, with Darcy looking every inch the gentleman. She finally lets go of me. If she's noticed the chain mail underneath my coat, she doesn't say so.

"My sweet sister," she says. "Whatever might you be doing here?"

"Hi there," I say. "Long time, no see."

"Is it truly you?" she asks. "How ever did you get here?"

"I would be happy to explain," I say, with a sidelong glance at Mr. Darcy. "Perhaps in a more private setting."

"Of course," she says. "But first, I have to introduce you to Mr. Darcy. Mr. Darcy, this is my sister, the Lady Ashlyn."

"Pleasure to meet you," Darcy says. He does not look happy to see me, but it is hard to imagine anything bringing light to his arrogant features. "Faith, I did not know that the Lady Penelope had a sister, let alone one so fair. If, perhaps, somewhat rustic."

I stifle a *you did not just say that to me*, and give Darcy my dimmest smile.

"Dear Mr. Darcy," Penny says, "May I trouble you for a few minutes alone with my sister? We have not seen each other in ever so long, and it would be so lovely to talk for a few moments."

This sounds like a great deal to me. Darcy frowns so hard that I am afraid that he is going to cause himself some damage.

"As you wish," Darcy says, with a notable sneer in his voice. "But only for a few moments. Cook will have dinner on the table soon. And you might wish to find your dear sister some more *appropriate* attire."

"Thank you kindly, my only love. We won't be long."

Darcy stalks out of the foyer, the hobnails of his heavy boots ringing on the floor. Penny takes my hand and walks me toward what I imagine to be some kind of parlor. It turns out to be a low-ceilinged room with worn beige wall-to-wall carpet and a window that looks out onto a scraggly woodland. It's all very familiar, just as though I have lived there most of my life, which is because I have.

"You took my room," I say.

"Mom and Dad should have let me take it when you left," she says. "You like what I've done with it?"

"New furniture," I say. "Nice." The room—my room—is decorated in a haphazard way, with old movie posters stuck on the wall, and paper snowflakes hanging from the ceiling. "But why would you hang out in here when you could hang out with Mr. Darcy, at long last? I mean, you've spent so much time with your nose in *Pride and Prejudice,* and now here he is, big as life."

"Because I need a break every once in a while," she says. "I mean, look, I love Darcy, of course I do, but he's kind of clingy, you know? Maybe not that, but you know what I mean." Penny plops down onto the bed, and her velvet dress changes into jeans and a black T-shirt. Her carefully arranged hair resolves itself into its usual lank strands.

Arrogant and creepy is more like it. I sit down on a beanbag across from Penny. "What do you know about Mr. Darcy? Honestly, he seems like kind of a jerk."

"How can you say that about the love of my life? You've barely even met him."

"And as soon as I did meet him, he told me to get lost," I say. "Have you been here the entire time?"

"I have no idea," Penny says. "All I remember is that you were mad at me for hitching a ride with you to New York. And then I was looking at my phone, trying to figure someplace we could go for lunch after your job interview, and then something hit me over the head. I woke up in this huge four-poster bed, with Darcy sitting beside me."

"There was a car wreck," I explain. "Not my fault. I was sitting at the stoplight, and a van crashed into us. I woke up in the emergency room, and then they put me in surgery."

Penny sits up in alarm. "Seriously? Did we both die? Are we in Heaven? Because if this is Heaven, I'm going to have a second helping of Yorkshire pudding."

"As far as I know, we're both in the hospital." I rub my gloved hands together; I am still freezing cold despite the apparent warmth of the cottage. "My working theory is that we're both alive, just asleep and dreaming. But I heard you were in danger, so that's why I came to rescue you."

Penny, relieved to hear this, bounces up and down on her bed. "Rescue me from what? Darcy? Get real."

"They told me that you had been captured by an entity, someone who wished you ill." I saw no need to tell her that the pronoun *they* in that sentence referred to a talking rabbit and a large knight. "They said you were in danger."

Of course, they had *also* said that I was the chosen one who had to destroy the Dark Lord. Penny doesn't look as though she is in any danger of anything except being ravished by Mr. Darcy. If she is really all right, then I can walk out of here with a clean conscience and start worrying about when I am going to leave Summervale, and if Nicholas is telling me the truth about not being able to murder me.

"That's nonsense," Penny says. "I love Darcy. He's sweet, and he dances divinely, and he does whatever I want him to. No matter what." She lets a little fey grin cross her face. "Why would I want to be rescued from that?"

"I don't know. I'm not sure. I don't know if you're in any danger or not, actually. What I can tell you is that you're in a place called the Eastern Marches. It's not supposed to be safe."

"Darcy is perfectly safe. Well, maybe not *perfectly*, but safe enough. Ashlyn, listen, you don't need to hang around here if you don't want to. I don't need to be rescued. I'm completely happy here."

"I suppose there are worse places where you can be than in the pages of your favorite book. Well, then. If you wake up before I do, say hi to Mom and Dad for me, and tell them I love them."

Penny tilts her head. "Wake up? You don't understand. I'm staying here."

I feel my body shiver, and not from the cold.

"What do you mean, you're staying here? You have to wake up eventually."

"Who says? I only have your say-so to prove I'm not dead. If I am dead, I don't have anything to worry about, and I can stay here with Darcy forever. If I'm unconscious, I also don't have anything to worry about, and I can stay here with Darcy as long as that lasts. I'm not planning on going back, if I have any say in it."

"You're not *dead,* Penny." I have to believe this, because if Penny is dead, I must be, too. "We're somewhere else, in a place called Summervale. We need to figure out how to leave here and get back to the real world."

Penny crosses her arms and pouts. "You can do what you want. I'm staying right here."

Nicholas said that Darcy is a siren and that his hold on Penny is strong. I now understand just how strong. I bang my fists together, trying to come up with a good argument to persuade her to leave.

"I can't let you do that. We need to figure out how to get out of this place, together."

"Don't talk to me about sisterly togetherness. You were ready to ditch me just this morning."

"This is a different situation, Penny."

"That's right," she says. "This is a totally different situation. And I like it. Do you want to know why?"

"Penny, listen to me," I say. "We need to— "

"*No*," she says. "You need to *listen to me*. You know why I like it here, you're just too afraid to acknowledge it."

"Penny..."

"I like it here *because I can breathe*. That's all. We've been sitting here arguing, and you haven't heard me cough, not once. I get up in the morning, and I don't have to cough out ten pounds of phlegm. I don't have to wear that stupid jacket or have Mom and Dad wake up early and pound on my back to help me get rid of the other ten pounds. I don't have to take one single pill, not one. I can go anywhere I want and not worry about getting infections. I don't have to feed my face to make sure I get enough nutrition. I can walk. I can *run*. I can *dance all night long*. And other things. Do you understand me?"

This is not going well. We need to get out of here. I need to calm her down, and she is not calming down, and we have to get out of here, and I don't know what to do.

"Okay, look," I say. "I know..."

"No. You *don't know*. You think you know because you watch me go through all of it, but *you don't know*. CF didn't happen to you. It happened to me."

"You think I had it easy? I had to be the responsible one. I had to look after you, make sure you were okay. Do you have any idea how much of my childhood I lost because you were sick? Everything I had to give up? You can't sit there and tell me you were the only one who suffered. We all did. Not as much as you, but we did, just the same."

Penny's face is red, and she glares at me as though I have struck her.

"Maybe you did suffer, a little. But you had options. You could go to sleepovers. You could go to summer camp. You could *go to college*. Pretty soon, you're going to leave for good. But I am stuck here. I'm not going anywhere. I'm not going to college. I'm not going to get to grow old."

"I know that, Penny, and I'm sorry, but staying here isn't going to solve anything."

"It solves *everything*. Don't you get it? I'm *happy* here. If you want to leave, if you want to go back to reality, that's great. I hope you do. Enjoy yourself. I want to stay here. And if you make it out of here, tell Mom and Dad not to wake me up."

"Don't say that. You can't mean it." Had I crossed the bridge to rescue Penny just to lose her for good?

"Maybe I'm dead. I am fine with that. I've been getting ready for that all my life. Maybe I'm on a respirator, breathing through a tube, and if that's true, I am going to enjoy it as long as it lasts. If that's the rest of my life, that's fine with me. I'm happy here. I don't want to wake up."

I have battled a fear-beast and crossed into the Eastern Marches to rescue Penny, and now I am losing her—not to the car accident, or the disease that is slowly claiming her life, but to a vicious siren offering her an unreal fantasy. That, and her own stubborn nature. "I don't know what Darcy is telling you, Penny, but you can't turn your back on everyone you love for him. I need you. Mom and Dad need you. You have to believe me."

"You don't need me. You never did. I am your sick little sister who ruins your life. But I'm not sick here. I'm healthy. Not just healthy. I am *awesome*. And I want to be this way for as long as I can."

"It's an illusion, Penny. It's not real."

"I don't *care* that it's an illusion. Why aren't you listening to me? Darcy *loves* me. We go riding out in the countryside—for real, not just that therapeutic riding stuff. We go on picnics. We make love under the stars. Well, I mean, what he calls 'making love.' It's very Regency-era and weird, but it's nice."

"It's not reality, Penny. Darcy isn't real. He's a—"

"Aren't you listening? I don't care if it's not real. It's better than real, because reality stinks. I'm not leaving, and I will fight you if you try to take me out of here."

"I'm listening to you, Penny," I say. "But that doesn't change the facts. You can't stay here forever, and you shouldn't want to. Darcy doesn't love you; he's not capable of it. He just *wants* you, wants to use you for his own selfish reasons."

"Can't I want him, for my own selfish reasons? Besides, you're a fine one to talk. Think about all the boyfriends you've had. How many of them did you use?"

"None of your business," I snap.

"Right. None of my business. Well, this is none of your business. I am not your responsibility anymore. I didn't ask you to rescue me, and I don't want to be rescued. So if all you can do is sit there and judge me, you can do that somewhere else. You understand me, Ashlyn?"

She is the beat of your heart, Lachesis had said, *and you are the breath in her lungs.*

"There's no way I can stay here," I say. "And I don't mean *here* as in this room, or this house. I want my life back, the one I had before the accident." I take a deep breath, because this is my best argument, and I want to make it work. "And I want you to be a part of that life. So I am not leaving here without you."

"In that case," Penny says, "then you need to get used to wearing a corset, because you're going to be here for a long time."

HIC SUNT DRACONES

I know Penny hates being sick. When she was little, she screamed and cried whenever Mom and Dad whacked her on the back, again and again, trying to get her to expel as much mucus as she could. She would beg them not to, just this once, but it had to be done every single morning, no matter what, or she would choke to death on her own secretions. I got recruited, early on, to help hold her down, and to hold her hand and calm her down afterward so everyone could get out the door and go to school or work. It was just something that had to be done, a part of the daily routine, no matter how horrible it got. Penny eventually grew into an understanding of why she had to take all of her medication, endure the hospital stays, and undergo the daily compression treatment, although she still hated it. And the treatment options got better—she has a vest now that she uses to do the lung compressions, for one thing. She still complains about the disease—anybody would—but the complaints are more about how the cystic fibrosis limits her options than the pain and indignity of it all.

I just assumed she had become reconciled to it, as people do. I never dreamed that she was harboring some secret rebellion against herself, that she would

128

willingly destroy what remained of her life to escape into a passive dreamscape. Yet that is what she is doing, and it is what she says she wants, and I can no more talk her out of her self-deception than I can rewrite her genetic code.

"If you're going to stay," Penny says, "we're having dinner shortly. You need to put something on that's era-appropriate. I will meet you downstairs. Please don't be late. Once you have the chance to meet Mr. Darcy, you'll see how happy he makes me."

As she stalks off, I look around what used to be my room. I check the closet, and it is stuffed with Regency dresses. I do not think that any of them would look good with chain mail. I take my coat and gloves off, and my hand reaches for my sword belt.

I don't have any way to persuade Penny to leave. But maybe I have a way to persuade Darcy to leave her alone. If she won't listen to reason, maybe he will listen to steel. I try to draw Dyrnwyn from the sheath, but I can't do it. Every other time, the sword has come out freely, but now it is stuck there as though it has been nailed in place.

"What the hell is going on?" I say, asking no one in particular.

"I can explain," a mocking voice says. "You are in my home, and I allow no one to draw a dangerous weapon in my home."

I look up and find Darcy leaning against the door frame of my room with his hands behind his back.

"How long have you been there?" I ask. "And how did you open my door?"

"To answer your second question first, this is my home. I go where I will. And I have been here long enough to know that you intend to take Lady Penelope away from here by force. I do wish you would stop. It is quite tiresome for me, and it is a waste of your time."

I long to wipe the arrogant look on the siren's smug face, but I suspect he could flatten me if I even try.

"You don't get to decide what Penny does," I say. "You don't have any right to warp her mind."

"When Lady Penelope came out of this room, she asked me if she were dead. She was very concerned, and I had to reassure her that she was not deceased. Who is it that is warping her mind?"

"You've convinced her to do whatever it is you want. She needs to be with her family. You have to let her go. She doesn't really want to stay here."

"On the contrary. Lady Penelope is quite sensible and quite clear about what she wants," Darcy says. "I work hard to make sure that's exactly what she gets. Right now, what she wants is you to come downstairs for a quiet family dinner. There is a lovely green velvet gown in the wardrobe that should fit you nicely. At any rate, it will flatter your complexion more than that martial getup."

"I am not going. You understand me?"

"Of course you are going. Your sister is waiting for you."

"I refuse," I say. "I am not dressing up for you, and I am not staying here one second longer. I want to leave, and I want to leave now. And I want you to let Penny go, whether she wants to or not."

"You have no power here," Darcy says. "You may not compel me in any way. More importantly, you should not set yourself in opposition to me. Not when I am the only one here who can keep your sister safe."

"That's not true," I say. "You're keeping her prisoner."

Darcy lets out a most ungentlemanly yawn. "Perhaps I am, but it is a prison of her own design. And here, in my home, she is under my protection. I assure you, if she leaves, she will have no such guarantee. She would enter a literal nightmare."

"I don't care. I want my sister back. I want my family together. You are keeping that from happening. You need to help her wake up."

Darcy's smug face transmutes into a vulpine grin. "You are incorrect. I do not need to do anything, except have a lovely dinner with the beautiful Lady Penelope. Won't you join us?"

I leave my room—or the room that Penny hijacked from me—and make my way into the foyer. I am wearing the plainest dress on the rack, a dark blue number without any lace or ruffles. I have the mithril coat on under it, and the sword belt over it, so I look like the Pirate Queen of New Jersey. I look ridiculous, but I will play along for a while if it means I have another chance to convince Penny that she is in danger.

Penny and Darcy are sitting across from each other at the dining room table, staring deeply into each other's eyes. "Mr. Darcy," Penny says, "did anyone ever tell you that you were a schmoopie?"

"Why no, Lady Penelope," he says. "I do not believe that I have had that pleasure."

"Because you are a schmoopie."

I roll my eyes, hard, but neither of them notices.

"No, Lady Penelope. I perceive that it is you who are a schmoopie."

That tears it. I slink into the kitchen, unnoticed, and start poking around cabinets and drawers. Maybe I can sneak up behind Darcy and brain him with a frozen leg of lamb or something. Then I hear a scrabbling sound at the back door. I open it, and Nicholas is on the back porch.

"How are you faring?" he asks.

"Terrible. She's not coming with me. She likes it in there."

"I am very sorry to hear that," the rabbit says.

"You were right about the siren being male," I say. "Penny is in there with Mr. Darcy, from *Pride and Prejudice*. That's a book," I explain. "Darcy is her favorite character, and he's convinced her that she's better off asleep than awake."

"You could not persuade her otherwise?"

I knock my fists together in frustration. "No, I couldn't. Besides, it's not just Darcy that's the problem. She's convinced herself. If it was just Darcy, maybe I could do something about it, but while she's asleep, she doesn't experience her symptoms. I don't have anything to offer her that's better than that." *Not even love.*

"What will you do now?" Nicholas asks.

"I don't know that there's anything I can do other than picking her up and dragging her outside, which you already said wouldn't work."

Nicholas twitches his whiskers. "What are they doing now?"

"Penny wants us all to have dinner. She's at the table now, sitting and staring at Darcy, and they're making googly eyes at each other. It's disgusting."

"Lady Ashlyn, as much as it pains me to say this, you should leave now. If you cannot rescue your sister, you will inevitably fall under the siren's power if you stay here. I regret that you could not rescue your sister, but you have to look to your own safety."

"I can't just leave her here. I can't just sneak out. I have to try again. I have to get her out of there."

"I am sorry, but it cannot be done."

"It can't be done by fighting or fair words, no. So it will have to be done by means of a trick. And this trick, Nicholas, is going to be devised by you."

I have, at long last, succeeded in making Nicholas look flustered.

"What the hell is going on?" Penny is in the doorway of the kitchen, wearing an even more ridiculous Regency-era dress than any in the closet. "Who are you talking to out there?"

I open the door a little wider so that she can see Nicholas waiting outside. "This is my friend, Nicholas. He is a Talking Rabbit."

"Good day to you, Lady Penelope," Nicholas says. "I hope you are well."

"Great," Penny says. "A Talking Rabbit. Adorable. Are you coming to dinner as well? Or are you late for a very important date?"

Nicholas, to his credit, ignores the sarcasm. "I have done as you have requested, Lady Ashlyn. Your parents are waiting for you both outside in the garden."

I cover my mouth with my hands, partly out of shock, and partly because I can't keep a straight face. My gesture is wasted, however, because all of Penny's attention is locked on Nicholas—who literally could not have said anything else that would have driven Penny around the bend any faster.

"You are joking, Mr. Rabbit," Penny says. "Or you had better be."

"They are waiting for you outside," Nicholas says.

Penny whirls toward me, crinolines and ruffles flaring. "Nobody asked you to bring them here. What the absolute hell are you thinking?"

"If you're going to stay here," I say, "I think you at least owe them the courtesy of saying goodbye."

"Courtesy! As though you know anything whatsoever about it. I invite you inside, instead of leaving you out in the snow, and the first thing you do is bring *Mom and Dad into it?* What is *wrong with you?*"

"Fine. I'll just go outside and tell them you don't want to talk to them because you're too busy playing footsie with your new boyfriend."

"You wouldn't *dare.*"

"Watch me, sister."

Penny takes a deep breath and stalks outside, nearly tripping over Nicholas on the way out. I follow her outside, closing the kitchen door behind me. We are in the large, formal English garden that backs up to Darcy's house. The snow on the stone paths is beginning to pile up in drifts.

"Where are they?" Penny says.

"I apologize, Lady Penelope," Nicholas says. "They must have stepped away for a moment."

"What a cheap trick," Penny sneers. "Weak. I'm going back inside. Alone. You understand?"

"Perfectly," I say.

Penny reaches for the handle of the kitchen door and pulls, but it doesn't move. She gives it a yank, hard enough to dislocate her elbow, but nothing happens.

"I am afraid, Lady Penelope," Nicholas says, "that you will not be able to return inside."

Penny cuts loose with a string of expletives that would cause a Marine drill sergeant to take a cautious step back.

"Okay, wait," I say, when I can get a word in edgewise. "I didn't know you couldn't go back inside."

"What the living hell do you mean, *you didn't know?* You lied to me, just to get me out here, and separated from Darcy for just a minute, and now I can't go back? Holy Christ, Ashlyn, what is *wrong* with you? Are you just that jealous of me being happy? Is that it?"

"Nicholas, did you know she couldn't go back inside?" I ask.

"All I did was to follow your request, Lady Ashlyn." Which is not helpful, and not what I asked.

"I can't believe you had the nerve to pull a stunt like this," Penny says, anger flashing in her eyes.

"Wait one second. You can't believe I had the nerve to pull a stunt like this? You're the one who snuck into my car in the first place and forced me to take you with me to a job interview, and you think I'm the one who is pulling stunts?"

"I never *lied* to you. You lied and said Mom and Dad were out here. And if they were here, they would be on my side."

"The way they always are, you mean?"

"Jealousy," Penny says. "I knew it. You are jealous. I can't believe it. You. The pretty one. The athletic one. The *smart* one. And all you are is mean, and awful, and jealous."

"You don't understand. I came here to rescue you. I learned how to fight with a sword. I fought a great, big, huge panther thing. I walked across the bridge. And that last one might not mean anything to you, but it was a big deal for me. I'm only here because I thought you were in danger, and I wanted to rescue you. Because you're my responsibility."

"No one asked you to be responsible for me. Not me, anyway. I would have been a lot better off if you wouldn't have been so responsible."

Nicholas—who is prudently hiding under a marble bench—chooses this moment to pipe up. "Lady Ashlyn, you need to think about what you are doing, and control your anger."

"I need to control my anger? What about her?"

"I am doing an *exceptional* job of controlling my anger," Penny says. "Because if I wasn't, there wouldn't be enough of you left to fit in a pie plate."

"I implore both of you to step back, take a deep breath, and control your anger."

"Not going to happen, Mr. Talking Rabbit," Penny says.

"And you know what?" I reply. "I think I'm *perfectly fine* feeling a little anger right now. I think I'm *entitled* to feel that way. I had a van fall out of the sky and drop onto me while I was on my way to a job interview. I ended up in the hospital and got stuck wherever this is. I got sent on a wild-goose chase to rescue a sister who didn't want to be rescued, and it turns out that my only friend is the literal personification of my own actual death. Okay? If all that makes me a little bit angry, so be it. I'm angry."

"I implore you, Ashlyn. Calm down. Control your emotions."

"And what if I don't?"

Nicholas doesn't answer, but instead darts off into the woods surrounding Darcy's garden. "That's right," I yell after him. "Take off. Run away. I don't need you anymore, Mr. Bunny..."

There's a rushing sound overhead, coming from behind me. I turn just in time to see the immense jaws of a dragon, veering from above.

"Get down!" I shout, and I hope that Penny hears me.

A dark crimson jet of flame rushes toward me, and I barely get my shield up in time to block it. Fire engulfs me on either side, the taste of sulfur and smoke burns the back of my throat.

I lower my shield when the fire subsides, and see the dragon rising in the evening sky. The blue velvet dress I took from Darcy's house is scorched, but I have withstood the original assault. I look around, but I can't see Penny anywhere.

"Are you okay?" I ask.

"What in the hell is that?" Penny yells. I glance over, and she is rolling on the turf of the garden, trying to put out a small fire on her skirt.

"Stay low. I'll try to drive it away. If it comes after me, run. Don't stop until you reach the edge of the forest."

The dragon is maybe twenty feet long from snout to tail. Its leathery wings and thin snake-like body give it an almost cruciform shape. The scales are a bright electric blue, the color of a natural-gas flame. It is making a slow loop in the sky, taking its time on the ascent, circling back toward me. I am ready for it. A deep anger rises within me, blazing hot and dangerous. I smoothly draw Dyrnwyn from its sheath, and it blazes into brilliant light.

"Ashlyn! What are you doing?"

"I am not going to run. I am going to fight."

I am not quite sure *how* I am going to fight, but if this dragon wants a piece of me, it is going to have to earn it. I raise the flaming sword over my head, building up the tension in my arm, ready to spring. The dragon hovers for a split second in the sky and then dives.

Once the dragon commits to its angle of attack, I lower my sword arm, crouch down under my shield, and rush towards it. I can feel the heat of the dragon fire behind me, but I've made it miss. I raise Dyrnwyn just in time to catch the dragon's tail as it lashes back against me. The blade slashes against the dragon's thick hide but clatters against the scales. The dragon flicks its tail, which smashes against my shield, driving me onto my back. The dragon once again takes to the air as I catch my breath and try to get back upright.

"Come on, Ashlyn. We need to get out of here," Penny says.

"You need to run," I say. "Don't think. Just run."

"I'm not leaving without you."

"Don't be stupid. Save yourself. I'll be fine."

My shield is scorched and dented, and likely won't withstand another attack. I sheathe my sword and try a Frisbee attack with the shield, like they do in the movies, but either I don't have the strength to throw it that high, or the inverse-square law is kicking me in the teeth again. The shield falls miserably to the ground. The dragon wheels in the cold winter air and dives back at me through the curtain of falling snow.

This time, I think I have it figured out. When the dragon is halfway through its descent, I pull my wand out of the sword-belt and shout, "*Conjunctivo!*" I aim the spell right for its eyes, and the dragon's head jolts back with the impact. I sprint to my left, just in time to avoid three tons of airborne dragon crashing down on top of me. The dragon, stunned by the pain of the Conjunctivitis Curse, slams into the ground face-first.

I avoid the bulk of the dragon's body, but I can't run fast enough to avoid the outstretched wing, which hits me at knee-level. I trip and fall, with the dragon's wing passing over me.

I can hear Penny screaming, but only for a moment. I scramble to my feet, just in time to see her run into the safety of the forest. The dragon has managed to raise itself up on its spindly legs as well. Have I blinded the dragon, or just seriously torqued him off? I put my wand away and draw my sword and take a tentative step in the dragon's direction. The dragon shakes his head, the same way that a horse would, and sends a jet of fire in my general direction.

I throw myself to the ground, and the fire passes over me, the snow beneath me melting, my body hot like embers. As I clamber upright, a crackling sound behind me sends me into high alert. I glance over my shoulder and see that the dragon's fire has hit Darcy's house squarely. The wood-shingled roof is ablaze. I let loose a sigh of relief. Whatever else happens, Darcy is likely to be a little too busy to go after Penny. My body is aching, my lungs are scorched from the dragon fire, but at least my sister is safe.

A curtain of brilliant blue scales falls before me and crashes into me like a battering ram. I fall backward, backward, and then I am enveloped in blinding white light.

EARLY POST-TRAUMATIC SEIZURE

Kingman knows what's happening as soon as he sees it: early post-traumatic seizure. It's not uncommon, maybe twenty percent of people with traumatic brain injuries have one within the first week after the injury. Ashlyn Revere's sleeping body goes stiff, and then her legs jerk under the hypothermia blanket.

Kingman gets on top of her, holds her down. Ashlyn's eyes are open for the first time, but her expression is vacant. Dawson rushes over from across the room to check her airway. Kingman feels the chill of the hypothermia blanket beneath him and the irregular rhythm of Ashlyn's shuddering limbs. He curses a blue streak under his breath. The longer the seizure goes on, the worse it will be. One minute, then another, and then her body goes slack and still.

"Pulse-ox is good," Dawson says, and that is at least an isolated bit of good news; Ashlyn hasn't been suffocated by her own feeding tube. "Heartbeat and blood pressure are going back to normal, and intracranial pressure is unchanged."

Kingman takes a deep breath and then checks the EEG monitor. There is a great deal of activity recorded in the last hour, and then the telltale spike of the seizure. Now the readings show the slow waves of deep sleep.

"Anything we can do?" Dawson asks.

"Hope that she doesn't have one of those again," Kingman says. One seizure is not uncommon, but two means epilepsy and all that will do is complicate her recovery. "She's resting quietly, so just continue to monitor and let me know if she has another one, or if her pressure gets any worse. I've got a consult with Dr. Myres upstairs in ten minutes, so I need to go."

Kingman hears a thrashing noise, and looks down at Ashlyn, hoping that she isn't having another seizure, but she is lying still and peaceful. It is the sister, in the next bed, and she is kicking and clawing under her bedsheets, and Dr. Drew Kingman has no idea how he is going to explain this to their parents.

FIRST BREATH AFTER COMA

I can't breathe.

This is not my normal day-to-day breathing difficulties—this is something else, and it takes me a moment to realize that I am on a ventilator and am in no actual risk of dying on the spot. But I don't like being unable to breathe, never have, not even after a lifetime of dealing with CF. I can't call out for help with a ventilator tube down my throat, but I can try to get someone's attention. I start kicking my bedsheets, trying to make as much noise as I can. I bang my ankle on a rail, and that's how I know I'm in a hospital bed, and I hate being in a hospital bed. The ventilator forces cold air into my lungs, and I open my eyes and instantly wish I hadn't. The light lances into my brain, resulting in what feels like the world's biggest ice cream headache. I try to wrap my arms around my head, and I can't move them, and that means some idiot has put me in soft restraints, and I *hate* soft restraints.

There is a doctor nearby, thank Christ, and he very calmly explains what is going on. He tells me I am on a ventilator, which I already figured the hell out, thank you very much, and a gastric tube. He says that if I calm down, he will unhook the ventilator and the tube. This is a surprisingly reasonable attitude from a doctor, and if I could talk, I would be very interested in where he went to medical school, just for future reference. It takes me a little longer than I think we both would like for me to calm down to that point, mostly because my head feels like a copper pot that's been bashed by an energetic toddler for hours.

"You've had a concussion," he explains. "So your eyes are sensitive to light. We've turned off the lights over your head if you want to open your eyes."

I open my eyes, slowly, and see the doctor hovering over me. He looks short, with thinning brown hair and dark circles under his eyes: not McDreamy, nor McSteamy, but maybe McTired. "Nice to meet you," he says. "Dr. Drew Kingman. This is Dennis Dawson; he's the ICU charge nurse. We'll get these tubes out, and then we can talk a little, if you're up for it."

Dawson knows his stuff, which is a damned relief. Spend enough time in hospitals as a little kid, and you learn a hell of a lot about how hospitals really work, and how to spot a good doctor or a good nurse. Dawson is gentle and careful, and I only gag once and that wasn't really his fault. Kingman pours me a cup of water while he does this, and I like him better for doing that; most doctors wouldn't get you water even if they'd just set you on fire. Kingman is a young guy; he hasn't been around long enough to convince himself that he's God's gift to medicine. He's got kind of a weird accent, sort of Southern, I guess, but not quite. I decide to suspend my usual anti-doctor prejudice and give him the benefit of the doubt. I take a long, cool, sip of water while Dawson props me up with pillows, and it unlocks my tongue.

"What happened?" I ask, and it comes out with a slur, but they understand me anyway.

"What do you remember?" Kingman asks.

"Mr. Darcy and I were in the dining room, right before dinner. Darcy was pouring some wine. And Ashlyn was there, and she'd brought a black rabbit, and the rabbit said my parents were there. So I went outside to talk to them, to convince them to let me stay with Darcy. Except they weren't there. It was a trick. So I had a big fight with Ashlyn, and then this dragon attacked her, and I ran away. That's when I woke up."

"Mr. Darcy?" Kingman asks. "From Jane Austen?"

"Yeah, that's him."

"This was in a dream?"

I take a moment to process what I have just said, and realize, for the first time, just how ridiculous it all sounds.

"Yeah. But it felt real."

"I understand," Kingman says. "Do you remember anything before the dream? Like how you got here?"

I drink another mouthful of water. I try to think, but thinking hurts. "Can't remember," I say.

"Do you remember your name?" Kingman asks.

"Penelope Dawn Revere," I say, automatically. "Call me Penny."

Kingman nods and looks relieved.

"If you had said your name was Elizabeth Bennet, we'd be having a different conversation," Dawson the nurse says.

"You're not helping," Kingman says.

"What actually happened? And, you know, what hospital is this?"

"Robert Wood Johnson in New Brunswick," Kingman says.

"That's a new one," I say. "I've been in and out of CHOP"—Children's Hospital of Philadelphia—"ever since I was little, and Goryeb in Morristown, and Cincinnati Children's for a research study a few years ago."

"I know," he says. "I've been through your file. Try to focus. What were you doing the day you were injured?"

"I was in the car with Ashlyn, my sister. We were going to New York. Is she okay?"

Kingman won't answer. It's bad when they don't answer.

"She was in the dream. She said we were in a car accident. Is that true? What happened to her? Is she still alive?"

"Yes," Kingman says. "She's still alive." But he sounds sad and tired when he says it, and I know something is up.

"When can I see my parents?" I ask. Because they're here. I know that. One of them is always with me in the hospital. And Dad will tell me the truth; he always does.

"Soon," he says. "Let me talk with them first."

ICU. Kingman said I was in ICU. They do not put you in ICU if all you have is a concussion. Well, maybe they do if you have CF, although I would bet good money that they don't really cover treating patients

146

with concussions who have CF in medical school. If I'm in ICU, and Kingman knows how Ashlyn is doing, my guess is that Ashlyn is here, too.

"Is she here? In the ICU?"

"Yes," Kingman says.

I take my first deep breath.

A DARK LORD

I wake up to a dark world, dark and furry and smelling more than a little rank. I decide that I don't care. It is a soft, warm place, and there aren't any dragons around, so that's a definite plus in my book at this point. I luxuriate in the warmth for a long as it lasts, but then I find that my feet are cold, along with the rest of me. I pull myself a fraction of an inch up from whatever I am lying on, and then decide that maybe that was too much effort.

"Good morning, Lady Ashlyn," a voice says.

I make a vague rumbly noise that could charitably be described as a grunt.

The voice is male, distinctly male, warm and deep enough that it could be poured out of by your local barista. I look blearily in the direction of the voice and see a dark, fuzzy outline, consistent with the rest of the world.

"How are you feeling, Lady Ashlyn?"

I am feeling as though I have taken on a very large dragon, and lost. More to the point, I am feeling markedly awful, and if people actually are capable of throwing up in Summervale, then I am in danger of doing that all over the nice man's boots.

"You have been asleep a long time."

Point one for Captain Obvious. I am struggling to say anything, and am certainly not capable of saying something as complex as "I am sorry, but I am currently unable to undertake any sort of conversation at this time, could you please come back later, preferably with a hot cup of coffee, two sugars, no cream." I settle for thinking this as loudly as I can.

"I said, you have been asleep for a long time."

Persistence, I think, *is an admirable trait, except when it isn't.*

I swing my legs over the edge of the bed, if that's what it is, and manage to sit up. I expect to feel lightheaded, but I do not. My head feels incredibly heavy, and it is a strain to sit upright. I focus my eyes toward the dark outline of my interlocutor, and he is picture-book gorgeous. Black hair, long and wavy without being frizzy. A generous dusting of dark stubble on a perfectly proportioned face. Broad shoulders, covered by a black leather mantle. And he's wearing a *mithril* chain-mail surcoat, nearly a twin to my own, but his is trimmed with gold at the collar. Part of me resolves not to swoon, while the other part wants me to do other things that I'm not actually able to do at the moment.

"All right! I thought you were awake. Cool. I've, like, been sitting here watching you, all this time, and I kept thinking you were going to wake up, but you were still asleep. I was a little worried, I don't mind telling you."

The voice, which had been warm and rich, is turning quick and chirpy—and grating.

"So, like, what do you think of my place here?" He waves expansively, and I follow his motion. We are in a tent, rather a nice tent, with walls of dense felt, and the occasional tapestry. There's a large cabinet in a far corner, with a shiny black lacquer finish. A warm fire blazes merrily in a pit in the center of the tent, and the top of the tent is vented to let out the smoke. It doesn't stop me from shivering, though, and I wrap myself tightly in what I am guessing is a bearskin.

"Great. So. Introductions. You are Lady Ashlyn, of course, but you knew that, so I'm not sure why I brought it up."

I stare dully at him and note that his hair is scragglier than I thought it was, and that his leather coat is worn at the cuffs. He might still be attractive if he would be quiet, but that does not look as though it is going to happen soon, if ever.

"And that makes me T.J. Valentine. Like Valentine's Day, I mean, spelled the same way. I'm not going to shoot you with an arrow or anything like that, honest. And I don't have any chocolate, or I'd give you some, because you look like you might need it."

"Hi."

"So, I'm like, the Warden of the Eastern Marches. It's not the coolest place, the Eastern Marches, but I kind of like it. It's got a really subtle charm."

I give T.J. my blankest expression, the one I save on idiots who are trying to hit on me.

"I'm talking too much. I get that a lot. Trust me, you'll get used to it, everyone does, eventually. So, like I was saying, probably the easiest thing to do is just chill. Not much to do in the Eastern Marches, anyway, you know? Other than, you know, fight dragons and stuff, but I figured you just got clobbered, so maybe you want to give that a rest for a moment. Although if you want some tips on that, I can maybe help out."

The last thing I want in this world right now is for him to mansplain about what I could have done to fight that dragon, so that of course is what he does, at length. "Of course," he concludes, "I mean, I don't have all that much power to, you know, really *fight* dragons on a regular basis. The Dark Side is pretty powerful, I grant you, but you don't want to push it."

"Dark Side?"

"Yeah, of course. Dark Side, all the way. Only side worth fighting for, if you ask me. Only way to have any fun, you know? I mean, the other side fights dragons too, I guess, but they're *serious* about it. I just do it for the fun of it. The pure joy of the sport."

"Wait. Does that make you the Dark Lord?"

"Me?" he asks. "*The* Dark Lord? No. No, no, no. I mean, like, *a* dark lord? Yeah, okay, maybe. But I'm not *the* Dark Lord, if you catch what I'm saying. I'm like the regional branch manager of the Dark Lord franchise for the Eastern Marches."

I am suddenly consumed with a fierce desire to lie back down and go to sleep, but I do not think that will make him stop talking, and if I could figure out what would make him stop talking other than beating him to death with my shoe, I would do that. I put my hand down on the bearskin, feeling the soft fur, and am momentarily startled. "Nicholas?" I ask.

"Huh? No. T.J.'s my name. The initials stand for..."

"No. Not you. My friend. Atropos. Looks like a little black rabbit."

"Atropos? Man, that dude is bad news. I'm Dark Side, but he's *dark,* you know. Seriously high on my do-not-tangle-with list, you know what I mean? I don't think he'd hurt anybody, but he's got a lot of mojo if you get on his bad side. He's your friend?"

"Yeah."

"Haven't seen him. Don't know how to get a hold of him, either. Although if I do see him, I'll tell him you were looking for him."

I don't know whether it is good or bad that Nicholas isn't anywhere around. I don't think the dragon got him, so there's that. If he's not close by, that probably means that he can't murder me, so that's good. But at least Nicholas is capable of intelligent conversation, which T.J. is, well, not.

"So, how did I get here?" I ask.

"Well, I do a lot of patrolling, you know. It's kind of my job. I saw a big fire, so of course I went to investigate. Dragon tracks all around, so it didn't take long to figure out what had happened. I went around the back, and saw you there, lying on the ground, and I figured, whoa, this can't be good. So I picked you up and brought you here, safe and sound."

When T.J. says the word *safe,* I suddenly remember that Penny was there for the battle with the dragon. I know she went into the woods, but what else might have happened to her? "Did you see anyone else?" I ask.

"Not a soul. Was there someone else there with you? If there was, I would have tried to help them. I'm Dark Side, you know, but I'm not a bad guy."

This is not helpful, one way or another, but at least I rescued Penny from Darcy. I don't know how well she is faring out in the woods, though. So that means I need to find her. If T.J. knows, he's either not telling me, or is lying to me. And it is probably not a good idea to underestimate T.J.; just because he sounds like an idiot doesn't necessarily mean that he is an idiot. That means I need to protect myself, and I reach for my sword belt, and it isn't there. All I feel at my waist is velvet, which means I am still wearing that idiotic blue velvet dress I picked up at Darcy's, and since it got scorched pretty badly by the dragon, that means I look like a wreck. I am too tired to think of what might be appropriate to wear in a yurt in the Eastern Marches, so I switch to my comfortable Carolina-blue hoodie and jeans, with the *mithril* underneath.

"Hey, cool. So, where you work, do you have Casual Friday?"

"I'm not working at the moment," I say.

"Right, yeah. Touchy subject. Like the Penn State game."

"What about the Penn State game?"

"Okay! Okay! Calm down, Lady Ashlyn. Like I said, touchy subject."

"Why are you bringing up the Penn State game?" I ask. Nicholas had done that, too, when he was trying to get me to control my emotions. *Why is this idiot asking me about the Penn State game?*

153

"Well, you know, it was one of those times you really lost control of your emotions. It's a big deal around here when you do that, you know, even when you're awake."

"The other time?"

"Yeah, you remember? Not that long ago? Great big blue dragon showed up? That's what happens when you lose it and get really angry, you know. Dragons. Sea monsters. Big scary scaly things coming at you."

"Wait a second. I *created* the dragon?"

"I don't know about *created*, I mean, but something like that always shows up when you get mad. So I don't want you getting mad at me, you know? Like, tell me if you're starting to get mad, so I know to duck."

"You mean, like now?"

T.J. takes a step back and starts edging toward the door. "Yeah, like now. Or any time. You understand how this works, right? You get mad enough, a dragon shows up. You get scared enough, one of those slinky black panthers shows up. You can't control your emotions, you can't control your environment. Lose too much control, you end up like the Penn State game."

"Can we please stop talking about the Penn State game?" I ask.

"Okay, but it's the best example of what I'm saying. You were *so* mad after that game, and all sorts of chaos were going on around here. Dragons. Griffins. I think I saw a manticore. And then you punched the wall, and that must have hurt, because everything went red for a little bit."

"What are you talking about? I didn't punch any walls."

"Sure you did, in the locker room. And then you lied about it! That was so awesome. It was really Dark Side of you, you know? I didn't expect that you had it in you."

I stand up, for the first time, and tap the idiot in the center of his broad, massive chest with my finger. "I didn't punch any walls, and I didn't lie."

"Oh, wow. You managed to convince yourself. That's the best thing, when you tell a really big lie. Everybody thought you jammed your wrist on that last play, and nobody saw you punch that wall, so everybody believed you when you lied about how you really got hurt. That's the great thing about being on the Dark Side, doing something like that, and getting away with it."

I feel the surging of anger in my chest, and remember the heat of the dragon fire, and try to calm down.

"Because you would have lost your scholarship if anyone had found out how you really hurt yourself. That's what you told yourself at the time, right? It was a lot of money, and you knew your parents wouldn't have had the money to send you out of state if you didn't have the scholarship. I understand. It was the sensible thing to do. But it was a dark thing for you to do, Lady Ashlyn. I respect that."

I take a deep breath. Nobody knew about me punching that wall. Nobody saw me, and everyone believed me when I lied about it. T.J. shouldn't know about it, I wouldn't think, but if Nicholas was right then T.J. is a part of me, so he would know—maybe better than anyone.

"It wasn't just about the scholarship money," I explain. "When I punched that wall, I hurt myself. But I hurt my team, too. I was out the rest of the season with my arm in a sling. I couldn't face my teammates and tell them that I punched some stupid wall, and I couldn't play anymore. That's why."

A stupid grin splits T.J.'s stupid face. "Awesome. Guilt *and* shame. That's real Dark Side material, there."

I take a step back, the better to paste T.J. a good one on his jaw, but I happen to look over his shoulder and see my sword, propped up against the felt wall of the tent. I try to dodge around him, but he is too quick for me.

"Hey! Hey!" he says. "You want to maybe take it easy for a second? I know you want your sword back, but right now you need your rest before you start trying to ventilate me."

I try to give him a hard punch, the way I did with that wall in State College, but he catches my wrist before I can connect. "Seriously, Lady Ashlyn. Relax. You want to have a sword fight; I'd be happy to oblige, but not right now. You had a seizure. Give yourself some time."

"I had a *what?*"

"Early post-traumatic seizure, is what I heard."

"You heard?" I ask. "Does that mean that you stopped talking long enough to *listen,* you overbearing blockhead?"

"That's a mean thing for you to say. And yeah, you had a seizure, on top of every other medical thing that you have wrong with you."

"What, exactly, do you know about that?"

"A lot more than you do, apparently. Want to find out?"

"Find out *what?*" I ask.

"You see that wardrobe back there in the corner? Open it up. You'll find out."

The Face of the Enemy

"You want me to go inside the wardrobe?" I ask. "Seriously? What's in there, a scared little faun and a lamppost?"

T.J. looks hurt. "I thought you would appreciate the literary touch."

"So what is in there?" I ask.

"There's a door at the back. If I'm right—and I'm not a hundred percent sure about this—then if you walk through, you'll see yourself. It's like an exit from this place."

I feel the hair on my neck stand up. "You mean I can get out of here? Seriously?"

"No! No, no, no. Sorry about that. Didn't mean to get your hopes up. All you can do is observe. Like a ghost. Not that you *are* a ghost, you understand. You're not dead, because then I would be dead, and man, that would be depressing. But you can walk around, and nobody will see you or know you're there. Or I think so."

"How do I know you're right about that, Mr. Dark Lord?"

"I keep telling you, I'm not the Dark Lord. I'm a regional representative. And I'm trying to help."

"How do I know you're not trying to trick me?" I ask. Nicholas had tricked Penny—come to think of it, he had tricked me, too. And both Sir Roland and Lachesis had conveniently neglected to explain that Nicholas was the incarnation of death. So far, there is not one person in Summervale that I can trust, and even if there were one, it wouldn't be T. J. Valentine.

"Hey, look. I'm Dark Side. I get it. If you don't trust me, that's cool. I'm not trustworthy. On the other hand, I don't have any incentive to harm you. I don't even have any reason to tick you off—it's not like I want you calling up any more dragons."

"Let's suppose I believe you, and I go in there. What will happen to me?"

"Nothing," T.J. "Nothing will happen, except that you'll learn the truth about what your actual physical condition is. When you are ready to leave—shouldn't take too long—all you have to do is walk back through the door. Clear enough?"

"What happens if I don't go inside?" I ask.

"Nothing. If you're up to it, I will give you your sword back, and you can go on your merry way. If you want, you know, I can escort you back to the bridge, back to the Western Marches. Or wherever, I mean, I'm just making a suggestion. But if you want to know the truth, all you need to do is step inside."

I do not want to go into that wardrobe. I do not want to do anything this maniac wants me to do. I want to go home, but I don't know what I am going home to. The most powerful argument to go into the wardrobe is that it contains the truth, or at least T.J. Valentine's version of the truth. And I know that having knowledge about my condition could warp my judgment, and make me do things that I would not otherwise do.

There is no good reason to do this, and just one bad reason to try. But I have to know. I have always been the child in our family who sneaks peeks at Christmas presents, who looks under every rock in the backyard. I want to know whether my body is going to recover or not. I need to know. And only T.J. Valentine, regional manager for the Dark Lord, can tell me, which is the stupidest thought I think I have ever thought in my life.

"If anything bad happens to me when I'm in there," I say, "I am coming back here, and I am not going to stop until I have jammed my sword all the way down your throat."

"Metal," T.J. says. "That's a real Dark Side sentiment. I love it."

I have another reason to go through the wardrobe, and that is to get away from this idiot. I open the door and take a tentative step inside. There is another door at the back, and I push it open.

Inside the door, everything is bright reflections of fluorescent light. The floor underneath is gleaming white tile, with a dull-blue stripe on the floor. The nurse's station is on the left, with a bored-looking occupant filling out some paperwork. There are three patients in the beds to the right, and the plastic guest chairs are all empty. Everything is quiet, save for the beeping of the various monitors and other medical equipment that I cannot name.

The people in the first two beds are men: one has a long gray beard and one has thick black hair on his arms. I don't see Penny anywhere, and I don't know if this is a good sign or a bad sign.

I am in the third bed; I must be. The first thing I notice is my right hand. It is swollen and bruised, but the scarlet polish is still on my fingernails. My entire left arm is encased in a cast below the elbow. My right arm lies limp and bruised on the yellow fabric of my hospital gown. The rest of my body is wrapped in an odd-looking blanket, and I can't think why.

I check out the monitors, which seem to be chugging away. I am hopeful that this means that my heartbeat is steady and strong, but I don't know how to interpret what I'm seeing. There is a sinister-looking tube coming out of my chest.

It takes me a long time to look myself in the face. Everything that is not bruised is swollen. There is a white patch over my right eye, and I send up a brief prayer that I am not half-blind under there, or scarred.

"That's a saline IV drip, if you were wondering," a voice says from behind me.

I spin around, fist outstretched, trying to do as much damage as I can to whoever has snuck up behind me.

I don't know who this is; he's no one I've ever seen before. He is plain-looking, short and balding, with a face seamed with worry and regret. His eyes are pale green, like the first spring leaves. He jumps back just in time before I knock him flat.

"Easy now," he says.

"What are you doing here?" I ask.

"Well, I'm trying to explain what you're seeing. To be helpful."

"You are not helping, not one bit."

"Be that as it may. As I was saying, they're using the saline drip to reduce the swelling in your brain. You're in what's called a barbiturate-induced coma, which means that they're using drugs to keep you sound asleep while they try to drain all the excess fluid out of your skull."

"Are you a doctor?" I ask. He's wearing a sober gray pinstripe suit, not hospital scrubs, but I can see a conservative doctor wearing something like that. Unless he's an undertaker, and I try to scrub *that* thought out of my mind as soon as I can.

"No. Just an observer, like you."

"So how long have I been here?" I ask.

"Two or three days," he says. "They're measuring your brain activity on that monitor over there, and they seem to be pleased about it. But that's all the good news so far."

"And the bad news?" I ask.

"Left arm and wrist are shattered—you raised up your arm to try to ward off the blow. Bad for your arm, but it absorbed just enough of the impact energy to keep you from having your jaw smashed. Right collarbone is broken, and five ribs on that side. They took you to surgery, if you were wondering, because there was a piece of your rib that was resting against your pericardium—that's the membrane around your heart. The surgery was successful, which means you're here in intensive care and not in the morgue. But the most serious thing is the brain injury."

I grit my teeth. "How bad is it?"

"The doctors say they cannot be sure," he says. "That's why they're trying the hypothermia treatment—you see the blanket? It's bringing your body temperature down, to try to reduce the swelling. So far, it's working, at least somewhat. That's why it's been snowing in Summervale, and why you feel cold all the time, if you haven't figured that out."

I hadn't figured that out, but I wasn't going to admit it. "What happens when I wake up?" I ask.

"Who knows? Obviously, part of your brain is working. Your higher thinking processes may be just fine. But what that might mean is that your motor functions may be impaired. You may be incontinent for the rest of your life, for one thing. Or in a wheelchair. Hard to say. Tricky thing, the brain."

I do not want to be in a wheelchair. I do not want to wear a diaper for the rest of my life. I want to get out of this bed, out of this room, under my own power, and I know that there is nothing I can do from where I am now to make that happen. I have to have faith in my doctors, and in God, but neither of them seems to be here just now. It is a long moment before I can say anything else.

"And Penny?" I ask.

"Lucky her, she was in the back seat. No broken bones. I think there's some soft tissue trauma in her neck, but nothing too bad. But she was hit in the head, too, and she had a concussion. She's medically fragile, so they had to put her on the ventilator. And the only reason they knew she was medically fragile was because you told them, so you can take credit for that."

"But she's not here."

The man runs his fingers through what's left of his hair. "No. She woke up. She's okay now, although she has a hell of a headache. Light-sensitive, too. Long-term, she should be fine, although *long-term* isn't the word for her prognosis, of course."

I am immensely relieved to hear this, to know that I did manage to rescue Penny, and that she wasn't harmed by the dragon. Unless he is lying to me—and because he's telling me what I want to hear, I'm more likely to believe it.

"How do I know you're telling me the truth?" I ask.

"About your sister? You don't, I suppose, but I have no reason to lie about her. As for the rest, what I am telling you matches with your experience, does it not? You have been in this dream a long time now. And you can direct your actions in a way you cannot normally do in a dream. You can make choices. You can come up with plans. In a normal dream, nothing like that happens. And things are more vivid, more real-to-life than in a usual dream, correct? That's because of the drugs."

"And you know all of this how?" I ask.

"Because I'm the Dark Lord," he says.

I reach to pull out my sword, and once again, it's not there.

"Ashlyn. Calm down. Okay? I'm not here to hurt you, or do anything against you. This is just a conversation we're having. And if you don't mind me asking, how did you get here, exactly?"

"Somebody named T.J. Valentine sent me," I say. "I walked through a door in the back of a wardrobe."

"Valentine. That idiot. Double idiot, if he's reading C.S. Lewis on the job. Tell him if he starts on *The Screwtape Letters,* he's fired."

"Yeah, no. Not my circus, not my monkey."

The Dark Lord shrugs. "Suit yourself."

"What T.J. didn't explain was that *you'd* be here."

"At least he got something right, so I shouldn't say mean things about him behind his back. But I'm the Dark Lord, it's kind of in the job description."

"What else is in the job description?" I ask.

"I'll tell you what is not in the job description, and that's dropping Ford Econoline vans on young ladies on their way to a job interview. I hope you understand that I didn't intend all this, or cause it. If there was any way I could undo this, I would. I don't get any pleasure in seeing you here with your body broken this way. Or your sister, of course."

"Then why did you bring me here?" I ask. "What do you want from me?"

"I wanted you to know the truth," the Dark Lord says. "I know what you think about me, if you've bothered to think about me much. You probably think I'm the devil, and I did this to you for some reason. Well, I'm not, and I didn't. The devil wants evil for the sake of evil. I'm not an aesthete that way. Fear, anger, greed, shame, guilt—that's my stock in trade. I don't want you pinning the blame for random accidents on me."

"They wouldn't call you the Dark Lord if you weren't a liar. How do I know you're telling me the truth?"

"As much as it pains me to say this," he says, "I am but a humble construct. So is your idiot friend Valentine, and the red warrior, what's his name, Roland. And the rabbit. You figured out what he is, right?

"He told me," I say. "Eventually."

"I sense conflict. Good. Keep in mind, we are all a part of who you are, no more, no less. My advantage is that I am more in tune with your sensory nervous system than anyone else. I know your appetites, your desires, better than you do. Better than you ever could. I hear the things that you don't. I listen to the doctors when they work on you. All I know, I learn by listening, and it is amazing what you can hear when you listen—especially things you are not supposed to hear. Like when your doctors and nurses think that you are in a coma."

I take a long look at myself, watching the fall and rise of my breathing. My bad luck to show up now, in the middle of the night, when nobody is talking about me. Unless this is just another of his lies. Or unless he's lying about Penny.

"I would never lie to you about something this important," he says. "Give me some credit."

"You just read my mind," I say.

"I *am* your mind, Ashlyn. Part of it, anyway. And I wish you and your sister no harm, truly I do not.

166

Unlike a certain rabbit I could name. This should be a time of rest for you, rest and recuperation. Why not sit back and enjoy it? We could have fun, you and me."

"I don't want to have fun with you," I say. "Or anything like fun."

The Dark Lord smiles. "Depends how you define fun. Tell you what, I'll make you an offer. Take my hand. I've got a penthouse apartment in New York. Flatiron District. King-size bed, silk sheets, lots of pillows. Not anything lascivious, unless you'd like that. Just rest, for as long as you want. Then, tomorrow morning, you and I can sit down over a pot of coffee—not *real* coffee, you understand, but close enough—and figure out how to spend the time you have left here in relative peace and comfort."

This is the same arrangement that the siren offered Penny, and I saw what that did to her, and I don't want any part of it. "No deal," I say.

"You need to think about it," the Dark Lord says. "It's the best offer you're ever going to get. This world is mine, and I alone can give it to you."

"I don't want the world," I say. "I want my freedom, and you can't give that to me."

"Of course I can. Freedom is a choice, and you have ten thousand choices, if you would use them. We could, even now, be dancing on top of the Eiffel Tower, drinking champagne and watching the city lights twinkle until dawn."

"It wouldn't be real. It would be an illusion. I don't want that. I want the real world, even if it's painful. And I don't want you anywhere around."

"You have listened to a pile of propaganda," the Dark Lord says. "I am not evil, or corrupt, not the way you think I am. The didactic little construct of good and evil that you have in your mind does not encompass me. I admit to being lazy, and greedy, and lustful, and any other sin you can name. But evil? I know you, Ashlyn, and you do not harbor evil in your heart. Nor do I. Take my hand."

I give the Dark Lord and his pale green eyes and his outstretched hand a long look, and then look back at myself, lying near-motionless on the hospital bed. I know what I have to do, and where my loyalties lie.

"What would you rather do, Ashlyn? Where would you rather be? Say the word, and we will go anywhere you like. Sailing on the Italian Riviera, perhaps? Walking on a California beach at sunset?"

"No," I say.

The Dark Lord gives me an appraising look. "No, I can't tempt you with modern luxury, can I? You want something you can't have. Knights in armor and fair ladies, and desperate cavalry charges with pennants streaming. Very well. Take my hand, Lady Ashlyn, and I will fulfill your heart's desire."

"No."

"Why ever not?"

"Because the one thing you can't trade for your heart's desire is your heart."

The creases on his face rearrange themselves to something that is almost a smile. "You stole that line," he says. "It's out of some book or other."

"I am not here to talk with you, or negotiate with you," I say. "I am here to break you. You understand?"

"No idea what you're talking about. You can't break me. You can't lay a glove on me. And you shouldn't try."

"I'm not going to try. I'm going to succeed. Because this is war."

The Dark Lord's green eyes glitter with amusement. "You want a war?"

"I do."

"Bring it."

"I will," I say, sounding more confident than I feel.

The Dark Lord shrugs his shoulders. "Don't stay on my account, then. Door's that way."

"I'm going."

"Well, then. I'm going back to New York. If you want to look me up, I'm not hard to find. Oh, one more thing, though, if it's not too much trouble."

"Yeah?"

"Tell that idiot Valentine I changed my mind, and he's fired."

STREAM OF CONSCIOUSNESS

I am not quite sure what I expect to see when I walk through the door, but I absolutely do not expect to see T.J. Valentine sitting on my bed, trying to wrench the flaming sword Dyrnwyn from its scabbard.

"Put that down, you snake," I say. I am angry—well, not dragon-summoning angry, not yet—and I don't mind letting T.J. know it.

"Oh, wow. You came back. Wasn't, you know, expecting that." He tightens his hold on the scabbard.

"Really? What exactly were you expecting? Did you think the Dark Lord would, what, just swallow me up? And you'd inherit a new sword?"

T.J. has the partial decency to look a little shamefaced. "I had very specific orders from the Dark Lord. He gave me the portal—and said to make sure you went in there, and that you didn't have that sword. That's all he said, and that's what I did. He never said you'd come out again, you know. He's got a mean streak."

"So, you sent me in there thinking I'd just *disappear,* is that what you're saying? And that it's okay because you were just following orders?"

170

"Yes! No! Wait. So, how was it? I mean, the Dark Lord, did he sound pleased?"

"He said you were fired, if that's what you're asking."

"Fired!" T.J. throws up his hands, but not long enough for me to sneak the sword away from him. "That's gratitude for you. I built that big heavy wardrobe to put the portal in, and carried it around all over the place, just in case I ran into you. And I do exactly what he says, and he fires me? Unbelievable."

T.J. looks a little down about this, so I take a few steps toward him, to sort of pretend to console him, but he figures out what I'm doing and grabs onto the scabbard with both hands.

"Does this mean you're not a Dark Lord anymore?" I ask.

"No. Yes. I don't know. I'm still Dark Side, I know that. I'm riding Dark Side all the way. But I worked hard to get to be Warden of the Eastern Marches and to have that taken away from me when I didn't do anything wrong, that's tough. What are you doing?"

"Nothing." I am sidling toward the part of the wall of the tent where my sword belt is; T.J. took the scabbard off the belt, but I am guessing that he didn't notice the wand. All I have to do is to keep him feeling sorry for himself a bit longer.

"It's not fair. That's what it is. It's absolutely not fair. He's such a jerk to me. I didn't even get an invite to the Halloween party this year."

"Wait a second. T.J., do you know where the Dark Lord lives?"

"Yeah. Flatiron Building in New York. Been there a couple of times. Got ranked out the last time and sent here. Why?"

"Because I just declared war against him, that's why. Can you guide me there?"

"Ridiculous. Out of the question. What exactly are you doing, again?"

"I'm just putting my sword belt back on. I got used to wearing it. Are you going to give me the sword or not?"

"I can't. I'm not supposed to. The Dark Lord said not to."

"You don't work for him anymore," I say, buckling the belt on.

"Doesn't matter. I'm still Dark Side. Can't just give that up."

"Too bad for you." I reach down for my wand, but it isn't there.

"Looking for this?" T.J. pulls my wand out of the pocket of his jacket and then replaces it. "Naughty, naughty, mustn't threaten poor little T.J. with dangerous toys."

"You patronizing little git," I say.

"That's 'patronizing little git, sir,'" he replies.

I check the pocket of my belt, and Lachesis's silver bell is still there. I could use it to call for help. But I figure that if I can't take on a little toad like T.J. Valentine on my own, there's no way that I'm ever going to bring a real challenge to the Dark Lord. And Lachesis might decide to squash T.J. like a bug or wink him out of existence. I want him to *suffer*.

I take a deep breath, the better to keep my emotions under control. *"Accio Wand!"* I shout, and my wand jumps out of T.J.'s filthy pocket and springs into my hand.

"Hey!" T.J. says. "You're not supposed to be able to..."

I cast the first spell I can think of. *"Petrificus Maxiumus!"* T.J. Valentine freezes into place. I slip the scabbard out of his grasp, buckle it onto my sword belt, and take out the sword. *"Draw Dyrnwyn, only those of noble worth.* Translation: no Dark Side morons allowed to touch my sword."

"Thass cheating," T.J. mutters through his clenched teeth. "Nuh fair."

I am momentarily discomfited that my petrification spell doesn't fully shut T.J. up, but it's hard to see how anything could.

"You know what else isn't fair?" I ask. "Luring me into a confrontation with the Dark Lord. So I guess we're even. Lucky for you that I'm not willing to test the edge of my sword by using it to slice your head off. So can you help me get to New York?"

"Lemme go first."

"Not a chance, worm."

T.J.'s eyes bulge in frustration, and he mutters something that sounds like "Dark Side."

"Fine. Then I'm leaving, and you can sit there until you start growing moss. Or, you know, I probably do need some practice on my fire spells. I think this tent would burn really nicely if I can just figure out the right incantation."

"Nnnh."

"You want to find out, big guy? You want to see just how Dark Side I am? Either you help me, or we're going to find out what your melting point is."

T.J. twists his neck and works his jaw loose, which I suppose means the spell is starting to wear off. "You're bluffing," he says.

I am bluffing. Damn it. Okay, I would *like* to set T.J. Valentine on fire, but that's just because he deserves it; since he's not threatening me at the moment, I can't actually *do* it. There goes my Dark Side street cred.

"I'll talk. Let me go."

"About that. I kind of don't know the counter-spell. I think it's just temporary, so it'll wear off. Maybe after a week or so."

"Let me go *now*, or I won't talk."

"Okay, what about this. I conjure up a wheelchair, load you in it, push you through that portal you sent me through, and let the Dark Lord fire you in person. Sound like a good idea?"

The color drains out of T.J.'s face. "You wouldn't."

"Try me."

I watch him swallow a mouthful of rage. "The Dark Lord lives in New York. I mean, the New York here, not the one where you live. They're similar in a lot of ways, but not identical. He lives on the top floor of the Flatiron Building, guarded by a whole phalanx of evil creatures that will make your blood run cold."

"Too late for that," I say. "Okay. How do we get there?"

"You and what army?" T.J. asks.

"Good point," I say. "What army?"

T.J., with effort, manages to wrinkle his brow. "That's what I said."

"Right. You said I need an army to fight the Dark Lord. Where do I raise an army?"

T.J.'s face wrinkles up in incomprehension. "So are you being sarcastic? I haven't known you very long, but you seem like the kind of person who uses a lot of sarcasm. I ask, because when you say things like *raise an army* and *fight the Dark Lord* it makes me think you're being sarcastic."

"I'm going to raise an army and fight the Dark Lord. Not being sarcastic, not one little bit. And you, T.J. Valentine, are going to help me do that."

"No. So much no."

"Well then. If that's your choice, I'll leave you out of it. And I'll be sure to let the Dark Lord know where you are, so he can come collect you if he wants. It's not like you're leaving here anytime soon."

"Are you crazy?" T.J. asks. "I know it's kind of rude to ask, but it would explain a lot. Only someone crazy would try to take on the Dark Lord. Why risk it?"

"Why take the risk?" I twirl my wand around my finger. "Because it's a matter of life and death. If I can't defeat the Dark Lord, I lose everything. And if I lose everything, so do you. I don't have a choice, and you don't, either. You can help me raise an army, or you can watch everything you know crumble around you while you sit here and rot."

"But you don't understand what you're dealing with, Lady Ashlyn. The Dark Lord is smart, and he's ruthless, and he never gives up. You wouldn't have a chance. Unless."

"Unless what?" All I have to do is keep T.J. talking, and considering that I can't shut him up, I ought to be able to do that.

"Unless you tell me what's in it for me."

"I don't know. Honor. Glory. You tell me."

"Turn me loose?"

"Of course."

"After that, I want my old job back," T.J. says.

"Done."

"And a badge."

"I think that's do-able."

"And maybe an office building. With a real office, not just a cubicle. And a coffee machine. A real one, not just one of those Keurig ones."

"I'll see what I can do."

"Um. Well. It just so happens I know a place you can raise an army. But it's kind of a long walk."

"Some of us," I quote, "are not nearly as fascinated by the prospect of trudging through the snow for hours as others might be. What happens if we skip the walking part and go straight there?"

"Oh. Yeah. I think I know a shortcut."

I release T.J. from his spell, and we leave the tent and take a dirt road through a frozen evergreen forest. We do not have to walk far before the trees give way to a sharp embankment sloping down to the highway below. The highway is wide and dangerous, with an endless flow of sedans and crossovers and eighteen-wheel trucks blaring by. A light snow is falling, but not enough to slow down the traffic.

"You realize," I tell T.J., "that it would probably be a good idea for you to explain exactly what this place is and how it helps me raise an army." *Nicholas, I think, would already have done that.* Nicholas is condescending and infuriating, but at least when he said something it was usually useful.

"Okay. You know Summervale is a big place, right? But all you've seen is the Western Marches, which is meadows and hills and forests and all kinds of pretty scenery. This is the Eastern Marches, and all the necessary stuff you don't want to put someplace pretty is over here. So that's where the highways are, and this is the main highway. And if you want to go to New York, you have to cross it."

"So does the traffic ever die down?" I ask. "Enough for us to cross?"

"That's just it. That's not traffic. Those are thoughts. Specifically, your thoughts."

"Say what?"

"What's on the highway is affected by what you're thinking and how you're feeling. Okay?"

"No clue what you're talking about," I say.

"Right. Okay, you want to raise an army to take down the Dark Lord. But he lives at the top of a tall tower, and every step of the way there, you're going to be fighting dragons and wyverns and griffins, and horrible things with no name—creatures that make me look like one of the good guys, okay? Close your eyes, think about how that makes you feel, and then open your eyes."

I follow his instructions and look, and there aren't any cars down there anymore. The highway is crammed with six-legged black beasts on a last-chance power drive.

"Oh, my God," I say. "There's thousands of them. Where did they come from?"

"They didn't come from anywhere. Those are your fears."

"Wait, my what?"

"Those are your fears. Right? You feel angry, dragons show up. You feel scared, those guys show up. And fears multiply. You have to take them on to make them diminish."

"They were cars before," I say.

"Because you were thinking about cars. Then you were preoccupied with your fears. That drew them here."

"Now I'm confused."

"Were you not listening? What you see on the highway are thoughts. Your thoughts."

"That's ridiculous," I say.

"Is it?" T.J. says. "Then try not to think about elephants."

"That doesn't work. When someone says, 'try not to think about elephants,' you think about elephants. Everyone knows that."

T.J. points a finger toward the highway. "Look."

I look, and sure enough, there is an elephant making its way southbound, with the six-legged fear-beasts rushing to get out of its way. I watch as the elephant disappears over the horizon, and then there is another, and another, and another, until all the lanes of the highway are filled with slow-marching elephants.

"So if I think of anything, it will show up out there. Elephants. Pop-Tarts. An eighty-foot-tall Justin Timberlake."

"Well," T.J. says, but it is too late. Justin Timberlake appears, eighty feet tall against the southern sky, and picks his way through the elephant herds. He is, I am unsurprised to see, eating a Pop-Tart.

"You weren't kidding about this being dangerous."

"It's not really a highway," T.J. says. "It is more like a stream. Get it? A stream of consciousness."

"You did not just say that."

T.J. lets out a loud sigh. "There is one safe way to cross the highway, and that is to clear your mind."

"How am I supposed to do that?" I ask, reasonably enough. It took me forever to cross the river to get here. I don't exactly have a lot of time to waste trying to cross the highway, not if I'm going to go after the Dark Lord.

"You calm down. You chill. You meditate. You clear your thoughts. And after a while, the traffic will calm down, and we can cross."

"I did meditation once in college. For about five minutes. It didn't work out so well. I got bored, and I started looking at my phone, and my friend Jenny texted me about this boy she was seeing, and that was pretty much the end of that."

"Try."

So I try. I sit on the embankment in what I think is a lotus position and try to clear my mind. I manage to get the highway back to looking like an actual highway, with cars, but the second I think of anything else, it appears on the highway as well, no matter what it is.

"This isn't working," I tell T.J. after a stream of Santa Clauses in bright red sleighs passes through.

"You're not trying hard enough. When I meditate, I just zone out, you know?"

I do not want T.J. Valentine to mansplain meditation to me. "Okay. What if it wasn't dangerous to cross? What if the dangerous things down there had something besides me to look at? Would that work?"

"A distraction? It might work. You would have to hurry."

"How about a really big distraction?"

I concentrate as hard as I can on building a memory. The first step is to imagine a median in the highway, which is easy enough—a big median, the exact size and shape of a football field, right down to the white lines and the Philadelphia Eagles logo on the fifty-yard line. Then I visualize a giant stage there in the middle of the field, with a huge giant Jumbotron, almost as tall as Justin Timberlake had been, with an earth-shaking speaker system on either side. The cars on both sides of the highway begin to slow, with the drivers rubbernecking to see what is going on there in the median. But the cars are still going by, and the stage is empty, and the speakers are silent.

I realize that I am too far away to do what I need to do, so I pick my way down the embankment to the edge of the highway. I stand right across the highway from the stage, and then I pull my wand out and say the magic word, "Formation."

I can barely see her on the stage, but everyone can see her on the Jumbotron screen. All the cars on the highway slam on their brakes as one, and all the drivers and passengers get out of their cars and flood toward the grassy median. I cross over the northbound lanes, and there I am, front-and-center at the biggest, baddest Beyoncé concert that there ever was. Queen Bey is at center stage, wearing a smart black leather jacket over a tight corset, with form-fitting fishnet stockings and bright scarlet knee-high boots. And she is *slaying*.

"Awesome," T.J. screams in my ear. I ignore him.

I'd gotten to go to the Beyoncé concert in Philly back in June—I'd saved up enough money from my on-campus job to buy myself a graduation present, and I'd gone with a couple of my friends from high school. We'd been up in the upper deck of the Philadelphia Eagles stadium, and Beyonce had been a little dot on the stage from up there, but it had been a great experience and a great memory. I'd remembered enough of it to create something that was close enough to the real thing to stop traffic.

I head left on the grassy median, through the Eagles end zone, and pick my way through the crowd. The spell is taking all my concentration, and it's hard for me to keep one foot in front of the other. There's another crowd coming from the other side, and I weave my way through the traffic, with T.J. a step behind. Queen Bey moves on to start singing "Sorry," and I love the song so much that I pause for just a moment, just to listen for a little while, which is a mistake.

"Oh, my God," a voice comes from out of the crowd. "Lady Ashlyn? Is that you?"

I turn, and there is T.J. Valentine. Except that it isn't. My T.J. Valentine has mussed hair and a sloppy beard. This T.J. Valentine has slicked-back hair and a pointed goatee. "I am so glad to see you," he says, "especially if I can rescue you from that idiot you're with."

"Get lost, A.J.," T.J says.

Great. There's more than one of them.

"Is that any way to talk to the new Warden of the Eastern Marches?" A.J. asks.

T.J. looks horrified at this news tidbit. "Since when?"

"Since you got your sorry self fired by the Dark Lord, of course," A.J. replies. "I'm here to..."

I never find out what, exactly, A.J. is here to do, because T.J. punches him in the jaw and runs off. I follow in T.J.'s wake, and we make our way to the edge of the northbound border of the highway. "This way," T.J. shouts, and then runs headlong into the car door of a white Mercedes. He falls senseless to the asphalt.

A.J. Valentine gets out of the Mercedes.

"How did you—" I ask.

"Not important now. You're coming with me."

"Not going to happen," I say.

"Or what?" A.J. asks. "You going to take that great big sword you have there and cut me in half?"

That sounds like a good idea to me. I unsheathe my sword.

The music switches off, and the big stage and Queen Bey and all her backup singers abruptly vanish. A.J. smirks an evil smirk. "You need to put that thing down, Lady Ashlyn, before someone gets hurt."

"I am warning you," I say.

"Yeah, yeah, yeah, blah, blah, blah. Look. It doesn't matter. You stab me with that thing, the Dark Lord will still find you. He knows you and that idiot you are hanging out with are here. If it's not me coming after you, it's going to be someone who's much, much worse. You understand? Come with me, and you won't get hurt."

"I warned you," I say, and swing my sword in his general direction. A.J. dodges to his left to avoid the blow, and I move to the space he'd vacated and run past him. The people who had been listening to the concert are headed back to their cars in the northbound lanes, so I infiltrate myself into the mob and follow them, elbowing people as I pass. If any of them are surprised to see someone in a UNC hoodie carrying a burning sword, they don't show it.

A.J.'s footsteps thunder behind me as I make my way across the highway. The cars are starting to move, and I dodge past a couple of them as I try to cross. The cars start going faster, their headlights shining in the iron dark. I am in the middle of the highway, with cars passing me on each side. I wave Dyrnwyn in the air, hoping that its burning flames will make me more visible, but the drivers in the cars don't seem to see me. I nearly get clipped by some insane person in a BMW.

A.J. Valentine slips in between two speeding cars and is standing astride the middle white stripe in the highway. "Come with me and you'll be safe," he says.

"I don't think so," I say.

"You can't escape. I can stop traffic; you can't. Drop the sword, agree to come with me, and we'll be at the Dark Lord's penthouse in two seconds."

"Come and take it," I say.

"What are you going to do, Lady Ashlyn?" A.J. asks. "You don't have a choice. There's nothing you can do to stop me."

"Maybe I can't stop you," I say. "But Justin Timberlake can."

A.J.'s white teeth glint in his goatee. "Yeah, right, like Justin Timberlake is going to save you."

"I don't need him to save me," I say. "I just need him to take one more step."

A.J. turns around just in time to see the bottom of eighty-foot-tall Justin Timberlake's white Adidas sneaker smash him into the pavement. I wave to Justin, who reaches down, picks me up in his hand, and deposits me on the far side of the highway.

184

"Thanks!" I say. "I'm a big fan."

"Not as big as me," eighty-foot-tall Justin Timberlake says. He smiles, and then he is off, stomping his way down my stream of consciousness.

I turn back to the highway, just in time to see T.J. Valentine vault over the hood of an approaching Chevrolet. He lands on his face, right at the edge of the highway, and then picks himself up and staggers over to where I am waiting.

"That could have gone better," he says. "What happened to my brother?"

"A.J. was your brother?" I hadn't thought that particular relationship all the way through, mostly because there wasn't a great deal of time, but now I am thinking maybe I should have done that.

"We're not actually that close," he says. "What did you do?"

"Well. He got squished."

"He got what?"

"He got stepped on by Justin Timberlake. I tried to warn him, but he didn't listen." I didn't try very hard to warn him, but maybe this is not a good time to bring that up.

"Remind me to listen to you if you tell me someone's going to step on me, then."

"I am really sorry," I say. "I didn't know he was your brother."

T.J. runs his fingers through his hair, rearranging it slightly. "Don't worry about it," he says at length. "A.J. was bad news. He would have reported us to the Dark Lord, and then we'd be hip-deep in fear beasts."

"And let's not forget he took your job."

"That, too. All right then. If I wasn't committed before to making sure you pulled this off, I am now. What do we do next?"

I give T.J. an appraising look. T.J. is a motormouth, and I have no illusions that he has a good heart, or that he's on my side for anything other than his own reasons. But I need allies right now, more than I need anything else, and he's the only one I have. For now. "Next, I build my army," I say.

"You need to figure out how you're going to do that."

"Way ahead of you."

PARENTAL LECTURE THIRTY-ONE

My dad shows up at seven in the morning because that is what he does. He gets up at five and drives to whatever hospital I'm in, when I'm in the hospital, which is more often than either of us would like. This was a major pain in the neck for him whenever I was in the hospital in Philadelphia; he would drive down to Philly, and then take Amtrak to where he works, right next to the MetroPark in Central Jersey. It was a huge sacrifice for him, and one day I'll tell him how much I appreciate it. I think he already knows.

At least Robert Wood Johnson hospital is a little more convenient for him, and he's there with a sack of Dunkin' Donuts from the little shop in the New Brunswick train station across the street. CF burns up calories like you would not believe, and that means you get to eat a reasonable number of donuts.

"Thanks," I say.

"I see hospital food is the same as ever," he says. Dad has been sneaking me food in hospitals since forever. Wawa hoagies and cheesesteaks from when I was in CHOP, and Graeter's ice cream in Cincinnati. (I never learned to like their chili.)

"Why would it change?" I ask. I take a huge bite out of a French cruller.

"Got something else for you," he says, and fishes a Kindle out of the pocket of his leather bag. "Yours had a cracked screen in the accident," he explains, "so I got you a new one, and loaded everything you had on it."

"Oh, thank God. I just assumed it had been lost," I say. "Thanks so much."

"When you get home," he says, "we are going to have a long talk about your reading habits."

"You're the one who told me it was all right to read genre fiction. Regency romance novels are every bit as legitimate as high fantasy."

"Regency romance novels are one thing. Regency were-dragon erotica is something else again."

"I stand by my choice of literature."

"Sure, call it literature, why not. How are you feeling?" he asks.

"It's a different experience," I say. "Usually, I'm in the hospital because I can't breathe. I'm breathing fine." As well I might after two days on a ventilator and nebulizer. "But I feel sick. I can't stand the light being on. I feel lightheaded when I try to get up. My neck is sore, and my head feels like the twins have been using it for drum practice."

"You may get the chance to make the simile come true; I think your mother is bringing them by later."

"Joy." I love my little brothers, I do, but if they make any noise at all, I am going to be miserable. Even the uneven hum of the air conditioning is painful to listen to.

188

"They miss you. We miss you. And Ashlyn, of course."

"How is Ashlyn? Really? Kingman won't give me a straight answer."

Dad suddenly looks far more tired than usual. "He's not giving me a straight answer, either, but I think that's because he doesn't have one to give. There's no way to evaluate how severe her brain injury is. But even if she didn't have the brain injury, she's looking at a lot of rehab ahead of her. All sorts of broken bones."

"I'm sorry," I say.

"You know that Ashlyn saved your life, right?" Dad says.

"Wait. What? When was this?"

"You were unconscious when you arrived here. Ashlyn was still conscious, and in a lot of pain, but she managed to tell one of the nurses that you had CF. The nurse told Dr. Kingman. Otherwise, he might not have figured it out in time."

"I didn't know," I said. I had seen her, of course, in my dream, and I'd shouted at her for trying to get me away from Darcy. Would I have acted differently if I'd known she'd saved my life?

"I'm so sorry about what happened to her," I say. One day I'll tell her how much I appreciate it, too. Assuming I get to.

"Yes, and about that," he says. "You get Parental Lectures Three, Eleven, and Thirty-One."

I wince. The first three Parental Lectures are "Don't Cheat," "Don't Steal," and "Don't Lie," and yeah, I lied to Mom about Ashlyn letting me go with

189

her. Lecture Eleven is "Don't Get Caught," and did I ever get caught. But the last number is unfamiliar. "What's Thirty-One?" I ask.

"Lecture Thirty-One is a new one. It goes like this; the only reason you're not getting punished is because there's nothing we can do to punish you that would hurt more than how you already feel."

I consider this as a stab of pain shoots through my cortex.

"Okay, keep in mind, I am not blaming you for what happened to Ashlyn. Okay? The driver of the van was going way too fast, but he died at the scene; there's no justice to be had there. The young woman who was driving the car that caused the accident made a mistake in pulling out in front of him, and she'll be charged with reckless driving, I think. I'm not pushing for jail time for her, if they ask me. It was a horrible accident, and you didn't cause it. But you shouldn't have been there in the first place, and you know that, and you'll have a headache for a good long time to remind you of what happened. And thank God it's nothing worse."

"I am really sorry," I say.

"I know. We all are. And trust me, you don't feel any sorrier than I am, because what I have to do is even worse."

"What are you talking about?" I say.

"Dr. Morton is back from his conference, and he's taking the train up here this morning." Dr. Morton is my pulmonologist; I've been seeing him for almost my entire life. "He'll be checking you out, making sure that you haven't had any ill effects."

"Okay, so what?"

"I asked him to check out Ashlyn, too. She had one of her lungs collapse in the accident; I want to make sure that she's breathing okay."

It takes me a moment to process this. Dr. Morton is a CF specialist. You wouldn't even catch him around a healthy pair of lungs, even if one happened to have recently collapsed. He'd be bored to tears. So why would he want to look at *Ashlyn's* lungs? Why would *Dad* want him to...and then I realize what this is all about.

"You're not serious."

"I am. We'll talk to Dr. Kingman, let him know."

"You can't do that," I say.

"I don't want to, and I know you don't want me to, but we have to be prepared."

"She's going to be okay. Right? She's going to be okay. You have to tell me that. You have to tell me she's going to be okay."

"Even if it's not true?"

I grab my blanket and clutch it close to me. "I don't want this. I don't."

"It's not your decision. It's not my decision; if it were, I'd decide the other way. It's Ashlyn's decision. And she's already made it."

"What? How?"

Dad's face turns as gray as his suit. "She signed the organ donor form when she renewed her driver's license."

Lungs

Kingman is having a good morning by far, at least by his usual standards. He went to sleep as soon as his head hit the pillow, a rarity for him. That meant that he got up twenty minutes before his alarm went off and that allowed him time for a nice leisurely breakfast—a healthy breakfast, for that matter: Greek yogurt and granola. He got a seat on the train and got to read a chapter out of a book he'd been working on intermittently for months—about the assassination of James Garfield, of all things, which had turned out to be very instructive from a medical point of view.

Kingman makes his way inside the hospital complex and finds an unoccupied elevator. He has a multiple sclerosis patient on the fourth floor who is bitter and lonely and edgy, and who thankfully is getting released today. He would drive her home if he could, just to get her out of range of the fourth-floor nurses, who have been unanimous and vocal in their desire to see the back of this particular patient. She is already in her wheelchair, and Kingman bids her adieu and tells her to take her medication regularly. She scowls at this but doesn't otherwise respond, and Kingman is happy to see her go.

As the reward for a job well done is another job, he wends his way to his office, intent on battling the morass of insurance paperwork before it becomes a quagmire. He makes it to his office, but his phone rings before he manages to actually sit down. It is Dawson, the ICU nurse.

"I have three different people down here asking about Ashlyn Revere," he says. "You mind making a quick detour?"

"Yeah. She OK?"

"Same old same old, but it's like a traffic jam down here."

There isn't much Kingman can do for Ashlyn Revere, but at least maybe he can help Dawson, who is an introvert's introvert and who wouldn't ask if he didn't need help. "Leaving now," Kingman says.

"Make sure you don't get lost," Dawson says.

Dawson is not wrong. Dr. Torrez is there, and he doesn't like what he sees. "We need to schedule surgery for her," he says. "Intracranial pressure isn't coming down."

"I would like to avoid surgery for as long as we can," Kingman says.

"It's been three days since the injury," Torrez says, "and the pressure hasn't gone down. You wait too much longer, and it'll get worse. Or else she'll get pneumonia or stroke out."

"The intracranial pressure isn't supposed to hover the way it's been doing. It should have either gone down or gone up. If it goes up, then definitely surgery. If it comes back down, then she'll be good. I don't think we should make the call on surgery until it does one thing or the other."

Torrez strokes his luxuriant mustache. "We'll do this," he says. "Brain CT first thing tomorrow morning. If the hematoma's still there, and intracranial pressure doesn't go down, then we'll make the call."

Kingman doesn't want surgery. He's not an accomplished surgeon, the way Torrez is. If he can bring the swelling down without drilling a hole in Ashlyn Revere's skull, that's the best way to handle it. But he's worked with Torrez for a while now and knows that despite him being a surgeon, he isn't eager to cut for the sake of cutting. It's the right decision, even if Kingman doesn't like it.

"OK," Kingman says. "I'll tell the parents. What time tomorrow for the surgery?

"Already on top of it," Torrez says. "OR 4, at one in the afternoon. If she turns the corner before then, well and good, but otherwise..."

One down, and now to deal with the rest of the traffic jam, which turns out to be Ashlyn Revere's father, and a graying, older doctor with pale green eyes, a big fleshy beak of a nose, and a gray pinstripe suit that makes him look like an undertaker. His name turns out to be Dr. Morton, and he's a pulmonologist from CHOP. "You're Penny's doctor, isn't that right?" Kingman asks.

"Yes, and I'll check on her in a bit. But right now, I'm here to evaluate Ashlyn, if you'll permit it."

"What for? Her breathing is fine." Outside of the initial scare involving the jagged ends of her broken ribs, Ashlyn hasn't had any heart or lung issues—in fact, she's breathing on her own. That, and the unusual activity on the EEG, is what gives Kingman the most hope about her recovery. "We're a little bit worried about her catching pneumonia or some similar infection, the same as you'd have with any long-term hospitalization, but she's doing just fine right now."

"I hate to be blunt," Dr. Morton says, "but I would like to evaluate Ashlyn as a potential organ donor for Penny. For a lung transplant."

Kingman is a neurologist; he is all too familiar with the grisly facts of organ donation. He has been the one, all too many times now, to tell a grieving family that their husband, or their child, would not recover from their serious brain injury and that they should prepare for the reality of organ donation. He has fielded dozens of calls from desperate nephrologists and ophthalmologists, asking, as nicely as they possibly could, about the status of near-dead patients. But he hadn't thought of Ashlyn Revere that way. Her injury was serious, all right—you can't have a fractured skull and not have it be serious. But he'd never seen it as life-threatening—that is to say, he's always looked at the picture of the bright field hockey player on his phone, and just assumed that she would return to something like her old self. If she doesn't recover on her own, Torrez will step in tomorrow, and Torrez is very good.

But the numbers on that surgery aren't ideal. It is a significant risk, although a necessary one. And yes, if things go wrong, Penny will benefit from a lung transplant. And yes, Ashlyn would be the best match possible, and the transplant would need to happen quickly. It would be almost irrational not to think that way. But Kingman doesn't have to like it, and he doesn't.

"Mr. Revere," Kingman says, "I came out here to tell you that Dr. Torrez has scheduled surgery for Ashlyn for tomorrow afternoon, which means her situation will resolve itself one way or another. Either the pressure goes down soon or we'll operate. We'll know in twenty-four hours, I think."

"How risky is the surgery?" Revere asks.

"I'm not going to give you odds. Your daughter is young, and outside of her injuries, healthy"—which makes her an even better organ donor, but Kingman doesn't say that—"and she has a good chance of making it through the surgery. I honestly don't think this is necessary."

"I hope that it isn't," Dr. Morton says. "But you hope for the best, plan for the worst. I would still need to see Ashlyn, if you'll allow it."

Kingman takes a deep breath. "I'll allow it," he says. "As a courtesy. But try to stay out of Nurse Dawson's way. He's having a difficult morning."

"Very well," Dr. Morton says. "It won't take very long."

"I hope and pray you're right, Dr. Kingman," Revere says. "This would be the last thing any of us wants. I would lay down my life for either of my daughters if it came to that. But if it's Ashlyn's time, and if she can help Penny, I know she would want to."

"I believe you," Kingman says. "Let's hope it doesn't come to that."

SETTING SILVER AGAINST BLACK

The key to building my army is re-imagining the highway. That, and getting T.J. to shut up long enough to let me do it. The illusion of the Beyoncé concert was effective because I had placed it in the median of the highway—working around the metaphor instead of reworking it altogether. But if I keep the highway the way it is, I'll get a mechanized force, with tanks and artillery, and I don't think I can lead that kind of army effectively. Everything I know about war and fighting comes from reading fantasy fiction, so if I'm going to lead an army to fight the Dark Lord, it stands to reason that what I need is an army of mounted knights. That means I have to change my perceptions, which is easy enough to do here, but also control my emotions, which is a lot harder.

So I manifest myself a coconut.

Two halves of a coconut, actually, and they appear in my hands and I put them together to make a clip-clop sound. *Clip-clop. Clip-clop.* I can see T.J. out of the corner of my eye, squatting in the grass by the highway, and I know he is just dying to say something sarcastic, but I keep on doing it. *Clip-clop. Clip-clop.*

One by one, without any sort of fuss, the headlights on the cars start winking out. The asphalt beneath them crumbles into soft black dirt. A light bank of fog settles over everything, and horses and riders begin to replace the cars. One of the riders pulls off the road and approaches me.

"Who goes there?" he asks. He is a tall man, with a beard, wearing a white surcoat over rusty chain mail.

"I have ridden the length and breadth of the land in search of knights who will join me," I quote.

"You're using coconuts," he says. "You're using two empty halves of coconuts, and you're banging them together."

"So?"

"Where'd you get the coconuts?"

"My dad made me watch this old movie about a hundred times," I explain, "about the Knights of the Round Table."

"Nicely done," the knight says. "King Arthur Pendragon, at your service. But you might want to get yourself a real horse, you know."

The King helps me round up a few more familiar-looking knights, and I am able to grab onto the bridle of a passing horse—a gray mare, just gentle enough for me to ride without embarrassing myself. I put on a surcoat of my own: a hunter-green one with a gold four-leaf clover, to wear over my *mithril* armor. T.J. finds a restive black stallion and begins doing some recruiting of his own. Between the three of us, we manage to gather a respectable band of armored, mounted warriors.

I tap my throat with my wand and say "*Magnavox,*" which I don't think is exactly the right spell, but it has the effect I want, with my voice carrying over the crowd. "Greetings, brave knights," I say. "I am Lady Ashlyn Revere, and I thank all of you for entering my service. We ride to New York, to topple the Dark Lord from his seat of power."

"A noble quest for a noble knight," Sir Lancelot says. He has wavy black hair and a thick Italian accent for some reason, and I have at least some idea of what Guinevere was thinking.

But not all the knights are convinced. "One does not simply walk into the Dark Lord's realm," one says, which is irritating, because I wanted to use that reference. I decide not to point out that we are all riding.

Another—not a knight but a barbarian, strong, shirtless, impossibly well-muscled—steps forward. "Why should we follow a little girl?" he asks, in a thick Austrian accent. "Who are you to command us?"

"I am in charge here," I say, sounding more confident than I feel. *If I am going to get these knights to follow me*, I think, *I have to take charge.* "This is my alternative reality. If you don't like it, you can go and do something else. But if you want to destroy the power of the Dark Lord, we need to go, okay? Let's roll."

"It's a suicide mission, then," one of the knights says. He looks a good bit like Sean Bean, but then a lot of them look a good bit like Sean Bean.

"I didn't sign up for a suicide mission," one of the other knights says. He is wearing a black hood and a black mask, which seems a little redundant, and a puffy black pirate shirt. "Even assuming we can make our way to this New York place, how do you know we can find this Dark Lord? And how can we defeat him?"

"With this." I unsheathe the flaming sword Dyrnwyn and raise it over my head like a torch. "This sword spells the doom of the Dark Lord. Who will follow me to glory?"

Not one of them stirs, the cowards, and I wonder how Joan of Arc managed it in her day.

"What ho, slugabeds!" I am heartened to see Sir Roland Hargrove, Warden of the Western Marches, make his way through the knights. "A fine lot of men you are, to fail to help a maiden in distress."

T.J. Valentine snickers. "Yeah, right. Maiden." I sheathe my sword and give him an elbow to the ribs, which causes him to yelp.

"Be that as it may," Sir Roland says. "Lady Ashlyn is a fine young woman. I trained her myself, I did, and she has been a credit to that training. I am pleased to add my sword to hers, and to fight with her under the banner of truth and justice."

Sir Lancelot and a couple of the others perk up to hear this, but most of my army looks restive. Before I can say anything, the loudmouth idiot chimes in. "I don't know about all this truth and justice business," T.J. says, "but I see a lot of my Dark Side homeslices out there, and if you're ready for a good fight, then me and Lady Ashlyn are ready to bring it on, Eastern Marches style. Am I right or am I right?"

"Lady Ashlyn," Sir Roland says, "is this young lout in your service? Because if he is not, I fear treachery."

"Okay, all of you, listen up," I say. I am grateful that my voice amplification spell hasn't worn off yet. "Some of you are Light Side, some of you are Dark Side. That's fine. This isn't a Dark Side versus Light Side fight."

"Whatever do you mean, Lady Ashlyn?" Sir Roland replies. "This is a fight against the Dark Lord, therefore it must be a fight against the Dark Side."

"No, it's not." Knights on both sides of the divide are getting restless; the two groups are starting to separate, and this isn't helping me one bit. "Hear me out, my good knights, and my not-so-good knights. The issue in this battle is not whether the Dark Side is better than the Light Side, or the other way around. The issue in this battle is what happens next to Ashlyn Revere. That may not mean a lot to a lot of you, but it should."

The knights are listening, but I haven't convinced anyone yet. "I was injured in a car accident," I say. "In my reality, I am lying in a hospital bed, unable to move. The Dark Lord showed me this reality in a vision. He offered me a choice. I could wake up and suffer, or stay asleep and surrender, and he would make whatever time I had left pleasant and agreeable.

I could lounge around in a penthouse apartment all day if I wanted to. Instead, I chose to fight."

"Hear, hear," says King Arthur, and several of the Light Side knights nod in agreement.

"I chose to fight—I choose to fight—because I have already been through rehab once. About a year ago, I hurt my wrist playing field hockey."

"She's talking about the Penn State game," T.J. stage-whispers to Sir Roland. I glare at both of them.

"I hurt it further when I tried to punch a concrete wall. It cost me the rest of the season, and I spent six months doing physical therapy to try to get my wrist in shape so I could use it again. I learned a lot about myself in those six months, and one thing I learned is that there aren't any shortcuts in rehab. You have to put in the work, and you have to put in the work every day. You can't just lounge around and hope to get better."

"*Ja,* that's right," the big barbarian Dark Side warrior says.

"The Dark Lord doesn't care if I get better or not. He offers me everything I want, in exchange for everything I am. He offers fantasy in exchange for reality, pleasure in exchange for pain. Well, that's not what I want. I choose to get better. I choose to put in the work. I choose to go through rehab and to make it through to the other side and get my life back. Not because of the Light Side, and not because of the Dark Side. Because of me. Because that's what I want for myself. The Dark Lord is standing in my way, and that means that I have to destroy him."

"It is not the Dark Lord alone that you should fear," Sir Roland says. "It is the Dark Side. To conquer yourself, you must conquer the Dark Side. No compromise with evil is ever possible."

"I am not asking anyone to compromise with evil," I say. "In the movies, Light Side against Dark Side is always good against evil. But that's not the way it works in real life. I'm not building a space station to attack peaceful Alderaan." I scan the crowd and see a lot of confused faces at that one. "The Dark Side— well, my Dark Side anyway—isn't evil, it's just negative. And if I'm going to get through everything I need to get through, I need the positive and negative aspects of my personality."

T.J. Valentine pumps his fist at that one, but for once in his life, keeps his mouth shut.

"Lady Ashlyn," Sir Roland counters, "are you not concerned about giving into temptation?"

"Temptation? Sir Roland, I *want* to be tempted, because that means I can choose whether to give in to temptation or not. There's a big world out there in reality, full of ice cream sundaes and lazy Saturday mornings and cute boys to kiss on Friday nights. I want all of that, and if it means I give in to temptation from time to time, well, that's my choice. I know you want the best for me, Sir Roland, because I want that for me, but I want the other things, too. You understand?"

"You are making a mistake," Sir Roland says. "You cannot trust the Dark Side."

"Maybe I am," I say. "But it's my mistake. It's my choice. And it's my life. That's why I am asking you to bend the knee and swear to serve me faithfully in this battle."

A look of utter incomprehension breaks over Sir Roland's broad face. "Bend the knee? To you? An untried girl? I will fight beside you, Lady Ashlyn, but I will not bend the knee."

"You tell him, Ashlyn," T.J. says, his eyes dancing with glee at Sir Roland's discomfiture. "Make him crawl."

"You as well, Valentine. Both of you. Bend the knee, and promise to serve me—and to work together in this battle."

"Alright, alright, alright. Say that again, because I don't think I heard you correctly. You want me, the Warden of the Eastern Marches, to bend my knee to you?"

"Former Warden of the Eastern Marches. And yes. All of you. Anyone who won't bend the knee is dismissed. Everyone who fights in this battle will swear loyalty to me. Period."

Sir Roland glares at T.J., and T.J. glares at Sir Roland, and for a long moment, no one says anything. Sir Roland moves his hand toward the hilt of his sword, just a fraction, and I start asking myself if this is really a good idea. I trust Sir Roland, but I can only trust him to do what he thinks is right. I don't trust T.J., but he can guide me to where the Dark Lord is, and I can certainly use his Dark Side troops. Having them both bend the knee will, or at least I hope, keep them from sniping at each other the whole way there. The other knights circle around Sir Roland and T.J.,

Light Side on the right, and Dark Side on the left. This isn't a conflict I can afford to lose.

From out of the crowd, a lone rider breaks into the circle and stands between the two would-be combatants. "I am Arthur Pendragon," he says, "King of the Britons, and wielder of the sword Excalibur. I pledge my allegiance to the Lady Ashlyn and will bend my knee to her command."

My heart leaps with joy. "I gladly accept your service, King Arthur, and appoint you the Marshal of all my forces, Light Side and Dark Side alike. Who will follow Dyrnwyn and Excalibur to victory?"

I glance over at Sir Roland, who looks horrified, and T.J., who seems to be having a coughing fit. Arthur dismounts from his horse, and kneels down, presenting me the hilt of Excalibur. I hand it back to him, and he stands next to me, tall and brave. Lancelot follows him, and Sir Robin, and a dozen others, including the tall barbarian. At length, Sir Roland tugs at his gauntlets, gets off his horse, and stands before me.

"You are making a terrible mistake, young lady," he says.

"He which hath no stomach to this fight, let him depart." I quote. "We would not die in that man's company, that fears his fellowship to die with us."

Sir Roland's face goes redder than usual, but he kneels down and puts his sword across his knee. I take his oath of service, help him up, and turn toward T.J. Valentine. T.J. is off his horse and is looking twitchier than usual. Sir Roland is glaring at him, all but daring him to challenge my authority.

"Okay, Lady Ashlyn, I mean, I get it. You want me to kneel, no problemo, but you gotta promise me something first."

"No promises, no conditions," I say. "Bend the knee or walk away."

"He is much too dangerous for you to allow him to walk away," Sir Roland says. "He will betray you to the Dark Lord, as he has before."

"Very well," I say. "Bend the knee, or I allow Sir Roland to use you for jousting practice."

"Hear me out, please," T.J. says. "I'm just asking you one thing, OK? If this battle goes sideways—and it's going to go sideways, things always go sideways when the Dark Lord's involved—promise me that you won't let us down."

"I'm not going to let you down," I say. "I'm going to fight, and I'm going to win."

"That's not what I mean," T.J. says. "I mean, don't let the Dark Side down. If it's necessary—and you'll know when it's necessary—don't be afraid to fight dirty. You understand? If all you do is fight by Light Side rules, you're going to lose, and lose badly."

I consider this. "Very well. You have my word."

T.J. bends the knee. "OK, like, I totally agree to serve Lady Ashlyn, and help her to defeat the Dark Lord, or, you know, whatever. Promise."

Sir Roland rolls his eyes so far back in his head that he has to be looking at his cerebral cortex, but it's official now, and that's all I care about. "That's everyone, then. All right, then, all of you, saddle up. We ride to victory, pitting silver against black, for the good of the realm of Summervale—to overthrow the Dark Lord."

"And may God have mercy on our souls," one of the Sean Beans says.

LIKE AARON BURR

"You keep your filthy hands off my sister's lungs."

Morton smiles. "How's my favorite patient?"

"Oh, it's *favorite patient* now, I see. The last time I was here, it was more like don't let the doorknob hit you in the butt on the way out."

"I will point out," Morton says, "that the last time we saw each other, it wasn't here. It was in CHOP. And I never said anything so rude or unprofessional to you, or even thought it loudly. You, on the other hand, have called me everything but a child of God."

Blast Morton and his pedantic brain and his cold hands. "Touch my sister, and you'll find out what exactly God has to say to you."

"I have examined your sister," he says. "Have they explained to you exactly what they are going to do tomorrow?"

"Surgery. For what, they haven't said, exactly, but it has to do with whatever brain injury she got when the van smashed into us."

"I thought as much. We have an agreement, you and I—one that I would like to extend to your sister's case, if I may."

"It's not an agreement," I say. "It is an absolute demand for total honesty on your part."

"Yes, coupled with my demand that you cooperate with me when I request it. That is what makes it an agreement. If you survive long enough to make it to law school, you'll doubtless learn about the distinction. May I continue?"

"I only threatened to go to law school so I could sue you for malpractice. It's not a realistic career path, not for me, anyway."

"We will know more about that tomorrow," he says.

"No, we won't, because as I said, you're not touching her."

"Be that as it may. Do you want the update on the surgery or not?"

"Kingman told me that they might not do it, if she got a little better overnight."

"Dr. Kingman is an optimist," Morton says. "Nothing wrong with optimism, mind you, but it can lead you down the wrong track. To put it bluntly, your sister's brain is being crushed to death by a blood clot. It's about the size of the palm of your hand, but there's not a lot of room inside the skull for even a small blood clot. Kingman thinks that the clot will break up on his own, and they won't have to operate. Generally speaking, from what I understand, that's almost always the way to bet. The statistics for total recovery are much better if you don't operate. What do you know about statistics?"

"I saw a Khan Academy video," I admit. "That's about it."

"Very well then. The thing that you have to remember about statistics is that they are based on something called the normal distribution. The various data points cluster around the mean—the average, you understand. Statisticians call it the bell curve because it's supposed to be shaped like one—bells are symmetrical, you know, they have to be, or they won't ring true. With me so far?"

"You're saying data points, plural," I say. "But Ashlyn's not a data point. She's a person."

"All the data points are people. Some of them are in the median, and you treat them that way. Some of them are on the right side of the distribution, and they turn out fine. I don't think Ashlyn is on the right side. I think she's on the left side—somebody has to be, or you can't have a bell curve."

"What does that mean?"

"I hate to second-guess another doctor," Morton says, "and Kingman seems like a sharp young man. But I think he should have operated on Ashlyn right away. It would have been risky, especially as she'd just come out of surgery to clean up that bone splinter. But he should have done it. That's what Torrez thinks— he's the neurosurgeon. Not saying that Kingman was wrong to wait. He played the odds."

"You play the odds, sometimes you lose."

"You play the odds, you're guaranteed to lose sometimes. Sometimes a lot. It's like playing the genetic lottery, which you lost."

"Don't remind me."

"I shouldn't have to. Anyway, the decision has been made, and it's too late to unmake it. First thing in the morning, they're going to do a brain scan. That's going to tell them two things—how big the clot is now, and where it is exactly. If it's shrinking, and the pressure inside her skull has gone down, well, that validates Kingman's decision not to operate. But if the clot is still the same size, or if it's getting bigger, then Torrez has an operating room reserved for her, right after lunch. You want your neurosurgeon to have a high blood sugar level before he operates."

I squirm a little under my thin hospital blanket. "What is the surgery going to be like?" I ask.

"It's what's called a burr hole procedure."

"Like Aaron Burr?" I might have listened to the *Hamilton* soundtrack one too many times.

"Don't believe so. It's just the name for a round hole that's drilled into a person's skull. It's actually a surgical intervention from ancient times, although they were mostly trying to let spirits out, or such nonsense. They drill the hole, suction out the blood clot, and then close up the wound. It's a simple enough procedure, and Torrez has done it many times."

"So that's good. Ashlyn has the surgery, she recovers, and I find another lung donor, who, you know, isn't actually my sister."

"Mind if I sit down?" Morton says. He looks tired, and his suit is as wrinkled as the rest of him.

"Be my guest."

Morton sags into the guest chair. "All right then. You know surgery is dangerous anyway."

"No kidding." I had to have two wisdom teeth out last year, and they couldn't give me anesthetic or even laughing gas because of the CF, and they had to use a local, and the extraction took forever and hurt like hell.

"Okay. So there are the usual risks of surgery, just for starters. Then there's the risk that removing the blood clot leads to more bleeding, which can get out of control and lead to a stroke. Or a heart attack—blood clots can leave the brain and get stuck in a ventricle, and you die on the table."

"Realistically. What kind of chances are we talking about?"

"Absolute honesty? She's young, so that makes it more likely she'll pull through. But the odds still aren't good. Even with the best possible care, twenty percent of patients die. So, there's one chance in five that your sister dies, and we do the lung transplant tomorrow. And even if she makes it through, she may need further surgery, which means that you're rolling the dice again, and the odds keep getting worse."

"Ashlyn isn't a data point, or chip on the casino table, or whatever else you seem to think she is. She's a person. She's my sister. And she's not going to die, and you're not going to cut her lungs out and put them in me. Do I make myself clear?"

Morton sighs—a deep, rumbly sigh that I have heard more often than I would ever have wished to. Although the last time he did that, if I remember right, was the time I escaped CHOP and took a cab to get pretzels and ice cream at Reading Terminal Market in downtown Philly.

"I know your sister," he says. "Don't forget that. She and I have had several conversations—she worries about you, and she thinks that she's responsible for you. I helped her with her college essay, and I bet you didn't know that. I even tried to get her to take a couple of pre-med classes, but she wasn't interested. Okay? I know she's a person. I don't want to go through this, any more than you do. I hope she makes it out of there, I really do. But—and this is something you have to understand—she's not my patient. She's Kingman's patient, and Torrez's patient if they decide to operate. You are my patient, my favorite patient, and you are in a hospital that does lung transplants, by God's grace. You are something like forty-ninth on the transplant list, but since it's your sister, you move to number one if she dies. I have to be prepared for that, and that means that you have to be prepared for that, which means that you need to get some sleep."

"If I stay awake all night," I say, "does that mean you won't do the operation?"

"Neither one of us is getting out of this that easily," Morton said. "It's going to happen regardless of what you or I might feel about it. Reality isn't a great respecter of our feelings; you ought to know that by now."

"Doesn't make it any easier," I say.

"There's only one thing you can do," Morton says. "And that is pray."

"You've got to be joking," I say. "Prayer never did anything for anyone."

"How do you know? Plenty of people have had good outcomes through prayer. I admit, it's not a substitute for actual medical care, but it never hurt anyone, and it can be beneficial."

"I would be surprised if anything I prayed for came true," I say. "I stopped praying a long time ago. My parents have prayed for me for years, and a fat lot of good it has done them."

"You survived a car accident that should have taken your head clean off," Morton says. "Maybe that was divine intervention. Who can say? All I'm saying is not to be so sure that prayer won't work."

"Unbelievable. You're the most cynical person I can think of, and here you are telling me to pray. It makes no sense."

Morton tents his hands together. "Did I ever tell you that I wanted to work in Boston?"

"I had no idea. Are you a Red Sox fan or something?"

"Orioles fan. I grew up in Baltimore, went to Johns Hopkins undergrad. I tried to get into Harvard, didn't quite make it. Tried to get into Harvard Medical—didn't make that, either, or Johns Hopkins. Somehow managed to get into medical school at Penn, though. Once I got out, I tried to get my residency at Mass General—it's one of the top pulmonology programs in the country. And I really wanted it. And I prayed to get in there. I wanted so badly to work in Boston, work for one of the top hospitals in the country."

"And you didn't get it."

"No, I didn't. I ended up with a residency down in Houston, at the Medical Center. I figured that was okay, Houston's a great place to practice medicine. But when I finished my residency, I applied to work at Mass General again. I even got an interview, which is farther than I'd gotten before. And the interview went really well, or so I thought. I prayed when it was over, and then all that next week. But I didn't get the job, and I ended up at CHOP."

"Lesson: prayer doesn't work. Big surprise."

"I thought that, too. I thought that for a long time. And then one day something happened; I'll never forget it. I was driving home one day. It was a tough day, because I'd lost a patient—little girl with pneumonia. She'd developed an embolism and died in minutes, couldn't do a thing for her. And I'm driving home on 76, trying to get across the Schuylkill River, and it hit me."

"What hit you, a truck?"

"No. I decided that maybe God heard my prayers, but someone else at CHOP who really needed help prayed for a doctor to help them, and God had sent me to CHOP to help that person."

"That's messed up."

"I thought so, too, at the time. Who knows. What I'm saying is that there's nothing you can do now but wait, or pray. You have to wait. You don't have to pray, but maybe it will help. Good night, and I'll see you in the morning."

"You're not touching Ashlyn's lungs," I say. "Let's be clear about that."

"If I may ask. Why don't you want the transplant? It would, literally, give you a new lease on life. There would be little chance of tissue rejection. You'd be able to breathe. What's wrong with that?"

I stare at him, as though he were some kind of eight-dimensional space insect that had been dumped in my room by a malfunctioning tesseract. "Because then every breath I took would be through my dead sister's lungs. And I'd never be able to pay her back for that, or even thank her, and I'd be reminded of what I owed her every second of every day."

Morton gets out of the chair, takes a long look at me, and shakes his head. "Good night, favorite patient."

"Get out," I say.

A nurse comes by with my dinner, and I eat it all, even the Jell-O. She takes my tray away and lowers the lights to as dark as it ever gets in a hospital. I stare at the ceiling. I want to help Ashlyn, and I can't think of a single constructive thing I can do except pray, for all the good it does. I have God's name on my lips as I fall asleep.

NEW YORK IN THE PRESENT TENSE

I always wanted a pony when I was little. I never got one, of course. But I did get to spend a little time on horseback. When Penny was about eight years old, my mom signed her up for this therapeutic riding class. That meant that I had to go with them, out to this horse farm in the next county, and sit around and watch Penny ride the same horse around the same paddock, over and over again, and it was the most boring thing on the planet. But occasionally, somebody else who had paid for the therapy wouldn't show up, or there'd be an extra horse around, and the people in charge of the class would take pity on me and let me ride, too. So, for a while anyway, it was like having a pony, and I loved every second of it.

So at least I have some small idea of what to do on a horse. But this time, I get to ride a horse that is going fast. I *love* it. It isn't just the speed and the exhilaration. It is the rhythm of the thing, the beating of my heart and the motion of the horse combined with the pounding hoof beats of a hundred mounted knights behind me. It is the feeling of the warmth of the horse under me, how it feels to trust my overall well-being to its gentle strength. It is the sun shining on a brilliant morning through the leaves of the sycamore trees flanking the roadway. When I see the first glimpse of the towers of New York in the distance, my heart falls, because I know that the furious charge will be over soon and the battle will begin.

T.J. Valentine is riding ahead of me, carrying my standard—the golden four-leafed clover, like the one stamped on the end of my wand—on a field of emerald green. He knows the way through the Eastern Marches, and puts up his hand when it's time to stop. "Here you are, Lady Ashlyn. The city of New York stands before you."

It looks different from what I remember, and yet the same. The Statue of Liberty is off to my far right, wearing the same familiar toga and spiky headdress. The green-topped towers of Ellis Island are on my immediate right, which puts the southern tip of Manhattan just to my left. The Freedom Tower glints in the afternoon sunshine and there appears to be new construction nearby for what looks like an identical building just to its north.

"That's where the Dark Lord's headquarters is," T.J. says, pointing uptown to a Flatiron Building that is something like quadruple its normal height.

"Is there, like, an all-seeing fiery eye on top of it?"

"No," T.J. says. "But it would be totally metal if there were."

"Very well. All we need to do is cross the Hudson and head north. Shouldn't be too difficult."

"I'm sorry, Lady Ashlyn—cross the what again?"

"The Hudson River, T.J. You may have noticed it. Large, flat body of water separating us from New York."

"Oh. You mean the Valentine River."

"Actually, that's not what I meant. Is that what it's called here? The Valentine River?"

"Well, that's what I call it," T.J. says. "It just seemed like a nice name, and it is the boundary between New York and the Eastern Marches. I figured I could call it whatever I wanted."

"This is ridiculous," I say. "Is there, you know, a Valentine Tunnel? Or a Valentine Bridge? Or an Eastern Marches Transit station anywhere close?"

"I have no idea what you're talking about," T.J. says. "I mean, not that it's the first time I've thought that. I get the sarcasm and all, I just don't understand what you're talking about."

"Let me put this as clearly as I can, then. How do we get across the river?" I ask.

"I have no idea," T.J. says. "I've only been there a few times, and that's because I was summoned. If the Dark Lord wants you in New York, then you're in New York. If he doesn't want you in New York, then you're not in New York. He never really wanted me in New York, you see."

"Sir Roland? Any ideas?"

"I don't know, Lady Ashlyn. How would you get to New York in your world?"

"Bridges and tunnels. Holland Tunnel and Lincoln Tunnel under the Hudson, and New Jersey Transit. George Washington Bridge farther north. Or the Tappan Zee, I guess, if you want to go that far out of the way. Ellis Island has a ferry, or if we can get over to Staten Island, there's a ferry there, too. You can take your pick. Do we have anything like that?"

"No, my lady."

"Is there a reason for that?" I ask.

"The city is a dark place, Lady Ashlyn, filled with temptations on every hand."

Great. Just great, I think.

"Lady Ashlyn," King Arthur says, "if I may inquire, what is it that you intend to do?"

"I don't know," I say. "If the rabbit were here, he'd just wave his paw and we'd be there."

"The rabbit?" the king asks, with a profound look of worry.

"Not that rabbit. Different rabbit. Friend of mine, named Nicholas. He could just build a bridge or something, and that would be that." I find myself wondering where Nicholas is, just now, and what kind of helpful advice he would have at this point.

"Well, you're better off without *him*," Sir Roland says. "I would keep my distance from Atropos. He is undoubtedly powerful, but he cannot be trusted."

"Concur, knightly dude," T.J. replies. "Atropos is high up on my do-not-mess-with list."

I decide to ignore this little colloquy; Nicholas isn't here one way or another.

"Lady Ashlyn," King Arthur asks, "you are a sorceress, I understand. Can you not bridge the river?"

"Let me think for a second." I rack my memory to see if I can remember Harry Potter or Harry Dresden building a bridge, but I can't. The Latin for "great

221

bridge-builder" is *Pontifex Maximus*, but I'm afraid if I use it I'll summon the Pope, complete with Popemobile, which wouldn't be terribly useful. Well, maybe something more modern. I pull my wand out of its sheath and point at the Manhattan skyline. "*Northeasternus Corridorus!*" I shout.

A low-slung railroad bridge appears across the Hudson, and an Acela train goes whipping past, roaring like a brace of artillery shells. The train makes it halfway across, but then a giant tentacle from beneath the Hudson stretches out and smashes the bridge, causing the bullet train to career into the river.

"The Dark Lord just unleashed the kraken," T.J. Valentine says. "Metal."

"You're going to need a bigger bridge," Sir Roland points out, helpfully.

"Good point. Okay, everybody, stand back. We're going to try this again."

I can do this. I built a replica of the Philadelphia Eagles stadium. I can build one lousy bridge. I cock my right arm back and cast the best spell I can think of.

"*Abracadabra Calatrava!*"

And just like that, a huge crystalline suspension bridge arcs into the sky, linking the Jersey marshes with Battery Park.

"Impressive," King Arthur says.

"Very much so," Sir Roland agrees.

"That looks like a Led Zeppelin album cover," T.J. says. "Wicked."

"We don't have a lot of time," I say. "Everyone hurry. We need to get across. King Arthur, you have the vanguard. You and Lancelot take a small cadre of knights and force a beachhead. I'll be right behind you. T.J., form a line of Dark Side knights behind me on the left, and Sir Roland, you do the same on the right. We'll form up on the other side of the bridge and hope there's not a lot of opposition. If there is, we'll just have to wing it. Understood?"

"No, Lady Ashlyn," Sir Roland says. "You belong at the rear. Let us clear the landing zone before you cross the bridge."

"Nonsense," I say. "I will not ask my brave knights to run risks I will not run myself. I will cross, and I will lead."

"If we lose you," Sir Roland says, "we lose the battle. You have to be protected at all costs."

"Very well," I say. "Assign me the barbarian as a bodyguard. But I will cross and I will fight. "

"I only request that you stay at the rear of the formation. You are a powerful sorceress; you can rain down fire missiles on our enemy from the rear."

This is annoying and sexist and stupid, and I can't stand the thought that Sir Roland is probably right. As impressive as my army is, I don't have any other magic users, and I've read enough fantasy novels to understand that we will ultimately have a better chance with me using my wand instead of Dyrnwyn. And only Sir Roland knows that my fencing skills are amateur-level at best—this is his way of letting me save face. "I would be a poor commander if I did not listen to the advice of my subordinates. Very well. But mark my words; I will fight this day. You will have need of my sword."

"I have no doubt of that," Sir Roland says. "We shall cross. May I ride with you, though, for a short way?"

"Of course."

As it turns out, there are several specific problems related to crossing enormous, gorgeous Calatrava-style crystal bridges over the Hudson River.

The first, and most evident, is that you have a steep uphill slope to run up to get to the soaring middle of the bridge. My gray mare trots her way slowly, pausing to catch her breath every so often. Even my *mithril* coat of mail feels like it is weighing down the poor horse. The other knights are struggling as well, but the bridge needs to be this high to keep the kraken from smashing it.

The second specific problem is that if you are crossing a crystal bridge, it is a bad idea to look down. I make that mistake and look down, and see the rolling Hudson below, ready to swallow me. I hold back nausea and look toward the city ahead. From the top of the super-sized Flatiron Building, a column of smoke is resolving into words. "SURRENDER ASHLYN."

"Nothing like the classics," I mutter.

"May I ask a question, Lady Ashlyn?" Sir Roland asks, riding beside me.

"As you wish," I say.

"When we were training together, not long before, you were not willing to fight. You could barely wield a sword. And now, here you are, leading an army into battle. What changed?"

"I learned the truth about myself," I say.

"Which is?"

"The Dark Lord showed me as I am now," I say. "Injured. Unconscious. Damaged. He told me that he could create a different reality for me—one where I had the choice to be whatever I wanted to be."

"You turned him down."

"I did more than that. I declared war."

"Why?"

The vanguard ahead has reached the far shore, and King Arthur's knights are fanning out. I stare impassively at our progress.

"Because the Dark Lord wanted me to stop fighting. I was telling the knights before about the rehab I did when I hurt my wrist. It hurt like hell, but I did the physical therapy every day until I ended up getting the full range of motion back in my hand. It meant a lot to me."

"I know," Sir Roland says.

"Well, that was like kindergarten compared to what I'm going to have to do to be able to function again. If what the Dark Lord showed me about my injuries is the truth, it is going to be the fight of my life, you understand? It is going to be an everyday struggle for...I don't even know. Years, maybe. And here the Dark Lord is, telling me to take it easy, to relax, to pretend like it isn't a problem."

225

"But why declare war?"

"That's the choice, isn't it? Life or death. Someone once told me there was no alternative. I choose life. And that means I choose war."

"And so has the Dark Lord," Sir Roland says. "Look."

FEARLESS GIRL

From the apex of the crystal bridge, the tactical situation becomes clear. The Dark Lord has placed his first line of defense at the far end of the bridge, blocking our path up Broadway. Three hundred Greek hoplites are standing there waiting for us, bronze shields glistening in the morning sunshine. I am temporarily heartened by this, as the Dark Lord could just as easily counter my medieval knights with a zombie horde or headless Thompson gunners or something else creative. The hoplites have helmets crested with dyed horsehair, and round shields with a big red Greek letter L for Laconia, which makes them Spartans, which means they can't surrender. Great.

The hoplites aren't making any aggressive moves, which suggests that they are the vanguard for a larger force waiting for us as we make our way through Manhattan toward the Flatiron. My knights ought to be able to take on this first obstacle, but there are going to be further surprises the closer we get to the Dark Lord. It's going to take more than brute force; I am going to have to be resourceful and cunning.

"Your orders, Lady Ashlyn?" Sir Roland asks.

"Hit them head-on," I say. "I'll provide the artillery and the air cover."

"The air cover?"

"No time to explain."

Sir Roland takes a long, searching look over the battlefield to come. "Remember," he says. "Control your emotions."

I am attempting to do just that. Alternating waves of anxiety and anticipation wash over me, driving the fear and the anger toward the back of my mind. The negative emotions may rise up, but they will not defeat me. I will use them—especially if I need to fight dirty, as T.J. thinks I will have to. But I won't let them use me. I will master my emotions, feeling them but not letting them run free.

I give Sir Roland a curt nod as he makes his way to the far side of the bridge. He and King Arthur and Lancelot lead the charge toward the hoplites. The opposition holds its ranks, resisting the initial thrust. I dismount from my gray mare and hold my wand at the ready. The Spartans, I remember, like to fight in the shade. That means magic missiles—but for some reason, I can't think of anything like a proper incantation. I finally decide to keep it simple and just say "Zap." And it works! My wand spits out a beam of light that resolves itself into a glowing rock that explodes when it hits the rear of the hoplite formation, scattering bodies and helmets and shields. I keep up the barrage, careful not to send my missiles into my own lines. I am able to thin out the enemy forces, but the front lines continue to battle, knights against hoplites. The Spartans have claimed a couple of casualties—one of the Sean Bean knights has been unhorsed and trampled—but the knights haven't yet managed to breach their line.

I had promised Sir Roland air cover, so I need to make good on that. *"Fortuna Intrepidus,"* I shout, and look hopefully to the Hudson to the left. Sure enough, in the distance, the bulk of the *USS Intrepid* separates itself from its pier and starts steaming down toward the Battery, flight crews swarming on the deck to ready a quick strike. I turn back to the battlefield, hurl a salvo of three magical missiles into the heart of the Spartan formation, and try to assess the forces arrayed against me. There still seem to be three hundred of them. Three hundred Spartan warriors. Three hundred *immortal* Spartan warriors that can't be killed.

Great.

Two vintage fighter planes, launched from the deck of the *Intrepid,* fly over the Spartans and lay down strafing fire. This startles my knights and the hoplites equally, and both sides take cover from the rain of bullets. But the bullets don't seem to slow the Spartans; they regroup and start pushing their way from their fortified position between two office buildings, moving my knights back into the intersection. The knights begin to unhorse themselves and make a shield wall to hold off the surge of warriors. Spears clatter against shields, with both sides pushing against each other, neither giving an inch. The *Intrepid* launches a second wave of fighters, but the Spartans are prepared this time and don't even bother to look up.

I decide that a change of tactics is in order. I wave my wand in the direction of the *Intrepid,* which is now halfway down the Hudson and putting on steam.

"*Semper Fidelis,*" I shout, and am heartened to see a couple of whaleboats being lowered over the side for reinforcements. If I can bring a cadre of Marines up to flank the hoplites, that will take some of the pressure off the knights, who are holding steady despite a couple more casualties. I pick out the Spartan with the fanciest headdress and send a petrification spell his way. To my delight, it works—and I follow it up with a magical missile, which blows the frozen Greek warrior to atoms. This causes the Spartan columns to take a couple of steps back, but it's not long until they recover in good order. I try the trick again, and it works, but it's a slow process and it's not doing much good to help my beleaguered knights.

I glance over to my right, where my barbarian bodyguard looms impassively. "Any suggestions?" I ask half-seriously.

"You might want to sink that boat before it gets here," he says. I look down—again, not a good idea— and the Staten Island ferry is making its way into the harbor. Or at least it's what the Staten Island ferry would look like if it were also a Viking longship, which happened to be crammed with Vikings. I direct a salvo of magical missiles in its direction, but they don't do anything but scratch the paint on the hull. "Damn the torpedoes," I say, which isn't really a magical spell, but whoever it is that's steering the *Intrepid* can either hear what I'm thinking or has figured out that the ferry is a threat. Two planes, a little larger than the fighters that were launched earlier, head toward the ferry and drop torpedoes that hit it amidships. The ferry starts taking on water and listing to its left, but it has enough momentum going that it keeps going until it crashes into the terminal, smashing the pier to splinters in the process. The Vikings scramble over and through the wreckage of the terminal and hit my knights squarely on the flank. The knights are forced to withdraw again, pressed on two sides by the Spartans and the Vikings.

The whaleboats from the *Intrepid* land over where the Liberty Island ferries dock, and disgorge two rifle companies of Marines, which head toward the knights and start laying waste to the counterattack. Braced by the Marine reinforcements, the knights battle back. The Vikings are tough and well-armored, but they're not legendary immortal Spartans, and my knights inflict heavy casualties. I send little balls of fire into the wreckage at the rear of the Viking lines and they begin to cough on the smoke.

I survey the battlefield, which has resolved itself into three distinct struggles. On the left, T.J. Valentine and his ruffian Dark Side knights are fighting a stalemate against the Spartans, with both sides trying to flank each other on a long, attenuated line. In the center, the mass of the Spartans is on the defensive, with King Arthur and Sir Roland leading a determined counterattack. The right is a confused mess, as the Marine rifle squads are out of ammunition and are fighting back the Vikings with fixed bayonets. The Vikings are bloodied, but they are fighting bravely with their backs against the wall of the ruined ferry terminal. I am concentrating magic missiles in the center, trying to give my knights some breathing space. The battle is in perfect equilibrium, with neither side able to flank the other or punch a hole through the line. I need a new tactic to recover the initiative, and I need it now.

"I should go to the front," I say at length. "The burning sword could make the difference."

"Stay here," the barbarian says. "You are doing more good with the magic than you could with the sword."

I take a deep breath. Throwing so much magic over such a long distance is tiring, and the barbarian is right—I'd be putting myself in too much danger, even with the burning sword in my hand. I scan the skies, hoping to come up with the bright idea that will turn the tide and win the day. In the sky over the super-sized Flatiron Building, a message appears, written in smoke. "PLAYTIME IS OVER."

"What does he mean by that?" I ask.

And then I understand. The long, strung-out line of the Spartans parts, for just a few seconds, and I hope for a moment that the Dark Side knights can break through and wreak havoc in the hoplite rear. But a giant bronze bull comes charging through the lines, bucking and snorting like a thing gone mad. T.J. Valentine is the first of the knights to see the gap and the opportunity it represents, and he is the first to encounter the bull's fearsome charge. The bull tosses T.J. into the air with its horns and he lands with a sickening crack of bones on the pavement. The bull rushes over to where T.J. is lying and crushes his ribcage with its front hooves.

I direct the hot blast of anger I am feeling at T.J.'s death into my wand. *"Fuego,"* I shout, and a white-hot fireball lances onto the battlefield. It strikes the bull right between the eyes, and I hope for a brief minute that it incinerates him. No such luck. The bull's bronze hide glows with the heat, but the spell doesn't do anything to stop its rampage. The bull crushes three of the Dark Side knights and gores another. A good number of the remaining knights scatter, with a few making a run to the northwest up Battery Place. The giant bull turns, headed toward the center of the line, with the Spartan forces in tow. The bull gains speed, its iron hooves striking sparks on the pavement. I have one chance to stop him before he turns the battle into a rout.

"Gulliver!" I shout.

A dozen stout ropes shoot out from the end of my wand and fly through the air, straight as arrows. They coil themselves around the legs of the bull on impact, checking its advance. The bull struggles against the thick ropes but can't break free. I follow up with a barrage of magic missiles; they do nothing but bounce off the bull's thick metallic hide. There has to be something I can do to stop the bull, but it's not obvious, and whatever I choose to do, I need to think of it fast.

Before I can decide, though, King Arthur breaks out of the melee with the Spartans and rushes at the great bronze bull, the great sword Excalibur unsheathed. The bull is still struggling with the ropes and that gives the king at least some hope of taking it down. I hold my fire while Arthur raises the sword over his head and brings it down on the bull's neck.

The sword makes a high, ringing sound on impact, but the blade shatters. Arthur is left holding the hilt, a look of incomprehension on his face. The bull snaps its head around, with the tip of its horn catching Arthur in the throat. The king's body slowly topples to the ground as the bull works his way free of the ropes.

Valentine's death had filled me with anger—I hadn't liked him, necessarily, but I'd gotten used to him, and he'd died fighting for me. But Arthur had accepted my authority unhesitatingly, and had fought and died like a hero. I had channeled my anger into a fire spell, but when I focus my hatred into my wand, it comes out as an unspoken curse. A green jet of flame leaps out toward the bull and hits it broadside. The fire lashes over the bull, leaving behind dark-red scorch marks. It only takes a moment for the scorch marks to spread over the surface of the bull's bronze hide and eat through to reveal the clockwork below. The corrosive effect of my emotions devastates the bull, turning it into a ragged pile of rust-colored junk. A lusty cheer rises from the remaining knights and Marines, and they lay into the Spartans, driving them back up Broadway.

Or all but Sir Roland, who glances over his shoulder and then flattens himself to the ground. I look up into the sky and see the electric-blue dragon, flapping his great wings over the Hudson. I am not a bit surprised. I am not in control of my emotions at the moment, but I've been able to use that to my advantage. I don't have to be afraid of the dragon. I can use it as a weapon. I point my wand toward the heart of the battle and shout, "*Dracarys!*"

The wand bucks and splits in my hand, consuming itself with fire. I drop it, and it falls onto the crystal walkway beneath me into a pile of ashes. The dragon, unaffected by the spell, swoops down over the bridge. And at that very moment, one of the undead Spartans throws a spear into the air, aiming for the dragon.

The spear strikes home just as the dragon reaches the apex of his flight. The dragon gives out a great cry of pain and then drops from the sky.

"Run," the barbarian says.

The dragon is falling, as gracelessly as a brick, and it is going to crash into the bridge. I hesitate only a second, and then turn and run for safety, the city and the battle and the Dark Lord at my back.

"Remember," the barbarian shouts behind me. "Only honor matters."

All I can see ahead of me is my gray mare, who is racing for the Jersey shore, well ahead of me. I feel rather than hear the dragon strike the bridge; the vibrations shake the fragile crystal latticework of the suspension cables. Even with the downhill slope in my favor, I am not going as fast as I need to be. The crystal bed of the bridge cracks beneath my feet just like new ice. I don't know if the bridge will continue to bear my weight, but there is no alternative. I sprint as fast as I can manage but the cracks in the crystal keep spreading ahead of me. There's an unholy crashing sound as the entire center portion of the bridge gives way and falls into the Hudson. I again make the mistake of looking down, and the glass beneath me is the same spiderweb pattern that my windshield had been right after the accident.

A piece of crystal about the size of a Buick gives way ahead of me. I leap to the right and grab one of the thick suspension wires hanging down from the central arch. The wires are made of some clear material, but it is not slick, and I don't slide off. I hold my breath and close my eyes, and hear again the sound of the remainder of the bridge floor smashing into the river below. I hang from a cable suspended two hundred feet in the air, with a deep and powerful river below me, ready to pull me under.

I grip the cable as tightly as I can. Other than a bit of swaying, it does not look as though I am going anywhere. I look up to see if I can climb any higher, but all that would do is strand me on the superstructure of the bridge with no good way to get down. I try to calm down and steady my breathing, but I can't. There is no way out but down, and I don't want to go that way, not at all, not at all, not at all.

I hear a distant beeping sound, faintly, in counterpoint to the rising sound of my own heartbeat. And then a voice, sharp and insistent.

Heart rate and blood pressure just went through the roof.

This does not sound good at all. I scrabble a bit with my feet and find a large bolt at the end of the cable. I am able to steady my feet against the bolt, which is a huge improvement, but it doesn't do anything for my predicament.

"All right," I tell myself. "There has to be something you can do. Don't panic. Don't panic, don't panic, don't panic."

The beeping continues, punctuated by the splashing sounds of the rest of the bridge falling into the Hudson. I scan the skies for a rescue helicopter, or one of Tolkien's eagles, but see nothing that is the least bit helpful. Even a Vogon Star Destroyer would be a welcome sight. If the starship *Enterprise* would only show up to beam me to safety, I would smooch everyone on board until my lips went numb.

Two milligrams of lorazepam, stat.

I reach for my wand, but it isn't there. There has to be another way out of this mess. The first thing that comes to mind is summoning a broom and flying away on it, but I cannot think of a more sure-fire way of hurtling myself into oblivion than trying to learn how to solo on a broomstick at two hundred feet over the Hudson. There has to be something else, some way out...

The cable above me parts. I am falling, falling, and I am not going to make it. I close my eyes and hit the water hard. When I open my eyes, everything goes silt-brown. I feel a bony hand clutch mine.

With my free hand, I reach into the little pocket of my sword belt. I pull out the silver bell and shake it. I do not hear a sound.

NOTHING ELSE YOU CAN DO

Kingman, for once, is at home, in his little apartment near the Rahway train station. He has been slowly and fitfully teaching himself to cook. Tonight, he has a nice little risotto on the stove, which he intends to pair with some of the leftover Andouille sausage from the previous week's effort at gumbo. Kingman hails from Plaquemines Parish, south of New Orleans, and went to LSU for college. He wouldn't say that he misses Louisiana, not after he worked so hard to get to where he is, but he wouldn't be human if he didn't miss his native cuisine.

It is a little past nine, and the risotto is almost done simmering. Kingman is getting the bottle of Crystal hot sauce out of the pantry when his iPhone rings. It's Dawson, the ICU charge nurse. "Torres took Ashlyn Revere into surgery just now," he says.

Kingman nearly drops the bottle of hot sauce but catches it while suppressing a string of Cajun curse words. "What happened?"

"She had a sudden spike in heart rate and blood pressure," Dawson says. "No idea what caused it. Dr. Torrez thought she was on the verge of stroking out, so he decided to operate."

"I can be there in half an hour," Kingman says.

"Wait one second." Dawson's voice drops off the line and all Kingman can hear is the ambient beeping of the ICU. "Dr. Morton wants to tell you something."

"I do not want to talk to that—"

"Relax, doctor," Morton says. "There's nothing else you can do. Either the surgery will stabilize the situation or it won't. You're not in a position where you can influence the outcome."

"She's my patient." Kingman is tired and hungry and agitated, but the last thing in the world he wants to do is to let Dr. Morton cut out Ashlyn's lungs as long as there's a chance.

"You're entitled to go home and rest every once in a while," Morton says. "The same as any of us. I would go home, myself, except that I have a transplant team on standby, and I can't leave until we know how the surgery goes. Eat your dinner and get some sleep. We'll talk in the morning."

"I don't like it," Kingman says. "I would rather be there for her."

"But what would you *do*, exactly, Dr. Kingman? Dr. Torrez can handle the surgery; there's no need for you to scrub in. He'll monitor the recovery and contact you once she's stable. And if she doesn't pull through, then there's nothing you can do there, either."

This is a good argument but not a persuasive one. Kingman understands just how much Morton wants to do the transplant; what doctor would pass up a chance to prolong his patient's life? But he's not ready to give up on Ashlyn Revere, not yet, and he hopes that wherever she is, she's not giving up, either.

"I want to be there if there's any way I can help."

Morton lets loose a pained sigh. "I just had this same discussion with my patient," he said. "And I advised her to pray."

"I'm not a faith healer, Dr. Morton. Neither are you."

"So we're not. But perhaps this is a situation where a little faith is warranted. Faith in your patient. Faith in Dr. Torrez. Faith in your other colleagues. And even though I may not have earned it in your eyes, faith in me."

"Faith," Kingman quotes, "is the substance of things hoped for, the evidence of things not seen."

"Yes, it is. And that is why we need it so badly. Please, for your patient's sake, eat some dinner and get some rest."

"I would feel better if I were there. I think..." But Kingman can't get the last sentence out, as it gets swallowed by a traitorous yawn.

"I think you need some rest. I promise to have Dr. Torrez call you when he's out of surgery."

"You do that," Kingman says. "No matter how late it is."

"I will," Morton replies. "And I am hopeful for a good outcome for your patient—truly I am."

Kingman hangs up and turns off the fire under the risotto. Even with the hot sauce, he can barely taste it. He washes the dishes and then turns on the last couple of innings of the Braves game, just to have another voice in the room while he waits for Torrez to call. But the call never comes, and sleep overtakes him midway through the eighth inning.

A CIRCLE OF FIRELIGHT

I fell asleep praying to God to help me save my sister's life. He sent me a horse. Typical. God must have it in for me—he gave me cystic fibrosis, after all.

At least He sent me a nice horse—a light-gray mare with a wise face. She isn't wearing a bridle or saddle; despite ten years of equine therapy, I am not experienced enough to try to mount her unassisted, much less ride bareback. So when the horse tosses her head and walks away, I don't have anything to do but follow her.

"Do you know where Ashlyn is?" I ask the horse. I figure, well, she *could* be a Talking Horse, you never know. But all she does is whicker knowingly. We walk on, headed to Ashlyn, or at least I hope so. Ashlyn had found me when she was looking for me, so it must not be all that hard.

In the distance, I see a line of fire across the western horizon, glowing yellow and orange. There is nothing else around, and the horse is heading in that direction, so I tell myself that the flames are there to welcome us rather than burn us to a crisp. There is nothing to lose at this point by being positive and the drawbacks of being negative simply aren't worth thinking about. I am going to find my sister and rescue her, and that's all there is to it.

As we get closer, the line of fire resolves itself into a circle—a circle of firelight, with an ancient ash tree at its center. The circle is made up of individual campfires, each circled by white stones. There is enough space between the campfires for me and the horse to enter the circle, and we slowly approach the tree.

There is a tall woman standing beside the tree, with golden hair cascading over her battle armor. She is leaning on a staff and staring impassively into the fire. I get the distinct impression that she could pound me into the turf without breathing hard, but she doesn't say or do anything. I am not sure if she has noticed I am here or not.

"Excuse me," I say, "I am looking for my sister? Ashlyn Revere? About five-ten, blonde, kind of athletic? Acts kind of bossy sometimes?"

"She is here," the tall woman says, gesturing to her right with the staff. I look where she is pointing and don't see anything, at least not until I look down.

There is Ashlyn, sitting huddled on the ground. Her head has been shaved, and she is wearing a thin hospital gown. She is holding what looks like a stuffed animal. Her face is pale and her breathing is shallow and quiet. I can see the tears drying on her face in the firelight.

I sit down beside her. "Ashlyn, are you all right?" I ask. She doesn't respond.

"What happened?" I ask the tall woman.

"She has fought a desperate battle, and lost," she says. "She needed help and I brought her here."

"And this place is, you know, not exactly a hospital," I say. "Because it looks like she needs a hospital."

"She is in a hospital," the tall woman says. "As are you, I believe. She is in surgery now."

I feel what I have always felt in my worst moments, the fingers of a giant hand constricting my ribcage. "She isn't supposed to go into surgery until this afternoon," I say.

"Time has little meaning here," she says. "And before you ask, I brought your sister here because it is my home. Where everything begins, and ends."

I look up into the spreading branches overhead. "You mean Yggdrasil?" I ask. "The world ash tree?"

"The same. You know of it, traveler?"

"Neil Gaiman. *Norse Mythology.*" You have to read something once in a while that's not a romance novel. "That makes you, what, a Valkyrie? Chooser of the slain?"

The tall woman's expression turns grave. "Let us hope that it does not come to that. I am Lachesis, and I have tried to help your sister as much as I can. But her life is in the hands of others now."

"Can you help me get her up?" I ask. "Maybe if we get her moving around, she'll feel better. Or something."

Ashlyn is still sitting there, barely breathing. She is petting the stuffed animal, which looks like a black rabbit. In fact, it looks exactly like the same black rabbit who tricked me into leaving Darcy's house.

"I am Atropos," the black rabbit says. "I am here to comfort your sister."

Atropos sounds stricken as he says this, as though he needs someone to comfort him as well. Ashlyn is still petting him, but she has a vacant glaze over her eyes, and she looks about ready to topple over. "I can see you're helping comfort her," I say. "But she needs more than that. How do we help her?"

"We cannot," the rabbit says. "As Lachesis says, it is out of our control."

The horse, who had been patiently eating grass this whole time, now comes over to Ashlyn and nuzzles her face. Ashlyn glances at me. "Unicorn," she says.

"Well, actually...sure. Unicorn."

"You brought me a unicorn," Ashlyn says.

"Would you like to, you know, ride the unicorn?" I ask.

"I can't," she says. "I'm not a maiden."

"Well," I say. "Good to know. We can talk about it later. Can you stand up at all? Maybe the unicorn can help."

I give Ashlyn my hand and manage to pull her to her feet. She doesn't feel as though she weighs anything. The rabbit jumps out of her lap in the process. Ashlyn leans against the horse, rocking unsteadily.

"Do you think you can walk at all?" I ask.

"I don't know," she says. "I've walked a long way. All the way to New York. But I'm tired now."

The circle of firelight is beginning to fade around me. The campfires are starting to burn themselves

244

out. I do not know what the rules of this little pocket universe are, but I have a strong suspicion that if I can't get Ashlyn away from this place, out of the circle, that she will die.

"I know you're tired," I say. "But we need to get out of here, okay? Can you make it just a little way?"

"I need to say goodbye to Nicholas, first."

"Okay, wait, who is..."

Ashlyn sinks to her knees, and I am afraid for a moment that she is going to pitch over, but she is just getting down to talk to the rabbit. "I need to go now," she says. "My sister is here."

"Are you sure that's a good idea?" the rabbit asks. "Stay here. It won't be long, now."

"No. I have to go. I have to try, anyway. I just wanted to let you know that you have been a good guide, and a good friend. I am sorry I yelled at you before, and told you that I didn't need you."

"It was true, though," the rabbit says. "You didn't need me. You fought the Dark Lord bravely, and you almost won. I am very proud of you, Ashlyn Revere."

"I am sorry I called you a bunny all those times."

"It is quite all right. Go now. We may see each other again someday."

Ashlyn slowly makes her way to her feet. "Thank you for bringing me here," she says to Lachesis.

"It is no more and no less than my duty. Be sure to perform yours, whatever it may be."

"All right then," I say. "Goodbye, everyone, we're leaving now. Come on, Ashlyn, let's get you out of here. Somewhere safe."

"There is no place like that here," Ashlyn says.

"Then we'll do our best. Come on."

Ashlyn leans against the horse, and I hold her other hand, and step by slow step, we make our way toward the firelight. One of the fires, off to the left, has gone out entirely, and another is just a few glowing embers under a pile of ashes. We don't have much time.

"We're almost there," I say. "We'll make it."

Ashlyn closes her eyes and shakes her head, as though something is deeply wrong, but I have no idea what it is. "It doesn't matter," she says. "Only honor matters."

"That's not true," I say. "Lots of things matter. Sunrises and sunsets. Going to the movies and going out for tacos afterward. Mint chocolate chip ice cream. Christmas and New Year's. All that stuff is important, and it all matters, and we need to start moving or you'll miss all of it. And I'll miss you."

Ashlyn gathers up her strength and takes a couple of steps forward, but she is struggling and I can only carry so much of her pain. "Why did you come for me?" she asks.

I give her a searching look. "You were responsible for me for so long," I say. "Just returning the favor."

We take a few more steps, and the fires are starting to go out. The horse takes a step forward, but Ashlyn doesn't step with it, and she leans on me. I hold her up and try to steady her.

"Wait," she says.

"We actually really don't have time for that," I say.

"I remembered something." She takes a step backward, and then another, and it is all I can do not to shout at her. The horse takes a step forward, and Ashlyn is now standing by her hindquarters. She reaches back to the horse's tail and removes a strand of hair.

"I almost forgot," she says. "I need this."

I have no idea what she needs with a strand of horsehair, but there are some things in life that you just have to accept. "Do you think we can get moving?" I ask.

"Where are we going again?" she replies.

"Home."

Ashlyn takes three tentative steps forward, making her way to the front of the horse. I hold her hand and give her what support I can. The closest two fires are still burning, giving us just enough light to see. The horse guides us to the path between the fires.

"Thank you," Ashlyn says. "Thank you for coming for me. I will see you when we get home."

"I will see you tomorrow, when you wake up," I say.

"I'm very tired," she says. "I was in a battle, and we lost, and everyone died, and it was all my fault."

"Don't talk that way. It wasn't your fault. You did the best you could. You always do. I need you. You're my sister. Don't give up now."

"I don't want to give up," Ashlyn says. "I love you. But there may not be time."

"Don't give up. Please don't die. I love you, and I don't want you to die."

We take one last step forward, out of the circle of firelight, and fall into the unknown darkness.

WE JUST DON'T KNOW AT THIS POINT

Kingman is wide awake now, and that gives him the advantage over just about everyone else in the room. Torrez was in the operating room for four hours and is working on maybe three hours of sleep. The hospital called the Reveres as soon as Ashlyn went into surgery; the husband and wife drove over from the little town where they live, and they've been up all night. So has Morton, who sits in the corner of the room, eyes hooded, like a malevolent hawk. Only Penelope Revere has had anything close to a decent night's sleep; she apparently woke up screaming at about three in the morning and the night nurse gave her a sedative. She is still out of it but it won't be much longer before she's awake. Kingman reckons that Penny has as much right to be in on the discussion as anyone, so they're meeting in her room.

Kingman is the most rested of anyone but he still had a rough night of it. He fell asleep in his recliner and didn't notice until about three in the morning, when he was woken up by a particularly obnoxious infomercial. Torrez had texted him at some point, saying that the surgery had been successful, and so he dragged himself to his bed and managed to get three more hours of sleep. He has showered and had a few bites of last night's risotto (which tastes much better the second day, or maybe he was just that hungry). Add to that two cups of early-morning coffee and he is ready to challenge the day. Today's challenge is Ashlyn Revere.

"Should we wake up my favorite patient?" Morton asks.

"Never a good idea," Mrs. Revere says. "Give her another minute. She's almost awake."

"Who's almost awake?" Penny asks, sleepily. She yawns, opens her eyes, and scans the room. Her face is a mask of worry.

"Ashlyn's still alive," Kingman says, which seems to at once confound and relieve Penny.

"Your sister underwent emergency surgery this morning," Torrez says.

"I know," Penny says. That sounds very odd to Kingman, but he doesn't interrupt her. "Although that doesn't explain what all of you are doing here." She lets loose a racking cough and spits up a massive glob of phlegm. "Unless it does."

"The surgery was successful," Torrez says. "My team removed the subdural hematoma—the blood clot, that is—that was causing the pressure inside her skull. Without the clot there, the pressure has gone down, which is all for the good. But she hasn't regained consciousness, and she's still on the ventilator."

"The question," Kingman says, "is whether she can breathe without the ventilator. I think that she can, and that we should take her off right away."

"And if she can't?" Morton says.

"Then we give her time to recover," Kingman says. "She was able to breathe normally before; there's no reason to think that she won't be able to breathe normally after the surgery."

"I think there is cause for significant concern," Morton says. "Ashlyn is not breathing on her own. She is not exhibiting the patterns of high levels of brain function that she had before. Whatever caused the high blood pressure that led to the spike in intracranial pressure that prompted the surgery may have caused further damage. I think we have to consider the possibility that she is brain dead."

Kingman shakes his head. "It is far too early to even think about that. She's only been out of surgery for four hours. The likelihood is that she's just sleeping rather soundly at the moment. The brain activity she experienced was usually accompanied by REM sleep, and we're not seeing that right now."

"What does that mean?" Penny asks.

"Before the surgery, the readings on your sister's brain indicated that there was a lot of high-level activity going on, usually during the time that she was dreaming. It's not uncommon to have lucid dreams when you are in a coma, especially when you are taking a lot of barbiturates, as she was. But she's not dreaming right now, and we're not seeing the same level of activity we were."

"It could be that she needs time to get the anesthesia drugs and the barbiturates out of her system," Torres says. "I agree with Dr. Kingman that it is far too early to jump to any conclusions. But Dr. Morton has a point. The damage to Ashlyn's brain may be so severe that she won't recover. We just don't know at this point, and there's nothing to do but wait."

"Can I see her?" Penny asks.

"No," Morton says. "You'd both be running too much of an infection risk."

"We haven't seen her, either, Penny," Mr. Revere says. "She's in sterile isolation. If she gets an infection, that could result in her needing more surgery."

Penny coughs again in what looks like a painful but necessary process. "Let me get this straight," she says. "My sister is down in intensive care, and all of you so-called doctors are up here, talking to me? Go take care of her; she's the one that needs help. For all any of you know, she's awake already."

"Penny!" Mrs. Revere says.

In the back of the room, Dr. Torrez starts coughing, trying to mask his laughter.

"Stop that," Mrs. Revere says to Torrez. "Penny, despite her customary rudeness, is absolutely right. I will stay here and help her with her vest. The rest of you, go check on Ashlyn, please."

"Yes ma'am," Kingman says. "We will keep you posted."

The doctors leave the room together. Morton heads down the corridor, presumably looking for breakfast. Kingman and Torrez take the elevator down.

"What do you suppose she meant by that?" Torrez says.

"Who?" Kingman asks.

"The sister. She said she knew that Ashlyn was in surgery."

"Did someone tell her?"

"I don't see how anyone could have. We made the decision so quickly. We didn't have time to call you, much less the family. How did you find out, anyway?"

"Morton called me."

"Oh, that schmuck. He probably told her, then. Which would be a stupid thing to do—why wake up your patient in the middle of the night? Go figure."

"Hard enough to sleep in a hospital, anyway."

"Tell me about it," Torrez says. "I'll look in on her with you, but then I'm going straight home to get some sleep. You honestly think Ashlyn has a chance?"

"I don't know," Kingman says. "You saw the brain; I didn't."

"It was ugly. But I've seen worse who survived and had at least some kind of recovery. She's young and strong. I think she has a chance, but the odds aren't good."

Kingman thinks the odds are better than that. He's seen the readouts. Ashlyn is somewhere in there, he thinks, generating all that weird brain activity. He just hopes he gets the chance to meet her.

NO PLACE LIKE HOME

"I recommend that you not try to get up," the voice says.

I open my eyes, just a crack, and try to raise my head. This instantly seems like a bad idea. Wherever I am, I am not going anywhere anytime soon. I am tired and disoriented, and I can feel the worst headache of my life forming like a storm system on the horizon.

"Sensible of you," the voice says. "For once. Do you know where you are?"

I turn my head to the direction of the voice. I see the fuzzy outlines of the Dark Lord. "Hell," I guess.

"Not exactly. You're in New York, in the penthouse. I wish you could get up—it's quite the view. And you are my guest, not my prisoner, you understand."

"How?" I ask. It is a struggle to focus enough to get even simple words out.

"You are recovering from emergency surgery," the Dark Lord explains. "You almost died. Apparently, your experience the last time you were here was unduly stressful and caused a dangerous increase in your blood pressure. You should be more careful. As for the question you didn't ask, you are in New York because I wanted you to be in New York. I think your friend Valentine may have mentioned that."

"Dead." It isn't a question.

"He is dead, and I killed him. I take no great pride in that, but he died bravely, as most of your force did. I give you all the credit in the world for creativity in that battle; bringing in the *Intrepid* was a stroke of genius. And, of course, I cheated a little bit."

I have no answer for this, but I let out a groan anyway.

"Because—you know this—the hoplites who fought at Thermopylae weren't immortal. They fought bravely and they died just the same. It was the *Persians* who were the immortals—they called themselves that, I mean. The Persians weren't immortal, either, but when one of their warriors died, he was replaced. So I cheated and made my hoplites immortal, and I am not sorry that I did."

I make a noise of frustration that is meant to sound like *get bent*.

"I am surprised to see that you escaped. I assume that the Valkyrie intervened, either her or the rabbit or both together. No matter. I have what I want and so do you."

I turn toward the Dark Lord and focus as much as I can. He has the sword Dyrnwyn resting across his knees. Just that much effort has made me completely exhausted; there is no way I am going to be able to take my sword back, much less do anything with it. If I didn't feel defeated before, I do now.

"I have your sword, and you have your pain, which is what you wanted. Unless you change your mind about that."

"Life," I say.

"Not so fast. There is an alternative available. Not the one I promised you before; that's not something I can offer. But you should know about your other option."

"No."

"Hear me out. Most of your life, you've been responsible for your sister. Hasn't always been easy. You've done a lot for her, and there's one more thing you can do."

"What?"

"You can die," the Dark Lord says. "I am not in favor of this, you understand. But you can choose to, you know, not wake up. And if you do that, well, you signed the organ donor card. There's a doctor here who is standing by waiting for you to do just that, so he can take your lungs and transplant them into your sister."

This sounds like a bad idea. I need my lungs to breathe. But if I'm dead, do I need to breathe? Don't think so. If I'm dead, I won't feel the pain I'm starting to feel in my head, and in my chest, and in what I think is probably my arm. There's a lot of pain coming at me in a lot of different directions. Even just lying on my back is a trial all its own.

But that doesn't matter. Only honor matters. Yes, it would be honorable to die and make the ultimate sacrifice for my sister. But it would be just as honorable to live, wouldn't it? Just more painful.

Dying now would make Penny's effort to save me—her selfless effort, as I now realize—all for nothing.

"Home," I say.

The corner of the Dark Lord's mouth quirks upward, just a little. "Farewell, Ashlyn Revere," he says. "You know what to do."

I click my bare heels together, three times, and close my eyes.

I hear the beeping sounds, the same ones I heard during the thick of the battle in New York but quieter and less insistent. I can feel cool air blowing and smell the old familiar hospital smell. I open my eyes to find a big square of fluorescent light and then close them to block out the stabbing pain. My mouth is dry and sticky and tastes unpleasant. I am breathing heavily, just the way I would if I were in the middle of a closely-contested field hockey game. My arm hurts and my head hurts and it hurts to even breathe, but I am not in the Dark Lord's penthouse, or the trackless wastes of the Eastern Marches, or in the circle of firelight around the spreading ash tree. I am home, wherever that is, whatever that means.

"Turn the light off," a quiet voice says. "I think she's trying to wake up."

My eyelids flutter open, and I see a slight man at my bedside wearing a white coat. He is on the younger side for a doctor, but he has the incipient worry lines and the receding hairline of a much older man. "Hi there," he says. "Dr. Drew Kingman. Happy to meet you, at long last."

"Where am I?" I ask, or at least I try to. It comes out as a low-pitched moan, one that I don't understand myself, although Kingman seems to.

"You're in intensive care at Robert Wood Johnson Hospital in New Brunswick," he says. "You were in a car accident and had a brain injury. You had surgery last night to remove a blood clot in your brain. It's nice to see you awake."

"Penny?" I ask. I manage to make the "p" sound, but the rest of the word comes out somewhere between a cough and a sigh. Maybe my mouth is dryer than I thought it was.

"Your sister?" he says. "She's fine. She's still in the hospital—she had a concussion, and with her condition, we needed to take extra precautions. You may not remember, but before you went into surgery the first time, you mentioned to a nurse that she has cystic fibrosis. That helped me out a great deal in treating her and I wanted to say thank you. She would tell you that, herself, but the risk of infection is too great for both of you."

I want to ask for water, just a little to get my mouth unblocked from whatever it is that's not allowing me to speak properly. I try to make a drinking motion with my left hand, but I can't move it at all. I try again with my right hand, and someone behind Dr. Kingman—probably a nurse—figures it out and gets me a cup and a straw. I drink a little and find that it helps.

"How long have I been here?" I ask, but it's still unintelligible. I am making sounds, but they don't sound like words and I am starting to wonder that it maybe isn't just that my throat is dry.

"Don't try to talk just yet," Kingman says. "I know it's difficult and you probably have a lot of questions about what happened. You may have some issues with your speech or other problems we don't even know about just yet. Now that you're awake, we'll be able to monitor them and figure out the best way to treat you. All right? If you give me a few minutes, I'll go upstairs and tell your parents that you're awake and that you want to see them. Good?"

I try to nod my head, but that hurts too. Kingman nods his head and is gone.

The nurse slides into my field of vision. "I'm the ICU nurse," he says. "My name is Dennis Dawson," he says. "Welcome home. And welcome to your first day of recovery."

Recovery. Family. Home. Simple words, but they ring like bells in my heart.

PARTS OF SPEECH

Click-whirr. Click-whirr. Click-whirr.

It is a bright and clear morning in late November, and I am driving my wheelchair down the corridors of the rehabilitation center in North Jersey where I have spent the last three months. I had my first experience in a wheelchair when they wheeled me out of Robert Wood Johnson, prior to putting me in the ambulance that brought me here. I wasn't a big fan of the experience. I would ten times rather have walked out of the hospital, but of course they don't let you do that and it's not like I could have, anyway. They won't let me walk here, even after all the progress I've made so far. And since I can't walk, I had to get pushed around by whoever was available to get to wherever I wanted to go.

That changed two weeks ago. The small glass company that owned the van that crashed into my car reached an early settlement on the insurance claim. Long story short, that meant that it was possible for me to have my very own wheelchair, complete with electric motor and joystick control.

As long as I am pointed in the right direction, I can make it down most of the corridors pretty smoothly. I can go from the cafeteria to my room and back without much problem, which is a real advantage—it is no fun at all to have to wait for someone to push me when it's time to eat and I'm hungry. But I haven't quite mastered how to make turns, and the path to the speech therapy area requires a bit more in the way of starting and stopping.

I am getting better at steering, though, and I make it to speech therapy eight minutes early—a new personal record. Speech therapy is a painfully slow and often frustrating process but it is absolutely necessary, and I am making real, measurable progress with it, which is more than is happening in other areas of my life.

Emily is my speech-language pathologist and in some other reality we might have been friends. We graduated from high school the same year; she went to Vanderbilt and was the runner-up in the hurdles in the SEC track tournament her junior year. Similar backgrounds, similar education, but she's going to go home at the end of the day and hang out with her boyfriend and have fun, and I'm going back to my room in my wheelchair and waiting for the next day. She is the young medical professional and I am the struggling patient, and that's no way to build a friendship.

"All right, Ashlyn," Emily says. "We're going to try the cards again, if you're ready. I'm going to show you an image and you're going to tell me what it is. Understand? Just relax and do your best."

The cards are designed for preschoolers; every card has a little cartoon and a word. This one has a soccer ball resting on green grass. "Ball," I say. It is one of the few words I can say consistently, along with "no" and "okay." "Ball" starts with a plosive and I do better with plosive words, at least the short ones.

I am learning a lot about speech-language pathology. There are basically two types of problems you can have. One is when you have issues with the parts of your body that make speech work—vocal cords, upper palate, lips or teeth or whatever. The other one is when all those speech organs work the right way, it's just that the brain can't communicate with your body the right way. This last part gets broken down into two specific problems—one called *aphasia,* where the name for the thing you are looking at has fallen out of your memory and you don't know what it is, and *apraxia,* which is when you know what the thing is, but you just can't get your mouth to form the word properly. And what is even more fun than this is when you have both of these things.

At first, they thought I had just aphasia. I could say "ball" but I couldn't say "fall," so they thought my brain was so damaged I couldn't understand what "fall" is. Except I did understand but I couldn't pronounce the letter F, which is a fricative and I can't handle fricatives just yet. Once Emily figured out that I had more apraxia issues than aphasia, she started treating me for the apraxia and I've made a lot of progress on that.

The aphasia is still there, though—it's part of the overall memory loss issues, which are another fun and unpredictable part of my life. I have been eating a ton of bananas since I got here—they're easy for me to chew—except one day they ran out and gave me pineapple, and I had absolutely forgotten that pineapples existed. Whatever neuron in my brain that had information about pineapples, and about my cousin Keith up in Toronto, and the whole business about how a bill becomes a law—all of that vanished and I have to reconstitute it. But since I don't remember what I don't remember, and I don't know that I don't remember it until the time that I need to remember it, it makes things a little confusing. When you add on that the fact that I still can't speak well enough to communicate high-level concepts like that, well, it gets kind of frustrating.

Emily turns over the next card: a picture of a baseball bat. It is another word that I can say, but not one that's very useful. "Bat," I say, trying to make it look easy and effortless. It is neither.

I have been told that my brain injury was not as bad as it could have been, and that it was a miracle that it wasn't worse. If it was a miracle, it was a crummy miracle. I can breathe normally, which I gather is what they were most concerned about after the surgery. I can control my bowels and bladder, which is a blessing, and I have most of my gross motor skills, or at least those that haven't been impaired by the damage to my bones and soft tissue.

Emily turns over the next card and this is not one I have seen. It is a long, sharp metal thing. The word starts with an *s*, which is a sound I can make if I think about it long enough. And then, just like that, it pops into my brain.

"Sword," I say.

"That's very good," Emily says. "You pronounced the sibilant correctly, and you didn't trip over the silent letter *w*, which is a big step. Can you say it again?"

"Sword," I say. "Sword sword sword."

"That's very good. I know you did field hockey; did you ever do fencing?"

"No." No way to explain how I learned to use a sword in my dreams, how I wielded one to slay a six-legged fear beast, how I lost it in the deep waters of the Hudson after a doomed assault on Manhattan, how the Dark Lord recovered it. I literally can't tell Emily anything about that, and if I somehow managed it, she'd think I was nuts. But I can say the word, and I do, with no small degree of satisfaction. "Sword," I say.

The next card is a picture of a Dalmatian puppy, with the word *spot,* and I can't say it. I ought to be able to, but I can't get the sibilant *s* and the plosive *p* to connect with each other. It is maddening to fail so quickly after a success and I make a little grunt of frustration.

"That's OK," she says. "You're doing fine."

Emily is unfailingly cheerful and patient with me, which makes matters that much worse. She is bright and energetic, with a long blonde ponytail and a perky smile. She has a cute boyfriend named Glen, and earlier this month she finished the New York City marathon in just under three hours. I don't want to hate her, but it is hard.

Now she turns over another card. This is not the one I have been waiting for—the one word that I desperately want to say—but it's close enough. The picture is of a brick wall. "Wa," I say. "Wa."

"Keep going," Emily says. "You're so close."

"Walk," I say, for the first time.

"That's close," Emily says. "Wall. You said 'walk.' But that's okay."

"Walk," I say. "Na wall. Say walk."

"You need to say what the card says, Ashlyn. Okay? I know this is difficult for you, but the only way I can evaluate your progress is for you to say what's on the card."

"Walk," I say, happily. "Walk."

I finish my speech therapy and go to another part of the facility to do occupational therapy, which is not quite what you think it is. They had me sorting money this time, which I can manage on an intellectual level—that is to say, I can tell a dime from a nickel from a penny—but is difficult when your fine motor skills have been affected. My left hand is still in a cast, so that adds a level of difficulty. Then it is time for dinner—macaroni and cheese, which I can manage independently, but with an aide at my elbow making sure I don't choke on it. Then the aide helps me change into my pajamas and I lie on my bed, staring at the ceiling.

I haven't slept much the past three months. I am not afraid to go to sleep; I am not afraid of anything. But it is difficult for me to go to sleep and often it's drug-assisted. I don't like it when they sedate me; I often dream that I am walking through a fog bank, wandering aimlessly and hopelessly. But the alternative is staying awake and worrying, and thinking about the accident.

I have not seen Penny since I left the hospital. She had a concussion and was out cold for a couple of days. They put her on a ventilator because of her cystic fibrosis, but she didn't have any broken bones and not much in the way of soft tissue damage. They wheeled me past her on my way out and we waved at each other, but that was it. They wouldn't let her come any closer because of the risk of infection. For that same reason, she isn't able to come to the rehab center. We can't talk on the phone very effectively, but she sends me long, chatty e-mails. I do my best to respond but even with an iPad, typing is a slow process, and of course speech-to-text doesn't work at all for me. I see Dad every morning; he got a new job with ADP in Roseland, which is just up the road from here. Mom drops by for a couple of hours every day when she can make it. But most of the time I am on my own.

It is nine o'clock and I am listening to the muffled sounds of the hospital. Tanya opens my door and sits down at my bedside.

"Do you have a minute?" she asks.

"Okay," I reply. I like Tanya, because Tanya is one of my physical therapists and my ticket out of here. Tanya is not a nice person. She is young and blonde, but she is not the least bit perky. She was a weightlifter in college and just missed out on the

Olympic team. I think she feels bad about this and is determined to take it out on the rest of the world, starting with her patients. I respect her like you would not believe.

"I had an interesting talk with Emily Parsons just now. She said you were saying something about wanting to walk."

"Walk," I say. I have been working on that word for Tanya. I want to let her know what my goal is. I am going to walk out of here, and the sooner the better.

"We've had this conversation," Tanya says. "It's not time for you to walk yet. If it was just the brain injury, that would be one thing. But you need to have both hands available to support you while you learn to walk again. Your collarbone is in good shape now, and you should get that cast off your wrist this week. But you still have balance issues, as well as muscle loss. You're going to be riding that wheelchair for a while longer. I'm sorry as hell about that, but you just have to be patient with yourself."

"Walk," I say.

"Not today," she says. "I want to see you back on your feet as soon as we can do it. But the risk of falling is too great, and a bad fall will set things back even further."

"Walk."

A grin splits Tanya's face, a horrible sight. "Emily is worried about you. She says you are trying to do everything too fast, and then you get frustrated and angry. She wants you to slow down and take it easy."

"No," I say.

"Can I tell you something?"

266

"Okay."

Tanya leans back in her chair. "I wasn't sure about you when they brought you in here," she says. "I mean, look. I have a lot of patients. You get an idea about people after a while. Most people talk a good game about physical therapy. They try, or at least they want to try. But they bitch about it. They say that PT stands for Physical Terrorist. They go through with it, but they don't really have what it takes. Not just to get better, you understand that? Not just to get back to where they were. To remake themselves. To become better. You understand?"

"Okay," I say, because that's all I can say. My heart is soaring, though.

"There's a difference between people. And that difference is determination. That difference is desire. Most people don't have that. I didn't think you had it. But I'm beginning to come around on that."

"Okay."

"I talked to your field hockey coach at UNC. She said you were kind of an average player most of the time. You had some talent, and you worked hard to get better, but you weren't always engaged. Do you remember anything about this?"

"S-some," I say, which is close to the truth. I don't think this is quite fair, but I'm not in a position to argue.

"Right. What she said was that when the team had the lead, you tended to get a little lackadaisical. Just a little bit—you probably didn't even realize you were doing it, consciously. The team was good enough that it didn't matter, most of the time. Except once in a while, you'd give up a goal or two and get behind. And then she said you changed at that point. You started fighting back. You would push yourself in a way that you hadn't before."

"Yeah," I say.

"She sent me a couple of videos. And I think she had a point—not that I know a lot about field hockey, mind you, but you can really see it if you know what you're looking for. You respond well to adversity. You know how rare that is?"

"No."

"It is very rare. You haven't complained once since you've been here, did you know that? And yeah, I know you have a TBI and you can't express yourself the way you want to, but I think you get it. I mean, you really get it. You want it. You want to come all the way back and set the world on its ear. Right?"

"Walk."

"That's the goal. Right? So here's what we're going to do. You listening?" She whips her mini iPad out of her canvas bag. "Okay. I'm reassigning you from Nancy to Gretel. You know Gretel?"

"No," I say, but I like where this is going. Nancy has been telling me to take things slow and easy, and *slow* and *easy* are the two worst words I know.

"Gretel is a doctoral student in physiology. She has a grip like a hydraulic press. You're going to love her. Unless you decide to hate her, and that's okay, too. Either way, she'll make you stronger. Another thing I'm going to do is, tomorrow, try to set you up on the rowing machine. I'd rather do the stationary cycle, but this is lower to the ground and you're less likely to hurt yourself if you fall off. Good enough?"

Definitely good enough. "Walk," I reply.

"You're damn right. You're going to walk. Not today, not tomorrow, but sooner than you think. I have faith in you, Ashlyn. I think you've got what it takes to walk out of here. All you have to do is work with me, and not be so hard on yourself."

"Walk," I say. "Walk."

Tanya squeezes my hand and leaves, and I am by myself in the darkness again. But not alone.

LONESOME STANDARD TIME

Dr. Drew Kingman is, for the moment, unemployed and homeless. Both of these words are accurate but at the same time gross overstatements. He has been named associate professor of clinical neurology at the Brain Institute at Tulane, which means he is going home. He has closed on a gorgeous white house with a pillared front porch on Henry Clay Avenue in New Orleans, a couple of blocks from Audubon Park, within easy walking distance to work. But the job doesn't start until January and the new house has some roof damage that won't be fixed until February. When he went to the Robert Wood Johnson HR department to turn in his notice, they told him, in the nicest possible way, that he wouldn't need to come in on Monday. It worked out; he got three months of severance pay, which will go a long way to pay for the roofers. And he was able to sell his condo in Rahway right away, on the condition that he move out right away. So all his stuff is in a grim-looking self-storage unit in East Brunswick, and he's house-sitting for a podiatrist colleague who is taking his wife and daughters on a Disney cruise to Norway.

Kingman has been spending the last week sleeping late and playing *NCAA Football 14* on the antique PlayStation in the guest bedroom and trying to start something like a workout routine. But this doesn't fill up his time very effectively, and like a lot of bored and lonely people, he's been noodling around on social media. He got a LinkedIn invitation from someone named Dennis Revere, an accountant at ADP, and didn't think twice about it until he got the message. *If you haven't left for Louisiana yet,* it said, *and if you have time, you might want to stop by and visit Ashlyn when you get a chance. She would love to see you before you leave for good.*

Well, how do you say no to that? Kingman can't possibly.

The rehabilitation center where Ashlyn Revere has been for the last three months sits on the foothills of the Watchung Mountains, across the street from a country club. It is a quiet place, probably a green place in the summer. It is now the last week of November and the skies have turned slate-gray.

Kingman checks in at the front desk, which as an unexpected, unannounced visitor takes him a little longer than he would have liked. He could have pulled rank and identified himself as a doctor, but that's not why he's here, not really. Ashlyn isn't his patient anymore; he's not here for any medical reason, or he hopes not. This is a social call; no need for a white coat or stethoscope.

A nurse picks him up at the lobby—one of those efficient, effective middle-aged women who have kept hospitals running since the Dark Ages. "You're a friend of the family?" she asks. "If she hasn't seen you in a while, she might not remember you. Try not to be disappointed."

"I helped treat her after her accident," I explain. "How is she doing?"

"Not bad, considering. She had a lot of damage. But she's coming along; it's just a slow process and she gets frustrated. It's getting close to her lunchtime, so I figured we'd just meet in the cafeteria."

Kingman considers this. "Food any good?" he asks.

This elicits the predictable eye-roll. "It ain't the Waldorf-Astoria. Stick with the soup."

"Right."

The nurse finds them a table out of the way, and Kingman gets the potato soup and a couple of yeast rolls and a diet Coke. The nurse returns after a couple of minutes, directing a young woman in a wheelchair to his table. Her hair hasn't grown in all that much yet, and he can still see the scar from the burr hole surgery. Her left hand and wrist are in a soft splint, which is a good sign. Her eyes are bright and it's clear that Ashlyn Revere is somewhere behind them, struggling towards the surface.

"King," she says, and it's almost intelligible.

"Pleasure to see you," he says, as the nurse aligns her wheelchair for the table and walks off to grab Ashlyn something to eat. "You're sounding very good today."

She licks her lips. "Walk," she says.

"They have you walking already?" Kingman asks. She would probably be able to walk by now, he thinks, if not for her other injuries.

"Naw," she says. "Want."

"Of course," he says. "Did your dad tell you I was going home? I got a job down in New Orleans, working at Tulane University."

"Yeah," she says. "Good. Work. Want work."

"I'm sure you do," Kingman says. "You're getting occupational therapy, right? So that ought to help with that, eventually."

That causes a brief look of something—disgust?—to cross her face, but it doesn't last long. The nurse has brought her lunch—Salisbury steak with mashed potatoes and squash, with a plastic cup of milk and a banana. The steak is already cut up and she digs in with a good appetite.

"Praxya," she says in between bites. Kingman doesn't understand and looks to the nurse for elucidation.

"That's Ashlyn-speak," she says. "You get used to it. What she is trying to tell you is that she has apraxia; she understands every word you say and you can talk to her like a grownup." Ashlyn drops her fork and puts her right index finger on her nose, which Kingman gathers means *That's right.*

"It looks like your appetite is fine," Kingman says. She has devoured half the Salisbury steak and is making a good start on the squash.

"Pro," she says.

"Right," Kingman says. "Protein to build muscles, so you can start walking again." Ashlyn touches her nose again and the nurse gives him a little smile. He is getting the hang of this.

"Why?" Ashlyn asks.

"Well, then. Why. I don't think anyone knows that. Accidents happen; statistically speaking, you were just the next in line to have one. There really isn't a reason. If you want the theological point of view..." Kingman stops, because Ashlyn has thrown a wadded-up napkin at him.

"That is also Ashlyn-speak," the nurse says, not overly helpfully. "It means something like *that's not what I was asking you, so wait a minute so I can figure out how to ask it the right way.* Either that, or she's still hungry."

"No," Ashlyn says, and then she pauses for a second. Kingman can practically see the metaphorical gears turning in her head. "La."

"La?" Kingman asks.

"No. La."

"No. La. Oh, wait. NOLA. You want to know why I'm going back to New Orleans."

Ashlyn smiles, touches her nose again, and starts going to work on the mashed potatoes.

"It's kind of funny. I never lived in New Orleans proper. I grew up in Plaquemines Parish—just downstream from there a few miles. I went to LSU for college, which is in Baton Rouge—the other side of New Orleans. Then medical school in Nebraska. Kind of lost the accent there. Then I did my residency at RWJ and stayed on there. Most of my folks left

Louisiana after Katrina, so I didn't have any real reason to go back. But...I don't know what to tell you. I have been working these crazy, impossible hours for years now and I haven't had much of a social life. Or any kind of life at all, when you get down to it. And when they called me and asked me to come home to Louisiana, I said yes."

"Home," Ashlyn says.

"When you get right down to it, yeah." Kingman takes a big bite out of one of the yeast rolls, which aren't bad for hospital food. "Did you get to go home? For Thanksgiving?"

"No," Ashlyn says, and her face gets dark. "Penny."

"That's her sister," the nurse says. "And...well, there are issues."

"I'm familiar," Kingman says. "They don't really think you're going to infect her, do they?"

"They're a little worried," the nurse says. "Penny moved up on the list for lung transplants. Any kind of infection and she might lose out on a new pair of lungs. That means Penny can't come here, and because Ashlyn is exposed to whatever viruses are going around while she's here, they can't see each other."

"That's no good," Kingman says. "You need to be connected to other people. I mean, that's why I'm leaving in a nutshell. I just get so lonesome here, sometimes."

Ashlyn nods, and doesn't say anything. Kingman very quietly kicks himself. However lonesome he is in New Jersey, it must be ten times worse for Ashlyn, stuck in a rehabilitation center all day long, trying to rebuild her life. She takes the last few bites of banana, drains the last of her cup of milk, and wipes her face with a napkin.

"You're really doing very well," Kingman says. "I'm serious about that. I didn't know what to expect when I got here. But you're feeding yourself independently. That's a big win, even if it's just soft foods. You can drink and swallow without choking."

"Most of the time," the nurse says. "That's why I'm here. But she manages all right, as long as she's not trying to talk and eat at the same time."

"I'm not trying to be clinical here, you understand, but you're able to carry on an adult conversation. Your higher brain functions seem to be working properly. As long as you keep working on your rehab and your speech therapy, you ought to just keep improving. And your dad says you're doing just that. You can be proud of what you've accomplished so far."

"Walk."

"I know. We need to get you out of that wheelchair, no doubt. It's not the ideal situation. But I have all the faith in the world in you."

"King," Ashlyn says. "G-g-good. Doc. Good. Doc. Doc." Her face goes red trying to move from the hard *c* to the soft *t* in *doctor*. "Doc." She leaves it at that. "Tankoo."

"More Ashlyn-speak," the nurse says. "She's trying to say that she thinks you're a good doctor, and she says thank you for taking good care of her."

"I understand," Kingman says. "I do."

Kingman walks Ashlyn to her next appointment, which is with a cast-iron Gorgon of a physical therapist with hands like meat hooks. "We'll have her whipped into shape in no time, Doctor," she says, and Kingman bids them both farewell. He would like to stay and watch, but she's not his patient and it's not his place, and he needs to leave anyway.

He makes it as far as the lobby before he breaks down. It's not like him and it's not professional, but he needs to unload the emotion and crying is a good way to do that. He finds a quiet corner of the lobby and sits there quietly and sobs.

After a while, a young woman comes over to him and sits down by his side. "Are you all right?" she asks.

"I'm fine," Kingman says, although he isn't.

"I'm Bernice Lynn," she says. "I'm a grief counselor here at the center. Would you like to come back to my office?"

"Oh, good Lord, no. It's not like that."

"Grief can come to us from directions we didn't expect. It's okay to have these feelings. Would you like to talk about them?"

"I'm a doctor," Kingman explains.

"It doesn't make a difference. People think that because doctors lose patients all the time, they're inured to death. Some are, but most aren't."

Kingman has a sense that this conversation is getting out of control. "Okay," he says, "can I explain a minute without sounding too full of myself? I am—well, I was—a doctor at RWJ in New Brunswick and I have a former patient here, and I came to see her. She's doing very well, better than I expected, and she said thank you, and she said I was a good doctor."

A flashbulb goes off behind Bernice Lynn's pale blue eyes. "You're not grieving," she says. "You're happy."

"I wouldn't go *that* far," Kingman says, "but I'm not grieving. I don't know what happened. All of a sudden, I had a lot of feelings to process."

"You said you *were* a doctor?"

"Yeah. It's complicated. I quit—not because I wanted to stop being a doctor. I got a new job at Tulane, down in New Orleans."

"Oh! I went to Tulane. Isn't it a gorgeous campus?"

Kingman looks at Bernice Lynn, really seeing her for the first time. Like him, she is on the short side, with a heart-shaped face and long brown hair. "I'm from Louisiana," he says. "South of New Orleans. Belle Chasse."

"I know where that is," she said. "I'm from Metairie. You're going back home?"

"Yeah, in January. Tulane Brain Center. I'm going to be a professor."

"Lucky you," she says. "I was there through Katrina, but I left to go to Rutgers for grad school in social work and I ended up here. I love what I do but it's kind of lonesome sometimes. I go back home every year for Jazz Fest and Christmas, but it isn't the same."

"I feel the same way. It's one reason why I'm going back."

"Hey, listen," she says. "Let me make it up to you for jumping in like that, okay? There's a place in Woodbridge—it's more a Mexican place than anything else, but they make a decent etouffee."

"I know the one you're talking about," Kingman says. "It's kind of hard to get into. There's always a wait."

"I know one of the hostesses," she says. "I can get us in. If you'd like to have dinner, you know. We can compare notes."

"I'd like that," Kingman says.

Boots and Saddles

"You need to get your boots on," my mom says.

"These are boots," I say. "They're on my feet and everything."

"Not those boots, Penny. Your riding boots. Change into them and get in the car. We're going for equine therapy."

"We're doing *what*?"

"Equine therapy. With horses and everything."

"What if I get an infection?" I ask. That's been her answer for everything since the accident. *You might get an infection.*

"You and I both need to get you out of the house for a change," she says. "If you wear your mask and keep your distance from everyone, you ought to be okay for a little while."

"I have been asking for *weeks* to get out of this house, and you want me to leave *now* for *equine therapy?*" I am just very slightly outraged about this. When I left the hospital and came home in mid-September, Dr. Morton somehow managed to get me moved up on the transplant list for new lungs. This has led my parents, who are usually super-paranoid about health care in general, to double down on every annoying and irritating behavior. Every time one of their phones ring, they're convinced that it's the transplant team wanting to get me down to Philadelphia to get my lungs swapped out with new ones. I've been under virtual house arrest—I can't see Ashlyn, or my friends, or go to the mall, or even drive to Five Guys for a cheeseburger, because any of these things might result in me catching a cold. And now—without any warning—we're going for *equine* therapy, when I haven't been on a horse in, what, three years now? This is crazy. Something is up.

"You're not going to catch pneumonia from a horse. Come on. Get your riding boots on and get in the car."

"What about Ashlyn?" I ask. "This is the time of the day where you usually drive over there and leave me here all by myself."

"Penelope Dawn Revere," she says. "You will get in the car, now, with your riding boots on, or I will take every single cheap historical romance novel off your Kindle and replace them with SAT study guides."

"Equine therapy," I say. "Wow, Mom. That sounds like fun. Just a second while I change my boots and I'll be right with you."

"Your sarcasm does not impress me."

"It isn't meant to."

I figured that there was a scam of some sort going on, and I was right. There in the parking lot is a minivan with the name of the rehab center where Ashlyn is staying. "Popular day for equine therapy," I say.

"I figured both of you deserved a little surprise," Mom says. "Try to say something nice. She puts up a good front, but all of this is hard for her, and it would mean the world to her if you would say something nice. For a change."

"I think I can manage."

"You can understand what she says if you try hard enough. Don't just ignore her or pretend you didn't hear her, because she will throw something at you. Or worse."

"I just want to talk with her. That's all I want." I've been sending Ashlyn the occasional chatty e-mail, but she never responds, and of course they haven't let us near each other, not for Thanksgiving, even. I want to see my sister and I'm going to, and my heart is light for once.

They have loaded Ashlyn up to the platform they use for kids who have mobility issues, and are loading her onto a horse, slowly and carefully. The equine therapy center is set up for this kind of thing but they're always super-cautious. The main person who's helping her is from the hospital—I can tell because she's wearing scrubs under a short parka—and she looks like she could bench press a musk ox. I go over to the stables, where they have a gray mare saddled up for me. I put on my helmet and my mask and climb aboard, remembering my horsewomanship, and guide the mare over to where Ashlyn is.

"Hey sis," I say. "What's up?"

"Penny!" she shouts, or at least something that sounds like *Penny*, but it's close enough, and it's good to see her happy.

"You going to stand around all day, or are you going to ride?"

Ashlyn makes the last straining effort to throw her left foot over the saddle horn, and then she's done it and we're riding together. The early winter wind stings a bit, but I don't care. The sun is shining, our horses are gentle, and my sister and I are doing something together. What more could one ask for? Other than a pair of handsome cowboys to lead us around the corral, I suppose, but they seem to have gotten stuck in traffic.

"Sick?" Ashlyn asks, slipping a bit on the sibilant *s*.

"Me? No. Never been better. Occasional headache, you know, due to the accident. But I'm not light-sensitive anymore, so that's good. Dr. Morton says I ought to get a transplant next year sometime, if I stay healthy and all the breaks go right." By which he means *if someone with a similar genetic profile to mine has a massive head injury*, but I try not to dwell on that.

Ashlyn taps her chest, twice. "Mine," she says.

"I don't want *your* lungs, sis. You still need yours to breathe and stuff."

"Yeah," she says. And after a long pause, she tries another word starting with an *s*, but she can't spit it out.

"I think she's saying *sorry*," says the hulking woman from the hospital, who is holding the lead rope of Ashlyn's horse.

"Don't be sorry. I want you to have your own lungs. I don't want you feeling bad for me; I've never wanted that. I'd rather have you as my sister than anything, even a new pair of lungs."

"S-still."

"I know."

We ride on, slowly and quietly, the yellow fall leaves outside the corral silently lowering themselves to the ground.

"Room," Ashlyn says, drawing out the *r* like a badly-tuned motorcycle.

"Oh, for God's sake. I have *not* taken your room over. Not that I don't *want* your room, but they won't let me. You know what they're like."

"Good."

"What I think I heard them say is that they're going to put in a stair glide, you know, to help you get up and down the stairs, when you do come home. The twins are all excited about it; they're probably going to wear it out."

"No," Ashlyn says. "Walk."

"I hope so."

"S-soon. Walk."

After the therapeutic riding is over, Mom follows the van back to the highway. I figured that we would separate at that point, but we don't. Instead, both cars end up in the parking lot of one of the mini-malls on Route 22 and Mom goes into the Five Guys. "Wait here," she says.

"Grilled cheese and two strawberry milkshakes," I say.

"I know what your order is, sweetheart. And your sister's."

There's a seat next to Ashlyn's wheelchair in the van and they let us have lunch together. Ashlyn inhales the sandwich and Mom gets her another one. I am telling some funny story or other about the twins, and Ashlyn starts laughing and nearly drops her shake. I help her with it and she gives me a smile.

"Tankoo," she says.

"Think nothing of it."

"An'... tankoo."

"For what?"

"Unicorn."

I take a sip of my shake, mostly to help me retain my composure. "You remember that?" I asked. "With the ash tree, and the circle of fire?"

"Unicorn," she says.

"They told me you were dying," I said. "In the dream. You were holding onto this rabbit for dear life."

"Nick'las."

"Yeah. I figured you needed to get out of there, and we started walking. You remember that? I mean, it was all in my dream, so I didn't know it was in your dream, too."

"'Member. Tankoo."

"You're welcome." I wipe away some rogue moisture from my eyes; I have no idea how it could have gotten there. "I love you, Ashlyn. I couldn't just let you sit there and die. I know you're having a hard time now, and I wish I could make it better for you. But I knew you were dying, and I was the only one that could help, so I did."

"Know. Tankoo, Penny. Love you too."

Mom shows up then, with another sandwich for Ashlyn. "Nice to see both of you getting along," she says.

"Yeah, we're getting along just fine," I say.

I don't start bawling my eyes out until we get in the car.

THE JOB INTERVIEW

It is Monday morning after a busy week. I am up early because my dad is here early on Monday morning. He has a very welcome sack of McDonald's sausage biscuits—there is nothing wrong with my appetite, at least, and I can use the extra protein. I have physical therapy scheduled for after breakfast, where I will be working with Gretel. She is strong and tireless and utterly contemptuous of weakness or doubt, and we get along wonderfully. I am still not good at doing anything with my left hand because it's still in a cast, but Gretel rigged me up with some resistance bands, and I'm starting to see some results.

Dad tells me that he can't stay for long, but that he will be there later in the evening with a visitor, which is something to look forward to. I don't have a lot of visitors. Most of my high school and college friends have sent cards or GoFundMe donations, and I appreciate that, but they don't want to come here. When I look in the mirror, I understand why. My hair hasn't grown back yet and my face still bears the scars of the broken glass from the accident. And of course, I can barely say anything, which makes conversations awkward. But a few people have made the trip and I am grateful for those who've made the effort.

Dr. Kingman came by to visit last week—I expect my dad had something to do with that—and we had a nice lunch, and he was nice enough to not notice the smear of mashed potatoes on my cheek. (I would like to blame the accident for this, but truth be told, I have always been kind of a messy eater). Then Gretel took me out of the building for what I thought was some kind of shopping trip but turned out to be equine therapy, and Penny was there, and we got to see each other for the first time in months, and finally have something close to a heart-to-heart talk. That was awesome. And when we got back and Gretel was wheeling me through the lobby, some random person—Gretel tells me she is a grief counselor here, which I didn't even know there was—stops me and gives me a big hug and tells me thank you for something I didn't even do. So it's been an odd week.

After a long day of PT and a better-than-average dinner of rehab-center lasagna, I am in my bed fooling around with my new iPad Pro, which is mounted to my bed. There is a knock at the door, and Dad walks in with the promised visitor. He is a stranger, tall, with a lined face and sandy hair turning to gray. He has on a tweed sport coat over a black polo shirt. He grasps my good hand.

"Pleasure to meet you, Ashlyn. My name is Gary Baxter, from Berserker Books. We were supposed to talk back in August."

"Okay," I say.

"Your dad called me that evening, after your accident. I was awfully sorry to hear about what happened." He has a mid-Atlantic accent and a warm smile, and I am sorry that I disappointed him by not showing up for the interview. "I know that you're still recovering and that you can't talk very well at the moment. I understand that. I'll do my best to keep up both sides of the conversation."

"Tankoo."

"Good. What I wanted to tell you was that I was supposed to interview three finalists for that job. You, a young man from Cornell, and a young lady from Bryn Mawr. You, of course, were unavailable. The Cornell grad got a better offer from Ballantine. Well, these things happen. I hired Amanda from Bryn Mawr. She was ideal for the job, in every way but one."

I wait a heartbeat; he is clearly expecting me to say something, but all I can think to say is *what might that be* and I can't quite put that together. Eventually, Baxter figures out that, as he said, he ought to hold up both sides of the conversation. "Yes, well," he continues. "So Amanda did everything I asked her to, except for the one thing I didn't want her to, and that was to fall in love with my marketing director. Young people, you know. Even that would not have been all that terrible, except that my marketing director decided to desert me. He got a job in Amazon, of all things, in Seattle, of all places. And to make matters worse, he is taking Amanda with him. They just sent me a wedding invitation in the same envelope as their matching resignation letter."

I make the little grunting noise that I make that sounds like *oh*, just to show I'm listening. I have no idea where this is going or why I should care.

"When I go to human resources to ask for a replacement for Amanda, all they can tell me is that there's a hiring freeze. It's all very tiresome, but they are telling me I cannot hire anyone at all until next October. Ridiculous, of course, but there you have it. What they *are* telling me is that I *can* hire an intern, on a part-time basis, and I am here to make you an offer."

"No," I say. The entire idea is ridiculous. I can't even walk yet—I mean, I am *going to walk*, sooner rather than later, but even if I could get up and walk around the room that isn't enough mobility to make a publishing job in New York reasonable. Dad, at least, has to know this, and you would think he has explained it to Baxter.

"Let us not be hasty, young lady," Baxter says. "All I am asking you to do, at this point, is read. No editing, no proofreading, nothing like that. Nothing you can't handle at this point. All you would have to do is read the book—an electronic galley, to be specific. Your father tells me you have an iPad, which is splendid. If you can read the books I send you and let me know your honest opinion, that is all I can ask at this point."

"It is quite the opportunity," Dad says.

I understand that and I want to take the job, but I want to earn it, not have it given to me as a charity. I can only have one answer. "No."

"I want to make sure that you understand the situation," Baxter says. "I could find another intern. I know enough people at enough MFA programs to hire a hundred interns if I want them. But none of those people are going to care about fantasy literature, at least not enough to take it seriously as a genre. I decided to interview you because you wanted to make a career out of it. And I hope you still can. Your father says that your thought processes weren't damaged. If that's so, then there's no reason why you can't use your knowledge and passion to help build a career. And it will help me out immensely."

"Walk," I say.

Baxter, for the first time, looks confused. "I'm afraid I don't understand."

"That's a new word, Ashlyn," Dad says. "Isn't it? I don't remember you saying that before."

"Walk."

"Right, then," Dad says. "If I understand her, she would like to take the job—right?" I nod in response. "But she's focused on learning to walk again. And talk again, for that matter."

Baxter clasps his hands together. "Oh, then. Understandable. But, well, can't you do *both*? I am not asking for that much time, here. Whatever you can spare. Obviously, you want to walk again. Naturally. I wouldn't think of standing in your way. But you can manage a little leisure at the same time, can't you?"

I want to say no, that I can't take his job, but I can't find a hole in his argument. Reading is the one thing I can do independently, although I am reading slower than before and I get headaches sometimes. And Baxter looks like a nice person, and he came all this way to see me, and it's not as though the rest of the publishing world is lined up behind him to offer me even so much as an unpaid internship. And the new iPad means that I won't have to struggle with physical books.

"Okay," I say.

"Then it's settled. I have just the book for you, too, to get you started. It's young adult—not that I'm saying you can't read anything more complicated but that's what I'm working on at the moment. I'll e-mail it to you in the morning. Deal?"

He reaches out his hand, and I take it. "D-d-d-d," I say, which is as close to *deal* as I can manage.

"Thank you so much, Mr. Baxter," Dad says. "I think we need to let Ashlyn rest, now."

"Very well then. Good night, Ms. Revere. I look forward to hearing back from you about the book."

Dad gives my hand a squeeze and flashes me a proud smile, and they are gone. I lie back on my bed and stare at the darkness and wait for sleep to come.

WHAT YOU KNOW ABOUT YOURSELF

I wake up sitting on a low bench, staring into a huge stone fireplace. The room has wrap-around windows, looking out at a vast evergreen forest. The only sound besides the crackling of the fire is the soft gurgle of a nearby creek. I am alone, wrapped in a soft wool blanket. I am exactly one cup of coffee away from complete contentment.

"Don't feel as though you have to get up," a voice says.

"Not planning on it," I reply.

An old man in a tweed suit sits on one of the other benches in the room. He takes a poker and starts to stir the fire. His white hair perches on top of his head in flowing waves.

"I hope you like this place," he says. "It's one of my favorites. I'm afraid I don't live anywhere in particular, but this is as close to a home as I have."

"It's a very nice place."

"Thank you, Lady Ashlyn. It is a pleasure to meet you at last."

"You know my name," I say, "but I do not know yours."

"I am known as the Lord of Light."

"Nice to meet you." I don't know what else to say. I don't think there's anything he needs from me or that I need from him.

"You're not curious as to why I brought you here?" he asks.

"I am working hard on my rehab, and I have a new job, and I am kind of tired right at the moment," I explain. "If you have something that you would like me to do, I'm listening, but I am not in a huge hurry, either."

"Not even to lead an army against the Dark Lord?"

"I tried that already. I got my entire army killed. My wand was smashed to a thousand pieces. I lost my sword and the Dark Lord has it. And, not to put too fine a point on it, but I almost died in the process. I am not opposed in principle, you understand, but I don't like my odds right at the moment."

The old man smiles sadly. "You have suffered much and lost much. Let me see what I can do to help you repair your losses." He rummages around in a bin next to the fireplace, which has a stack of small branches that are used for kindling. He draws out a long stick of ash wood and hands it to me. "From the World Ash Tree," he says.

I take the branch and fish around in the pocket of my hoodie until I find the strand of unicorn hair. I had built my old wand out of little more than imagination and memory. This one is going to take a little more effort. The unicorn hair must form the core of the wand, I know that, but I don't have the kind of woodworking equipment I would need to hollow out the stick. I am going to have to wing it. With no other good options, I wrap the unicorn hair tightly around the outside of the ash stick and intone what sounds like a proper incantation:

Up and down
Away we go
Let the magic
Power flow.

I open my eyes, and there it is. A slender wand, slightly springy, with a silver spiral inlaid into the ash wood. I wave the wand, and a steaming cup of coffee appears. Perfect.

The Lord of Light eyes the wand carefully. "That is quite the powerful weapon," he says. "Dangerous in the wrong hands."

"Then it's a good thing that it's in my hands."

"What are you going to do with it?"

I consider this for a moment. I don't actually have a plan other than revenge.

"You said something about leading an army against the Dark Lord. Were you serious about that?"

"Are you?" the Lord of Light asks.

"Part of me wants to," I say. "The part that remembers what happened, how T.J. died, how Arthur died, how I was defeated. But there's a bigger part of me that wants to rest. To build up my strength."

"Why is that?"

"What happens here affects the real world," I say.

"Really." The corners around the Lord of Light's eyes crinkle with amusement. "Which is the real world, though? Here, or there?"

"Here, I only lost a battle. There, I almost lost my life. And I've already had one seizure, fighting that dragon. Two seizures mean an epilepsy diagnosis. They won't let me walk on my own for a long while if they think I have epilepsy. And they won't ever let me drive."

"Does that mean that you are passing on the opportunity to defeat the Dark Lord?" he asks.

"At the moment," I say, "that is exactly what I am doing. I want my revenge, don't get me wrong. But I am not yet in a position to take it. They say that it's a dish best served cold."

"That is wise," the old man says. "The Dark Lord feeds off negative emotions like hate and revenge. Your most powerful weapons against him now are not wands and swords, but love and forgiveness."

"Forgiveness? The Dark Lord killed King Arthur, and Sir Roland, and T.J., and my dragon. And the barbarian. Honor demands—honor requires—that I avenge them. You know. Eventually."

"No, it doesn't. Honor is what you know about yourself: no more, no less. You are no less honorable if you fight the Dark Lord with love than if you fight him with weapons. And if you can't consider forgiving the Dark Lord, you can perhaps start by forgiving yourself."

"Why do I need to forgive myself?" I ask.

"The answer should be left as an exercise for the student."

I huddle into my blanket and take a sip of coffee. "Well. Yeah. I took the battle to the Dark Lord. I called up my army. I led them into battle without really understanding what the Dark Lord could do. I didn't retreat when maybe I should have. And then I let my emotions get out of control when people started dying. That cost me my friends, my sword, and my honor."

"You did not lose your honor," the Lord of Light says. "Far from it. You know more about yourself now than you did, and you have used that knowledge well and wisely. You gain in honor every time you pronounce a new word, or row another stroke, or lift another weight. My advice is to seek honor where you know it may be found."

"You stole that line," I say. "It's out of some book or other."

"What if it is? Either way, that is exactly what you are doing. You will find your life again, Lady Ashlyn, and your honor, although the struggle will be long and painful."

"All right," I say. "I won't go after the Dark Lord—although if he comes after me, that's another story. What can I do *here?*"

"I understand," the Lord of Light says, "that the Western Marches need a new Warden. If you are interested, I can put in a good word for you."

"I don't know," I say. "Sounds stressful."

"I can give you an assistant."

I find the door that leads out onto the wraparound front porch, which juts out over the rushing creek. Nicholas is sitting on the porch, watching the water stream down the neighboring waterfall. I sit beside him and scratch between his ears.

"I am glad to see you again," he says. "What did the Lord of Light tell you?"

"He said I was the new Warden of the Western Marches, and that you were my assistant."

"Sarcasm," Nicholas says, "does not become you, Lady Ashlyn."

"Go ask him yourself, if you don't believe me."

"You are serious, then? Well. It will keep you occupied, and may keep you out of trouble."

"I've never been a warden before. It should be interesting."

"I certainly hope not."

We sit for a long moment and listen to the rushing waterfall.

"So, Lady Ashlyn, do you have a goal in mind?"

"Such as?"

"Your heart's desire."

I scratch the rabbit behind the ears. "I want to go home," I say.

"All you need to do is wake up to accomplish that."

"No, you don't understand. I'm in the rehab center, have been for a while now. I want to go *home*, where my parents are, where my family is. They won't let me—they wouldn't let me go home for

Thanksgiving. I want to go home for Christmas, if I can."

"I am afraid I cannot help you."

"Nicholas, I know you can't. But you asked me what my heart's desire is and that's what it is right now. I want to go home. Sleep in my own bed. Wake up with my brothers on Christmas morning and watch them open presents. Get some eggnog and pecan pie, and listen to my dad yell during the Jets game. That's my heart's desire."

Nicholas hops into my lap. "Well," he says. "I hope you achieve that, Lady Ashlyn. Do you have any short-term plans?"

"I was thinking we could sit here and watch the sun set."

"That will take some time," he says.

"Maybe not." I take out my new wand and point it in the general direction of the sun, moving it toward the horizon.

"Where did you get that, may I ask?"

"Eleven inches, unicorn hair core. The Lord of Light let me have a stick from the World Ash Tree."

"That was...an exceptionally dangerous and unwise thing for him to do."

"Maybe. We'll see."

"That amount of power in the hands of anyone would be hazardous. But to give it to you, of all people?"

"Nicholas?"

"Yes?"

"Let's just watch the sunset together, all right?"

I sit with Nicholas as the long shadows of darkness fall over the forests of the Western Marches. I close my eyes and wake up to the early morning half-light in my room at the rehabilitation center. It is twenty-four days until Christmas. I have a lot of work ahead of me if I'm going to make it home.

ABOUT THE AUTHOR

Curtis Edmonds is a writer and attorney living in central New Jersey. His work has appeared in *McSweeney's Internet Tendency, Untoward Magazine, The Big Jewel, Yankee Pot Roast*, and *National Review Online*. His book reviews appear on the *Bookreporter* website. He has written two novels, *Rain on Your Wedding Day* and *Wreathed*, as well as a flash-fiction collection, *Lies I Have Told*, and a children's picture book, *If My Name Was Amanda*, all published by Scary Hippopotamus Books. His most recent work, *Snowflake's Chance*, a collection of online humor columns, was published by Liberty Island.

A BRIEF FACTUAL APPENDIX

Writers don't always remember where or when they got their ideas, but I did this time. It was Thursday morning, February 18, 2016. I had spent the morning in Jersey City, in an administrative-law courtroom, representing a client on a Medicaid appeal. Both sides agreed to adjourn the hearing, and so I drove my black Hyundai Santa Fe back down Interstate 78, and then south down the New Jersey Turnpike, toward my office in beautiful downtown Trenton. And at some point between Newark Airport and the I-195 turnoff, I had the idea to do a novel set inside someone's dreams. I went home after work and did a quick little Google search, and found that there weren't all that many novels that took place in dream-space. *Alice's Adventures in Wonderland*, naturally, and *The Wonderful Wizard of Oz*. There was also *The Chronicles of Thomas Covenant*, which I remembered reading when I was a kid and not liking very much. I couldn't think of that many more outside of that list, for the sort-of-obvious reason that it's hard to tell a story that happens within a dream, and (as Robert Heinlein reminds us) it's also cheating to tell a story where the inevitable end is "and then the little boy fell out of bed and woke up."

But I thought I could do it anyway.

I started writing this novel on Saturday, February 20, 2016, because I had a little space between when the carpet-cleaning guy finished and when my wife and kids were getting back from the birthday party they were attending. I figured out the heroine's name—Ashlyn, an Americanized version of "Aisling," a Gaelic name which means "dream," and Revere, from the French word *rêver*, which means "to dream." And I found the name Penelope, which has the alternate meaning of "dream weaver." I was ready to start. (It is purely coincidence that the publication date for this book is February 20, 2020, but a neat one.)

Having said all that, I am quite at a loss in how I came to write this *particular* book. Without turning this into an infomercial, my first novel was meant to be in the literary fiction genre; it's about an old man coming to terms with the death of his daughters. That book got categorized, much to my shock and horror, as a *romance* novel, and since that label seemed to help sales, I figured I ought to write another one. The second novel is a mess, a "new adult" piece of chick-lit featuring an unlikeable borderline-alcoholic narrator with a social-media fixation who (not intentionally, I swear) alienated everyone who'd read the first book. And the one after *that* was an adorable rhyming alphabet picture book, which you should totally buy, but is a different species altogether. And the one after *that* was an absurdist piece of political satire.

So this is another completely different direction for me, which (considering the dismal sales figures for the other books) may be a Good Thing. It is probably a Bad Thing, in that one of the Things You Are Not Supposed to Do as an Author is switch genres all the time; that confuses people. (If you bought this book thinking that it was like the others, I apologize, but it didn't work out that way, sorry.)

The car accident actually did happen, although not quite that way. It was the morning of December 3, 2015 and I was in the left lane of Cedar Grove Lane, stopped at a red light, waiting to turn left on Easton Avenue and get on I-287 southbound to go to a supportive housing conference in Woodbridge, New Jersey. I was listening to a *Dallas Morning News* podcast about the health of the Texas Rangers pitching rotation going into the upcoming baseball season, when I saw a gray minivan going south on Easton launch itself into the air and land on its side in the center lane of Cedar Grove. Mercifully, there wasn't another car in either the center or the right lane for the van to crash into; anyone who had been there would have been squished the same way Ashlyn and Penny were. I got out of my car and called 9-1-1 and had a brief argument with the dispatcher about whether the accident had happened in Franklin Township or New Brunswick. Eventually, the dispatcher linked me in with the Franklin Township police, who came out to the scene. Other drivers got out and tried to help the driver of the van—she apparently told them that she was uninjured, but I don't know that for a fact. The other drivers were trying to tip the van over and I told the police, and they said not to do that, which I passed along. The police finally came and had everyone get back into their cars and clear the scene, and that's all I know.

I had to make Ashlyn Revere a geek. I am not sorry about that at all. I had to give the reader a frame of reference for everything Ashlyn was dreaming about, and the most relatable way to do that was through the lens of popular culture. I had no choice. I could have, I suppose, given Ashlyn a deep well of life experiences that she could have drawn from to enhance her own dreams—and I hope I did that, too—but honestly, the best way to tell the story was to have Ashlyn construct it from a mélange of popular culture clichés and tropes. I am not the least bit sorry. (If you're going to blame anyone for this, blame Ernest Cline, because he did almost the same damn thing in *Ready Player One*, which sold a million billion copies and was made into a movie by Stephen Freakin' Spielberg. Ask Cline if *he's* sorry, preferably as he's getting out of his DeLorean.)

There are a lot of references in this book. Here are some of them.

The interview that Ashlyn doesn't make it to is with a fictional subsidiary of Macmillan, which (at the time the story was written) was headquartered in the Flatiron Building. (I actually got to interview for a job with Macmillan at the Flatiron Building in 2017, which was a neat experience, even though I didn't get the job and I am *not the least bit bitter about this,* and it's just coincidence that's where the Dark Lord lives, honest.)

Ashlyn gives the rabbit the name "Nicholas," because that is the name of the rabbit in the classic board book "I Am a Bunny" by Ole Risom, illustrated by Richard Scarry. (If you have little kids, you know this already.) Although Nicholas is a Talking Rabbit, he is meant to sound a bit like the Professor in *The Chronicles of Narnia.*

Sir Roland Hargrove is named in part after Mike Hargrove, my favorite player on the awful Texas Rangers teams of my youth. Hargrove was known as "The Human Rain Delay" because of his penchant for adjusting his gloves between pitches, a nervous tic that Sir Roland shares. Sir Roland tells Ashlyn that "use makes master," which is a direct quote from Stephen Maturin in *The Hundred Days*, by the masterful Patrick O'Brian. He is also fond of saying "There is no alternative," which I lifted from Steven

Pressfield's history of the Six-Day War, *The Lion's Gate*. (This book, like every book there ever was, is a big fat finger in the eye of Resistance. Take that, Resistance!) The sword Dyrnwyn is from *The Book of Three* and its sequels, by Lloyd Alexander—as is the line about honor that the Lord of Light quotes.

The original inspiration for the scene where Ashlyn uses orchestral music to invoke the sunrise may be found in *The Phantom Tollbooth* by Norton Juster. One of the songs that she uses is *Morning Mood* by Edvard Greig. (Google it and you'll recognize it from various Bugs Bunny cartoons.)

The silver bell that Lachesis gives to Ashlyn is of course the same sort of bell that Santa Claus gives to the boy in *The Polar Express*. And *Silver Bell* is a Patty Griffin album, of course.

Ashlyn briefly considers braining Mr. Darcy with a frozen leg of lamb, which is the murder weapon used in the classic short story *Lamb to the Slaughter*, which I looked up just now and was somewhat surprised to learn was authored by Roald Dahl. (And yes, a true Regency kitchen wouldn't have a freezer, of course, but the reference was too cool to pass up.)

The chapter title "First Breath After Coma" is the title of a song on the Explosions in the Sky album *The Earth is Not a Cold Dead Place*. Explosions in the Sky (you may remember them from the movie *Friday Night Lights*) makes my absolute favorite writing music of all time.

The Dark Lord is correct in thinking that Ashlyn stole the line about her heart's desire; it is to be found in *Memory*, by Lois McMaster Bujold. (I honestly can't say enough good things about *Memory*; it's the weirdest thing—it's in the middle of a very long and involved space opera saga, but it's incredibly well done. Most of the time, these kinds of series—looking at *you*, Honor Harrington—get more and more awful as they go along, but that didn't quite happen here, and all honor to Bujold.)

The chapter title "Lungs" is inspired by the Townes Van Zandt song of the same name. The book Dr. Kingman is reading is the excellent *Destiny of the Republic: A Tale of Madness, Medicine and the Murder of a President* by Candice Millard. (She was at Baylor when I was there, but I don't think I ever met her.)

Including the talented actor Sean Bean in Ashlyn's retinue of knights is of course a reference to his roles in J.R.R. Tolkien and George R.R. Martin adaptations, but is primarily my way of paying homage to Bernard Cornwell, who wrote the Richard Sharpe novels for which Bean starred in the movie adaptations. I am sorry to have killed him off yet again, but *come on,* you must have expected that. The Italian Sir Lancelot is of course Franco Nero, from *Camelot*.

Ashlyn's penchant for pseudo-Latinate terminology for spell-casting is of course inspired by Harry Potter, but also by the Harry Dresden series of urban fantasy novels by Jim Butcher. If the Dark Lord reminds you a bit of Gentleman Johnny Marcone, Baron of Chicago, well, there's a reason for that.

The chapter title "New York in the Present Tense" is a nod towards Mark Helprin's splendid *Paris in the Present Tense*, and it is not coincidental that Ashlyn's bridge ends where the Battery Bridge in *Winter's Tale* begins. The chapter title "Fearless Girl" is a reference to the statue of that name—which, as I was writing this, had been placed near the bronze bull statue on Wall Street, which plays a pivotal role in the conflict between Ashlyn and the Dark Lord.

The chapter title "Lonesome Standard Time" is drawn from the song and album of the same name by Kathy Mattea.

As I was writing this, I read *Draft No. 4* by John McPhee, which warns you against using stale reference points. I have tried to follow this advice, but not as well as I might have liked. So while I am not entirely sure that someone Ashlyn's age would know about Monty Python, as a child of the 1970s, I couldn't resist the reference.

ACKNOWLEDGMENTS

This book is dedicated to my daughters. While I was working on the manuscript for this book, I published a rhyming alphabet picture book, *If My Name Was Amanda*, and they lobbied hard to have that book dedicated to them. I knew I was working on *this* book, so I didn't dedicate *that* book to them. (I hope this is all clear.) So they get this book.

This book took forever to write, and that is largely because while I was writing it, I was also working on my master's degree in human resource management at Rutgers University in New Brunswick. So that's the main reason for the delay; I was studying hard and I had class projects to finish and papers to write— including a law review article that got published by a journal at Brooklyn Law School. (I am mostly saying this so you don't think I spend *all* my time sitting around eating potato chips and watching football games, like George R.R. Martin.) So thanks to the faculty and staff at Rutgers, and my fellow students.

As a contributor to the *Liberty Island* online publication, I was invited some time back to participate in a writer's conference. This book was nowhere near completed at that stage and I wasn't really looking to go to any more writer's conferences. But this particular writer's conference—the Taliesin Nexus conference, to be specific—had Mark Helprin as its guest of honor. Mark Helprin is America's greatest living author and I couldn't pass up the chance to meet him. (And I did meet him, in a hotel ballroom overlooking Times Square, which was at that time slathered in high-definition M&M ads, which was a surreal experience, and I thanked him for writing his novels, and he said that was a *mitzvah,* which gave me all of the feels and still does.)

I workshopped this book, which at that time was called—I think—*All We Know or Dream*, and featured an Ashlyn Revere who was a grumpy thirty-year-old librarian. The leader of our group was the super-talented novelist Anne Fortier (*Juliet, The Lost Sisterhood*), who basically ripped what I had to shreds. Which was fine! And then I re-wrote it and she liked that a little better, and then I re-wrote it again, none of which would have happened without her help and guidance. And I got to meet other talented authors, including Karina Fabian (to whom I apologize for not making the dragon in this book hyper-talkative, or sarcastic, or Catholic), Richard Walsh (*The Adventures of Seamus Tripp*), and Matthew Souders (to whom I should apologize for being hyper-talkative and sarcastic if not very Catholic), all of whom helped to make this a better, brighter book. And thanks to Patrick and the TalNexus team, and Adam and the *Liberty Island* team, for all they've done for me and other conservative authors.

I was very pleased to have the expert assistance of Erin McCabe (https://www.authoraccelerator.com/ erinlindsaymccabe) in developing this work and getting it into shape. I tend to struggle through revisions, mostly as a revolt against my own stupidity. I won't lie to you and say that this revision was *easy*, because it was like being hit in the face with a bag of oranges every day for three weeks, but I understood why I needed to make the changes.

Richard Yang (Neil Blade at the Deviant Art website -- https://www.deviantart.com/neilblade) did the cover art, and I think it just turned out fantastic. I highly recommend him, not least because he got the little details right in the book, and because he very patiently worked with me to get the artwork just right.

I got the final version of the cover art the same day that the estimable Duchess Goldblatt announced the cover art for her book, so I delayed the reveal out of respect to Her Grace. (I also think I need to apologize for not referencing Lyle Lovett somewhere in here; I don't know what I was thinking.)

One of the minor characters in this book is a nurse when Ashlyn goes into her first surgery; she is inspired by a nurse who helped my wife after our children were born. All too often, doctors and nurses in books like this are afterthoughts. In fact, in the first drafts of this book, the character of Dr. Drew Kingman wasn't there at all. Once I put in Kingman, I wanted to try—without detracting from the overall story—to make the doctors and nurses who treat

Ashlyn and Penny flesh-and-blood people, not just ciphers. Kingman is a good doctor, but he's often tired and homesick and fallible, and that's normal. All honor and glory to them for all they do for us.

Curtis Edmonds
Duckthwacket, New Jersey
September 2019

A Circle of Firelight

CPSIA information can be obtained
at www.ICGtesting.com
Printed in the USA
FSHW022333190120
66260FS